"I can't say enough good things about *Jar of Dreams*;
you'll immediately feel at home with these characters,
find yourself caught up in the drama they all face,
and loving every minute of it!"
—*Guilty Pleasures Book Reviews*, 4½ stars

"Enough depth to make the characters and situations real,
yet enough hope and heart to make you fall in love
with them and their community."
—*Book Sojourner*, 4½ stars

"Small town romance at its best!
It is filled with a cast of quirky, loveable characters
that I wanted to get to know in real life."
—*Harlequin Junkies*, 4½ hearts

"A compelling story that will put a smile on your face,
a tear in your eye, and love in your heart."
—*Book Raven's Reviews*, Recommended Read

"*Jar of Dreams* is another captivating and emotional novel
that fans of contemporary romances will not want to miss.
It is a charming story of family, healing, and love that will
resonate with readers. Liz Flaherty consistently delivers
realistic stories that will make you laugh, cry and rejoice as
the characters find their happily ever afters."
—*Book Reviews & More by Kathy*

Also available from Liz Flaherty
and Carina Press

ONE MORE SUMMER

Jar of Dreams

Liz Flaherty

carina press®

carina press®

ISBN-13: 978-0-373-00242-9

Jar of Dreams

This edition published by arrangement with Harlequin Books S.A.

www.CarinaPress.com

Printed in U.S.A.

Dear Reader,

I drank coffee for years—that was the easiest path to take when I married someone who I swear had coffee running through his veins in lieu of blood—but when I stopped smoking a lot of years ago, coffee lost much of its appeal. It was worth it a thousand times over to no longer be dependent on cigarettes, but I missed having a steaming cup at my elbow all the time.

That was when I got friendly with tea. It was easier on my stomach and I loved all the flavor choices. I've always been a morning person, but these days my favorite time is predawn, alone in my office with a cup of hot, soothing and caffeinated tea. Several cups, actually, but we don't need to go into my little self-indulgences here.

Even with my penchant for tea, I was surprised when Lucy's visit to Gert Taylor ended with the two women going into business together as the proprietors of a tearoom. Tea on Twilight is the setting for *Jar of Dreams*, where Boone, with all his endearing clumsiness, takes his first dragging steps out of grief and Lucy begins to believe that maybe, just maybe, some of the dreams she's stashed in the pickle jar on the counter will come true.

I was reluctant to leave the tearoom and its owners when the story came to an end. I hope you will be, too.

I'd love to hear from you. I can be reached at lizkflaherty@gmail.com, or stop by my website at lizflaherty.com and say hello.

Thanks for reading!

Liz Flaherty

Dedication

In loving memory of Elmer, Myrtle, and Gladys Neterer,
my grandparents and my aunt.
They would have liked Lucy and Boone.

And for Skyler, Shea and Connor Wilson and
Fionnegan and Eamon Flaherty, my grandboys.
You're my real-life cartoon and I love you all.

Jar Of Dreams

Chapter One

...Can you come home for a while? Aunt Gert's failing...

The two short sentences in the middle of his sister's e-mail had leaped out at Boone as if she'd typed them in bold black print instead of her usual girly green font. Just like she'd planned when she wrote them. She always knew how to get his attention. It must be the lawyer in her. Not that that was necessarily a good thing, but it had gotten him off his couch and his mind on someone besides himself.

Common sense told him if Aunt Gert had *really* been failing, Kelly would have been on the phone barking out commands in prosecuting attorney language and he'd have been on the next flight out of O'Hare. Instead, he'd spent a week preparing to be away for the summer before trundling down Interstate 65 in his Jeep this morning.

He sublet his apartment to a resident at the hospital nearby. He and Chris Fodrea had become friends after a rather violent racquetball game when the young orthopedist had told him his leg wasn't broken and that he didn't need painkillers—he needed exercise. Boone forwarded his mail to the house on Twilight Park Avenue in Taft, Indiana, and stopped newspaper delivery. He'd stuffed a backpack with shorts and T-shirts, tossed his golf clubs into the back seat and buckled his laptop into the passenger seat.

He couldn't bear the idea of Aunt Gert growing old. Well, maybe she was already old—she'd lied about her age so long he had no clue as to how long she'd actually been leaping headlong into life in her Birkenstock sandals and white bobby socks. She'd seemed old when he and Kelly had moved in with her and Uncle Mike, but they'd been young adolescents with pain dripping off them in hot and dark streams—so his memory was probably less than accurate.

The exit for Taft and the neighboring small towns that dotted the banks of the Twilight River jumped up unexpectedly—had the town moved and he didn't know it?—and he whipped the Jeep in front of an eighteen-wheeler to keep from missing the turn, waving an apologetic hand out the window. The trucker's response, immediate and absolutely unfriendly, didn't involve his whole hand.

Boone plucked his cell phone off the dash and spoke his sister's name into it, thinking voice recognition was probably a good thing for people who shouldn't talk on cell phones in cars but did it anyway. "Hey, Kell," he said, surprised when she answered her own phone, "what do you mean, failing?" He'd left her a message asking that same question on the day he'd gotten the email. If she'd called back, he didn't know it. He had a tendency not to check his messages.

There was a quiet moment in which he was pretty sure he heard the wheels turning in her head, bringing her mind back from wherever it had been—it was a shame that she'd gotten all the powers of concentration in the family. He'd been told frequently that he could do with a few himself. When she spoke, though, it was still his little sister's voice. Light and musical and, if you were her often-annoyed older brother, fretful. "She's just acting weird, Boone. Are you in your Jeep? It sounds like a hurricane. I really wish you wouldn't use the phone in the car. You're already the worst driver in three states."

He ignored that. Lawyers probably exaggerated everything—that was how they made so much money. "What would be weird is if she didn't act weird." He inserted just a hint of a sneer into his voice. "You know that. What's she doing exactly?"

"Well, she's practically adopted this kid, Jack, to help with the yard and the garden. She can use the help and I suggested him to her in the first place, but…I don't know, it's as though she looks at him and sees us when we were kids. For another thing, she has a renter. A woman. Young. With no apparent—I'll be right there, Bridget—past, no money, and a vehicle that should have been condemned in the last century."

"Does she need money? Gert, I mean, not the mysterious boarder. Or does she just want company? That's a big old house for just one person."

"No."

"No what?" He wanted to manage the conversation, really he did, because that was the best way to talk to one's bossy sister, even if she was two years younger and addicted to cosmetics and designer clothes.

"No, she doesn't need money—she's a freaking financial wizard. And no, she doesn't want company. Or, if she does, she's never said so, and you know very well Aunt Gert doesn't hold back."

They shared a dry and affectionate chuckle at that choice bit of understatement. Boone jerked the Jeep back into his own lane. *Watch where you're going, idiot.* "What else?"

"Well, she's gone into this crazy business thing, and when I tried to talk to her about it, she didn't take very kindly to my advice." Kelly sounded both prim and offended.

"Tell me you didn't use the word 'crazy' when you brought it up."

"I might have." Offended had become offensive—damn near whiny. "Because it is, Boone. I feel responsible—"

Boone turned a laugh into a cough. He might be absentminded and on the clumsy side, but he wasn't stupid. "Tell you to butt out, did she?"

"In so many words."

"Aunt Gert's been adopting strays for at least twenty-some years. This kid and this woman don't sound any different. The kid, as a matter of fact, sounds like a really good idea, especially if it means I won't have to mow the yard or weed the garden this year. So far you aren't giving me anything to worry about." *Which is good, but tell me again why I'm going to Taft for the whole summer.*

"She's actually... Okay, Bridge, I'm coming right now. Gotta go, Boone. Duty calls."

"Kelly—"

But she was gone. Off to do legal things, he supposed. Hard to believe his sister the homecoming queen was an attorney. He'd never seen her in court—the mere suggestion that he watch her in action had horrified her to the extent he'd let the matter drop—but he always imagined her approaching the judge's bench wearing a funny-shade-of-blue satin gown and a corsage of tipped-to-match chrysanthemums. She'd have one of those banner things crossing her chest that proclaimed her Miss Indiana At-Law or something. He'd never been to her office, either—the timing and logistics had never worked out right for him to visit her there.

He knew a moment's regret. Time was passing them by. He needed to see her more. Maybe this summer.

Taft was just ahead. One more big swooping curve around the Twilight River and the city limits sign would appear. *"Welcome to Taft, Indiana. Home of No One Special. Population 1841 counting cats, dogs, and the occasional parakeet."*

He'd forgotten how sharp the curve was—it bent instead of swooped—*oh, hell, what's that?*

He made it back into his own lane in time to avoid smacking into the lopsided blue van that came from the other way, but the other driver overcorrected and wobbled inexorably off the road. The vehicle came to rest with its rusty nose against the bank that reared up from the ditch.

"Shit. Super shit." Boone swung his car into a U-turn, coming to a jerky stop behind the van. He jumped over the side of the Jeep and ran to the driver's window. "Are you okay?"

The woman was young—younger than him, anyway. She had curly hair the color of butterscotch pudding and wide leaf-green eyes that were staring out at him in horror. She smelled… holy God, she smelled like butterscotch pudding too. *Aunt Gert's* butterscotch pudding, to be more precise. She always cooked it till it was damn near burnt—a process that gave it an extra flavor and aroma that were famous all over town. The sweet smell sent a surge of unexpected longing through him—it had been too long since he'd been to the house on Twilight Park Avenue that was the safest, warmest place he knew. Too long since he'd spent unhurried time with Aunt Gert.

But she'd kill him if he'd caused injury to someone because he was woolgathering. Or she'd threaten to, anyway. He and Crockett used to call her Aunt One More Time because those were the words that prefaced every dire warning of what was going to happen to them if they didn't straighten up.

Sometimes I'd give a lot for one more time to get it right.

But this wasn't the time or place for either remembering or reminiscing.

"Miss? Are you okay?" he repeated, wrenching open the door of the van.

The leafy eyes focused on him. Lord, she had

beautiful skin. "Y-yes." She extended a hand as though she was going to feel his forehead for fever, then withdrew it before she touched him. "Are you? I'm so sorry. My mind was wandering and I must have scared you to death."

She was sorry? It had been her fault? Oh, good. Aunt One More Time wouldn't even have to threaten him. "I'm fine. No problem at all," he said magnanimously. "Let me help you out and we'll see what we need to do."

"Do you have a cell phone?" She accepted his hand to climb out of the van. "I'll have to call Sims to come pull me out and I forgot mine. I'm always forgetting it, or else letting it go dead. My dad used to holler at me as I was going out the door."

She laughed shakily and Boone glanced at her. "You're okay?" he asked again.

Her nod was decisive. "I'm fine. Messy, though. Sims will never let me hear the end of this."

"He still runs the service station?" Boone sniffed at the stickiness she'd left on his fingers. He'd been right. It *was* Aunt Gert's butterscotch. "He must be at least eighty. He's been talking about retiring for years. I figured he'd at least have hired someone to manage the place."

"He's seventy-five." She was leaning back into the van, and her voice was muffled. "What a mess. I'll need to call Gert, too. It's a good thing she made extra."

The driver of the blue van was wearing denim shorts and a watermelon-colored T-shirt. When she leaned into the vehicle, the shorts stretched snugly across her backside. Boone had never realized he even liked green, but she certainly wore it well. Butterscotch pie filling was smeared all down her right arm. He wouldn't mind one bit licking it off. The very thought made him draw back. What on earth was he thinking? Nothing like coming home to toss you twenty years backward into puberty.

She said something, but his ears were buzzing. More retroactive pubescence. "Huh?"

"Do you have a cell phone?" she asked again.

"Oh, yeah." He sprinted back to get it, figuring up what he knew about the driver of the rusty van. Her eyes were the kind you could get lost in if you weren't careful, her nose slightly sunburned, and her fingernails chewed well into the quick. She wore tiny pale green earrings—no necklaces, bracelets, or rings. Especially no rings. She was pretty in denim and butterscotch pudding, smelled good and took responsibility for her own actions. Maybe his too. Boone wasn't sure about that and he really didn't want to dig too deeply.

So what did she have to do with Aunt Gert?

He handed her the phone and went back to watching her. She was easy on the eyes, not at all a bad first sight when coming home. Was this Aunt Gert's mysterious boarder, the one who had Kelly all tied up in bossy knots?

"Hi, Sims," she was saying. "I went off the road out here by Bowditch's farm. Could you come and… no, no one ran me off. I mean, there was another car, but…yes, he's tall with brown hair…I don't know, Sims, I can't see it. Do you want me to ask him?" She covered the mouthpiece of the cell phone and spoke to Boone. "Sims wants to know if you have a tattoo on your…er… A coonskin cap tattoo?"

Boone sighed. And nodded. The mechanic's next words were going to be "One more time." Aunt Gert wasn't the only one with the threat gene going on.

"Yes, he does. What does that have to do… Okay, I'll be here, but can you hurry some? I'm supposed to have four pies out to Mrs. Kline in a half hour and I'm wearing one of them… He will?" She shifted her gaze back to Boone, her eyes wary. He felt insulted. It had been at least fifteen years since Taft in general, and Sims in particular, had been terrorized by its own dynamic duo, Boone and Crockett. *Ah, Crockett…*

"I'll ask him. See you then." She disconnected the phone and handed it to Boone. "Sims says you'll run me on out to Mrs. Kline's while we wait for him. Could you?"

She grinned cheekily. The expression registered somewhere around a ten on his hormonal scale. "He says drive slow and pay attention to what you're doing. I take it you know each other?"

Boone grinned back. "Sure. She still live on Bumpy Road?"

"Yes." She reached into the van and came out with two flat white boxes. "Hold these, will you?"

He took the boxes, sniffing again and enjoying

the aroma. "I'm Michael Brennan. People generally call me Boone."

She emerged from the van with the third pie. "I'm Lucy Dolan. People generally call me Lucy."

He moved his laptop to the back seat of the Jeep and opened the door for her, setting the two pies he held on her lap. Now that the pudding was drying in her hair, he could see that the soft curls really *were* the color of butterscotch, matching the freckles that marched across her pink nose.

"Gertrude Taylor's my aunt," he said, swinging onto the road without remembering to check the rearview mirror until a horn honk reminded him. He raised a hand. He was doing a whole lot of gesticulatory apologizing today.

"I figured that out when Sims asked about the tattoo. I should have known it anyway from the pictures on the walls of the house and from your aunt talking about you and your sister and Crockett." Wariness lingered in her eyes. "Gert's my landlady."

"Thought she might be." Why was she looking at him like he'd just crawled out from under a rock when she was obviously the encroacher here? And hadn't she nearly run him off the road? "I never knew Aunt Gert to take in boarders before."

She smiled, although the pink color seemed to spread from her nose across her cheeks. "My van broke down in front of her house. I rang the doorbell to use her telephone because mine was dead and never left. There's Bumpy Road just ahead," she reminded him, a little late.

He took the corner at about thirty-five, far too fast, but it was either that or have the pickup that had been following them become a decoration on the Jeep's bumper. He had the feeling her answer was more evasion than fact. There would be time in the lazy summer before them to find out the whole truth.

"You might try turn signals sometime," she suggested, her voice sounding somewhat strangled. "You know, just as an alternative."

"I'll give it a shot." He saw Mrs. Kline's white farmhouse and dutifully turned on his signal, though no one followed or approached them on the gravel road.

Forty-five minutes later, after having his cheeks pinched by Martha Kline and his hand wrung by Sims, Boone followed Lucy's van into town. The city limits sign was still there, though the population number had been lowered by a hundred or so residents. Some of the cats must have died.

He drove through downtown, noting there were more empty storefronts than there had been the last time he was home. But the doors to the Methodist church were still painted fire-engine red and Down at Jenny's, the café, was still going strong. Three houses past a left turn onto Twilight Park Avenue, he pulled the Jeep into his aunt's driveway.

The house was the same, painted red and trimmed in gray and white. Flowers bloomed in multicolor profusion on either side of the brick sidewalk that approached the porch. A well-built teenager in a Taft High School T-shirt and ragged shorts pushed a lawnmower across the yard, his movements efficient. He lifted a hand in a desultory wave. This must be the kid Kelly was worried about.

Boone waved back, then stopped and squinted at the discreet sign that hung from the gingerbread work on the front porch. "Tea on Twilight?"

Lucy parked behind him and walked past him toward the house. He caught up with her, grasping her arm before she could mount the steps. He gestured at the sign. "What the hell's this?"

Not again. Boone Brennan's chocolate-colored eyes had the same expression of distaste his sister Kelly's always did when they focused on Lucy. It was a silent insult she hadn't earned and heartily resented.

"I believe," she said evenly, "it's a sign. Excuse me, please. Gert needs me to serve lunch."

She shook free from his grasp, but before she reached the door, Gert was pushing it open. "Boone, is that you? Haul your tight buns in here. I need help in the kitchen."

"Hi, Aunt Gert."

Lucy felt the hairs on her arm stand on end when he brushed against her skin. He stepped past her and swept Gert into a hug, then laid the old lady back over his arm. "Ah, woman, you've ruined me for anyone else. When are you going to marry me?"

"Why would I marry a fresh young pup determined to put my back out at every turn?" Gert straightened, swatted his shoulder and kissed his cheek in one economical motion. Then she hugged him again, drawing back and lifting the tail of his shirt to dry her eyes. "Did you meet Lucy?"

"We met." He met Lucy's eyes coolly. "What's going on here, Aunt Gert?"

"Lunch, as a matter of fact, and we're behind because someone ran the waitress off the road. I thought I was going to have to call Jack in from mowing the yard to don an apron. I can just imagine his reaction to that. It would be a replay of the Crockett and Boone show." Gert frowned at Boone at the same time as she took his arm in a fond grasp. "Sims called me," she said.

"Sims the busybody," he complained. He started to follow his aunt inside, then stepped back and motioned for Lucy to go ahead.

She went straight down the center hall to the kitchen, keeping her eyes to the front. She didn't care to witness Boone's reaction to the sight of both parlors, the dining room, and the former den filled with fifteen small cloth-covered tables.

In the big kitchen, Gert picked up a magnum of chardonnay and pushed it at Boone, smacking him in the stomach with it. "Open this," she ordered. "Lucy has trouble with that damn corkscrew every time. Lucy, those salads are for the front parlor."

"Wine?" Boone sounded shocked. "For lunch? In Taft? Does the sheriff's office know about this? Tom Simcox is still sheriff, right, or has the whole town been taken over by a syndicate from the big city that allows drinking in the middle of the day?"

"If you're going to be a pain in the tookus," Gert said, scowling over her glasses at him, "you need to go to your room and give some thought to your behavior."

Lucy didn't think she'd ever heard of a "tookus," but it seemed to have some effect on Boone. He went to work with the corkscrew. When she came back from the front parlor, she noted with no small amount of resentment that he apparently hadn't had any trouble opening the wine. That was as irritating as the snotty expression in his eyes.

"Aunt Gert, don't you think you might have mentioned this venture at some point?" he asked, filling the glasses Lucy set in front of him. "We talk on the phone a couple of times a week. For that matter, do I even *have* a room upstairs or have you opened a bordello, too?"

Gert frowned at him. "No, we're saving that for next year. Do you need hormones, Boone? You sound grouchy."

Lucy sped away with the tray of glasses without waiting for his response. She returned in time to hear Boone say, "...a stray cat. You can't just adopt people because you like their eyes."

"I liked yours and Kelly's and Crockett's twenty-some years ago, my boy," Gert said sharply. "Give the other tray of wine to Lucy and come over here and slice this pie."

"Do you have a license to serve this stuff?" He

handed Lucy the wine without meeting her eyes and stomped over to the slate-topped island, acting for all the world like an overgrown little boy in the middle of a tantrum.

"I have enough licenses and permits to open an agency of my own," Gert responded impatiently. "Your sister, remember, is an attorney. And as cranky as you are, I might add. She left absolutely no stones unturned." Her smiling eyes belied the irritability in her voice. "How long are you staying? Do I need to let Tom know you're back on the streets for a while?"

"All summer," he said diffidently. "If that's all right."

Lucy nearly stumbled on her way to the back parlor and had to do a swaying little dance with the wine tray to retain her balance without dashing the chardonnay against the wide floorboards of the hallway. All summer? She was going to encounter those disapproving eyes in that devastatingly handsome face every single day for the entire summer? Maybe he would stay with his sister in her townhouse… No, he'd already asked about his room upstairs.

She usually loved when the tearoom was busy. Even though the three hours during which they served lunch often left her with sore feet and numerous flavors of tea, coffee and wine spilled on her apron, it also left her clear-headed and hopeful. But today wasn't usual. The tables remained full from eleven until well past two and her apron pocket was bulging with cash, but the time seemed unending. Her feet were aching by noon and she'd changed her apron three times. She spent so much time mentally planning where she was going to go when Boone Brennan manipulated her ouster from his aunt's house that she had to count Reverend St. John's change back to him three times.

Eli told her it was all right—he didn't know how to count anyway. Lucy ended the transaction laughing. He had a habit of smiling down at his family from the pulpit and counting heads aloud. "There were only seven this morning," he would tell his wife Jessie, "and now there are nine. How does this *happen?*"

"When we got married," he often explained, "she had three, I had three, and we inherited three from someone else. The problem is, we can't remember who had which ones and we didn't save the receipts, so we can't send any of them back."

Lucy smiled with the thought of the St. Johns. Maybe she could stay with them if she had to leave Gert's—Eli would never even notice she was there and Jessie was too nice to tell him.

The grandfather clock in the hall chimed a quarter after two when she turned the elegant little "closed" sign toward the street and leaned back against the wall.

"Lucy, come and have some tea. I can hear your dogs barking from here," Gert called.

Lucy lifted each foot and stretched it, realizing for the first time just how tired they were. Her right arch cramped and she had to push herself away from the wall, biting back a groan. "On my way."

Gert was sitting on a bar stool at the island, counting receipts, her reading glasses balanced near the end of her nose. "Excellent day, Lucy," she announced.

"Good." Lucy accepted the glass of wine Boone offered. "Thank you."

She scrounged into her apron, pulling out the rest of the cash and dumping it onto the slate in front of Gert. "Here you go." She went to the counter that ran along the wall and dropped coins into the gallon-size pickle jar that sat there. A large white label on the outside of it said, "Lucy's Dreams." It was half full of money, business cards, and pieces of paper.

"What are you doing?" Boone's expression was scandalized. "You don't get to keep your tips? Shame on you, Aunt Gert, for taking advantage of the help."

Gert divided the cash according to denomination and laid the checks and credit card receipts in separate piles before she replied. "And shame on you, Boone, for speaking out of turn. Lucy's not 'the help.'" She totaled the receipts and handed the tape to Lucy before scowling at her nephew over the top of her reading glasses. "We're business partners."

Chapter Two

Two days passed before Boone connected with Kelly—days spent dusting hard-to-reach places for Aunt Gert, running the power-washer for Sims at the service station and learning abso-damn-lutely nothing about Lucy Dolan.

After sharing pizza, beer and some decadent breadsticks he'd brought from the tearoom, Boone sat in his sister's living room and glared across its width at her. "Why didn't you tell me what was going on?" Not that he was at all sure anything *was* going on. Lucy was as much a mystery as she'd been standing beside her car on the road into Taft. Jack just seemed to be a nice kid who worked hard—he was a whole lot more productive at the handle of a lawnmower than he and Crockett had ever been.

"Because Aunt Gert told me, in so many words, that she didn't want us to interfere." Kelly met his expression, scowl for scowl. "Maybe if you found your way here more than once a year, or maybe twice if you make it for Thanksgiving or Christmas, you could keep an eye on her sometimes too."

Boone opened his mouth, then closed it. He had no viable argument. When he and Maggie had been together, they'd made the trip almost every month, but the last two years had been different. Living in a swirl of pain was one thing—rippling that eddy out to everyone he knew and loved was something else again. "What do you know about Lucy Dolan?"

"Aunt Gert had a hissy fit when I suggested doing a background check on her." Kelly shrugged. "Our aunt's an adult, Boone. I couldn't treat her as incompetent even if she was." She sighed and sat on the white couch, leaning forward and steepling her fingers under her nose. "Truth be told, Lucy's been wonderful to her as far as I know. The only reason I don't like her is because I don't want to."

Something in her voice sounded wrong.

Defeat. That's what it was.

Suddenly *everything* about this scene seemed wrong. The glitzy townhouse and hard-edged voice didn't match up with the sister he thought he knew, although the perfectly cut silk suit was right up her wardrobe alley.

Her hair, which she must have run her hands through once too often, made him think of that first day they'd come to live with their mother's older brother, Uncle Mike, and Aunt Gert. They'd both been mired in the grief of losing their parents and the fear of whatever came next. Boone was angry and taciturn in ragged jeans and a T-shirt with a torn sleeve, but Kelly wore a carefully matched outfit with complementary socks and headband. Her braids, plaited by an older brother's impatient fingers, were crooked and loose.

It seemed as though he'd never gotten taking care of his little sister exactly right, but he was still trying. "What's wrong, Kell?" he asked. "This is about more than Aunt Gert, isn't it?"

She sat silent, staring out at the man-made lake that was the hub of the wheel of condominiums that had sprung up on Taft's east side in recent years. After a moment, she nodded—just a quick little jerk of her head—but didn't meet his gaze.

Trying to stifle impatience, he sat beside her and put an arm around her, leaning back on the sumptuous leather with her tucked into his side. "Tell me," he said quietly. He dropped a kiss on the top of her auburn-streaked dark hair, then rubbed his chin lightly over the spot he'd kissed. "There. It can't come off now."

Her soft laugh had a little hiccup in it, and he knew a moment's horror that she might cry. "Lucy's van broke down in front of the house when she came here, as you probably know, but this is where she was heading anyway."

Her shoulders stiffened under his arm before she went on. Her voice sounded splintered and brittle. "She came to Aunt Gert's because Crockett sent her."

The grandfather clock chimed just once when Lucy came down the stairs. She glared at it as she passed, as though it were to blame for the fact that she couldn't sleep through the night.

In the kitchen, she poured a glass of sweet tea and slipped out the back door as noiselessly as she could, walking around to the broad porch that embraced the front and one side of the house. She sat in a wicker chair and lifted her feet to cross them on the rail. Her robe fell away so her legs were bare, and she relished the breeze on her skin. The outside smelled like fresh-cut grass and lilacs, and she breathed deep.

The cool air seemed to sensitize her nerve endings in much the same way Boone's touch had. Remembering the brush of his arm, she rubbed a hand down the length of her own as though to eradicate the feeling he'd left behind. This was neither the time nor the place for man-woman feelings. She wasn't the woman and God knew Michael Brennan wasn't the man.

But what a man he was, with his slightly long brown hair and dark brown eyes that saw too much. A full eight inches taller than her five feet five, he carried his size easily. He was well-muscled, but not with the rippling definition of a man overtly conscious of his body. The jeans he'd worn today had been snug but not tight, his shirt loose enough to appear comfortable. His voice… Oh, yes, his voice. It was deep and soft at the same time, with music in it. The music of dreams.

It had been so long since Lucy had heard that kind of music.

"Guilty conscience keeping you awake?"

She jumped when the voice with all its musicality came from behind her. She nearly spilled her tea, and closed her eyes against the sting of his sarcastic question.

"Must be." She kept her voice light, but rubbed her stomach against the nausea that teased its edges. The fact that the man made her think she might throw up was conclusive evidence that she needed to avoid him.

"Mind if I join you?"

He was in the chair beside hers before she could think of any way to dissuade him, his long, narrow feet propped on the porch rail next to her short, stubby ones. He had a can of beer in his hand, and he lifted it to his mouth for a long swallow.

"So," he said, "where do you come from, Lucy Dolan? And what do you want?"

She relaxed. Straight-out nosiness was much easier to deal with than suspicious glares. Kelly Brennan had treated her as though she were a criminal for so long—from the first time they met—she'd almost come to believe she was one. It wasn't exactly a new feeling, but it wasn't one she'd ever gotten used to.

"I come from Richmond, Virginia," she began, "and I don't want—" She stopped. It wasn't true that she didn't want anything, but she didn't know how to explain. "I want a future," she said finally. "A place to call my own, enough money to pay the utilities before the shutoff notice comes, my own kitchen with a window over the sink." She smiled, caught up in the hope it was possible to feel in the middle of the night when the air was dark and soft and nothing seemed threatening. "A pickle jar full of dreams."

"How do you know Crockett?"

"He used to come into our restaurant for lunch sometimes. He's a nice man, a friend."

"Why did he send you to Aunt Gert?" His voice remained quiet, even friendly, but the question was more challenge than query.

Enough light from the streetlamp showed her that what she was starting to think of as "the look" was back on his face, and she forced herself not to shrink away. She lifted her chin. "I've done nothing to earn your contempt, so I wish you'd stop treating me as though I'd just come in on the bottom of your shoe."

His face cleared instantly. "I'm sorry." He turned away, facing where the full moon glinted silver on the Twilight. "Aunt Gert's been everything to Kelly and me. When our folks died, I was twelve and Kelly was ten and we were nobody's prize—we came fully equipped with tree-limb size chips on our shoulders. But she just came in and took us without so much as a blink. She didn't have to—our only connection was that she was married to our uncle—but she did it anyway. It's our turn to take care of her."

"I'm sure she appreciates that," Lucy said primly.

His laughter was a whoop, subdued by a hand over his mouth. "She abso-damn-lutely does not," he said. "She'd much prefer we just mind our own business the way she'll say she taught us. But there are a lot of bad people out there who prey on old folks."

Lucy recalled her family restaurant's unrepaired roof, its faulty eaves troughs, the cleaning service that had charged higher prices but promised a year's-end rebate that never materialized. She thought of the uniforms for the service personnel that had been ordered and paid for, but none, except the prototype, were ever received. She remembered her father's confusion, his hurt that people would do such things deliberately, and her hand curved into a fist. She pounded the arm of her chair with quiet and unspoken vehemence, anger roiling helplessly through her veins.

"Yes," she said, the bitterness flowing free through her voice, "there are. But I'm not one of them, Mr. Brennan."

"Good." His answer was instant, and he turned his head so their eyes met. "Why a tearoom?"

She shrugged. "It was what Gert wanted. I was going to try and get a job waiting tables at the café. It's what I've done all my life and I think Jenny would have hired me. The next thing I knew, Gert was on her hands and knees measuring the rooms of the house. She sent me into every attic in town to find tables and chairs. She'd applied for the beer and wine license and the local permits before I realized she was really serious about this."

"I just can't figure out what the secrecy was all about," he murmured. "I call her at least twice a week and email her nearly every day. She just visited me in Chicago three weeks ago. In all this time, she never mentioned you, a tearoom, or anything. Why not?"

"I don't know," she admitted. "I had no idea

you didn't know, but she may have been concerned you'd react like your sister did."

"How was that?"

"That's telling tales out of school." She shook her head, sorry she'd said anything. "Speaking of school, what made you become a cartoonist?"

He chuckled. "I've got a writer friend who about gags every time someone asks him what made him become a writer. He says no one in his right mind would be a writer if he could avoid it. He just was one and there was nothing he could do about it. Drawing cartoons is just the opposite."

"Why's that?" She tucked her hands into the pockets of her robe.

"Because you can be whatever you want to be through your characters."

She thought of the protagonists in the comic strip signed "Brennan," with a little stick figure drawn at the end of the name. It hadn't taken her long to recognize "Elmer and Myrtle" when she came to Taft. "You want to be Sims and Gert?" she asked mildly.

He shot her a surprised frown. "Most people don't catch on to that. It's not as though Elmer and Myrtle resemble them, other than Myrtle's Birkenstocks and Elmer's bicycle cap. How did you know?"

"When Sims came to tow my van in the first day I got here, Gert was on the porch and he yelled up to her to order some flowers because any vehicle that had lived as long as she had—meaning Gert, not my car—deserved a nice funeral. She told him he should know, since he'd been old enough to vote at her christening." Lucy tilted her head to face Boone. "It wasn't the same dialogue, but it was surely the same speakers. Gert and Sims love each other in the same way that Elmer and Myrtle do. Then when I met Kelly, she was obviously Daphne, Elmer and Myrtle's daughter, right down to her designer shoes."

Boone winced. "I hope you didn't tell her you recognized her. Kelly doesn't care a lot for Daphne."

Lucy raised a surprised eyebrow. "You don't think so? I think she's proud of her. Check out the wall in her office, the one across from her desk."

"You've been in Kelly's office?"

"Um. Gert sent me to pick up some papers." She kept her voice even. "It's a very nice office. I'm not overly excited about lawyers, but her surroundings put you at ease." *At least until she does that "get back to the gutter where you belong" thing with her eyes.*

Lucy wasn't sure, but she thought Boone saw her differently than his sister did. Not exactly trustfully, but not with total disdain, either.

Right now, he was frowning at her. "So what's there?"

She must have missed something. "Huh?"

"What's on the wall in Kelly's office?"

Oh. She lifted her glass and drained her tea before getting up. "You'll have to see for yourself."

Chapter Three

"When I suggested you come here, this wasn't quite what I envisioned."

Lucy started to tell the owner of the large Nikes not to step on her freshly waxed floor, but the order stopped in her throat. "Crockett!" Delighted, she came to her bare feet to hug the tall man with curly dark hair and a smile framed by the deepest dimples she'd ever seen. "What are you doing here?"

"Came to check on you, of course."

"Yeah, right. You knew I'd land on my feet, especially considering where you sent me. Gert Taylor wouldn't allow anything less on her watch."

Noah Crockett ruffled her hair and tapped the end of her nose. "And *have* you landed on your feet?"

"I think so. Gert's wonderful, and I like Taft. The tearoom's going like gangbusters. Gert even had to hire someone to mow the yard and work in the garden because we didn't have enough time to do it all. A kid named Jack that I've decided to keep for a little brother—I never had one, you know." Shadows darkened his blue eyes. The creases in his lean cheeks seemed deeper than they had only weeks ago. "You seem tired, my friend."

"I *am* tired. That's why I'm on vacation." But there was more in his shadowy eyes than weariness. He seemed wired with a tension she'd never seen in him before.

Suddenly, it was as though all the light had gone out of the room, though the sun still shone brightly through the windows' sparkling panes. Noah's attention strayed to a point beyond her, and the tension in him became almost a palpable thing.

She knew before she turned that Boone stood there. In the days since his arrival, it was as though she'd sprouted antennae where he was concerned. The good part of that was that it made it easier to avoid him. The bad part was discovering she didn't really want to. She liked rooms better when he was in them.

But this wasn't the loose-limbed man she was coming to know. This Boone Brennan stood tall and taut and dangerous, his dark eyes nearly black and his generous mouth set in a straight, hard line.

She didn't think she liked this Boone.

Crockett broke the noisy silence first. "Boone."

"Crockett."

"Lucy?" Gert's voice preceded her. Walking with her head down, she bumped into Boone's straight-as-a-board back, sending him slithering across the still-wet floor, his arms windmilling backward for balance. When he reached the portion of board that had not yet been waxed, his feet stopped abruptly, but his forward motion did not.

Crockett caught him before he fell, and for a moment the two big men stood suspended in an awkward embrace that would have been hilarious if there hadn't been such a big cloud of tension in the room. They withdrew from each other's touch, but still avoided eye contact like two little boys who had been ordered to apologize but didn't know how.

"Thanks," Boone muttered, and turned away.

"No problem." Crockett's eyes followed him for a few tortured seconds before he said briskly, "Hey, Aunt Gert, are you still going to run away with me when I grow up? I'll carry your knapsack and everything."

"Take a number," Lucy suggested, her gaze following Boone as Crockett went to hug Gert, skirting the wet wax. "Would you all get on out of here now, so I can finish this floor before we open on Monday?"

Her arm tucked through Crockett's, Gert led her nephew into the hallway. "Come into the kitchen. I'm baking pies and can't stop in the middle. You can tell me what you've been doing."

Lucy resumed waxing. Boone stood silent and moody by the window. "Are you all right?" she asked.

He nodded, and abruptly got to his knees beside her. "You got another cloth? I'll help, since you have to redo where I went skating."

They worked in silence for a few minutes, then Lucy said, "He's your best cousin, isn't he? And your best friend?"

"Cousins, no. Kelly's and my uncle married his

aunt when we were all little kids. All three of us used to visit for the same few weeks in the summer, so we sort of grew up together. Kelly and I came to live here when I was twelve and she was ten. A year or so later, Crockett's folks got divorced and rather than do the Solomon thing of splitting him up, they let him go altogether and he came here too." He stared into space, his lips lifted in a half smile. "Best friends? Once upon a time." The words were clipped, and he rubbed doggedly at the wood floor. "Aunt Gert needs to polyurethane these suckers if she's going to have everyone in town parading over them."

"Sims has told some stories." She didn't want him to stop talking about the family they had been.

"I'll just bet he has. Crockett and I both worked at the station when we were in high school. It's amazing the business survived." He reached the edge of the room and sat back on his heels. "We'd do our homework while we were there. Sims would check it when he came to close up. If it wasn't done, he'd dock our wages. Pretty soon he got wise to the fact that I did Crockett's English and he did my math. Then there was hell to pay."

"What happened?"

He pushed himself to his feet, his knees cracking. "We both graduated—not exactly at the top of our class, but not in the 'get 'em out of here, they're beyond help' category, either."

She knelt before the fireplace, her gaze reaching up to meet his. "I mean, what happened with you and Crockett?"

He hesitated, pain settling into the planes of his face, darkening his eyes to the point she could scarcely distinguish the pupil from the iris.

"We both loved the same woman," he said quietly, and left the room.

She was still kneeling motionless on the marble frontispiece of the fireplace when the front door opened.

"Aunt Gert?" Kelly called.

For a reason she couldn't have begun to explain, Lucy wanted to stop Kelly's advance, to warn her of Noah Crockett's presence. But before any words could leave her mouth, Crockett stepped out of the kitchen. Kelly came to a dead stop at the bottom of the staircase, the color draining from her face. She clutched the newel post, her knuckles turning white. Panic trembled from every rigid line of her slender body.

"Kelly!" Lucy came to her feet and stepped gingerly across the floor. "You're just in time to help me with…you know, with that thing we talked about. Come on up to my room."

She grasped Kelly's arm and pulled her along, chattering meaninglessly until they reached the second floor hallway. Opening the door to her room, she pushed the other woman inside. "Sit down," she ordered. "I'll get you some water."

When Lucy came out of the small bathroom that adjoined her bedroom, Kelly was sitting on the edge of one of the chairs at the window, her gaze aimed toward the river. She accepted the glass Lucy offered. Finally, several sips later, she spoke.

"Isn't it amazing how you can go for years existing on the same planet with someone and not see them even when they're right in front of you? I've always been able to avoid him. When he visited Aunt Gert, I'd stay away. When he came to the weddings of mutual friends, I sat on the other side and pretended he wasn't there. At Christmas or Thanksgiving, if he was here, we managed to be in separate rooms or at opposite ends of the table. Even at Maggie's funeral, when Boone was depending on us both, I didn't have to confront him."

The suffering in her voice was so intense it seemed as though one should be able to touch it and push it aside. Having no idea how to do that, Lucy sat in the other chair and chewed at her thumbnail. Kelly was Gert's dearly loved niece—far better for her to be angry than in this paralyzing pain. "I don't know," Lucy said. "Till recently, my future's always been my problem, not my past."

Kelly's gaze met hers across the cloth-covered round table that sat between the chairs. The brown eyes, so like Boone's, glittered with animosity. "Ah, yes, your mysterious past."

Lucy thought it might be kind of fun to slap the scorn right off Kelly Brennan's face, but that would be counter-productive. "Better the devil you know than the devil you don't," her father used to say. She knew and was used to Kelly's disdain even though she'd never grasped the reason for it.

But the memory of that almost palpable pain remained, and Lucy sensed the stilted climate of their relationship was a little bit changed. Even the return of the familiar contempt was tempered by those moments of human frailty.

"My past isn't a mystery," Lucy said. "It's way too much of an open book. I'm surprised you haven't discovered that for yourself. Isn't that what lawyers do?"

"Not when Gert Brennan's their aunt, they don't. They have to use an entirely different playbook." For just a moment, humor gleamed on Kelly's face, and the resemblance to Boone was uncanny.

Lucy hesitated. "You know, you could have just asked."

"I did. I asked Aunt Gert. She said it was none of my business."

The resentful tone in Kelly's voice made Lucy want to laugh. She shook her head. "I meant you could have asked me."

"No, I couldn't. Aunt Gert wouldn't let me. She gave me the look—you've seen that, haven't you, where she sighs and rolls her eyes?—and told me to leave it alone. She said that people are entitled to their privacy and she didn't pay all that money to send me to law school so I could be a two-bit snoop."

Lucy couldn't help it. The laughter burst free. She had been the recipient of "the look" herself, accompanied by hands on hips and Birkenstock-clad feet shoulders' width apart.

"I'm sorry," she said to Kelly's glare. "Really I am. But did you know you and your brother both do the whole eye-roll and sigh thing as well as Gert does? I'm not naturally quiet, but when any of you puts your hands on your hips, I just shut up and go on about my business."

A hint of a smile lit Kelly's eyes, although her features didn't relax an iota. "And what would that business be? Exactly what do you want from Aunt Gert?"

Boone's voice came from the open door. "Good question. I couldn't even have a piece of pie because Aunt Gert said it was 'yours'—after she smacked me with a spatula. Exactly what is it you need an entire pie for?"

He slouched against the doorframe, arms folded loosely over his chest. Lucy's heart tripped over itself in immediate response to his presence even as resentment rose into her throat.

She got up. "Well, there you have it. I'm going to get the pie analyzed so I can mass-market it. And don't you know, she's changed her will? I stand to inherit her entire wardrobe of Birkenstocks. Maybe the two of you can start drawing up whatever kind of document it is that contests wills." She stalked out of the room, pushing past him, anger and hurt at war in her chest.

It wasn't until she was in the parlor setting tables for Monday's lunch that she wondered why Kelly had been so upset by Crockett's arrival. And who was Maggie? Why had Kelly and Crockett been at her funeral and why had Boone depended on them?

Boone was waiting for her when she came out of the parsonage later that day. He leaned against the gate that led to River Walk—the cobblestone path that meandered beside the Twilight—and watched her approach.

"Why didn't you just tell me?" he asked.

Her glare took over her whole face. "Tell you what?"

He didn't know how she could stare down her nose at him when he was so much taller than she was, but she managed. He sighed. "That the pie was for the church supper and the reason Aunt Gert said it was yours was that you'd baked it."

Lucy walked past him, edging a little sideways so they didn't touch. "Because you'd pretty much already made up your mind that I was going to steal the recipe and become the next Mrs. Fields, only with pie instead of cookies," she said. "You and your sister have decided I'm a bad seed blown into Taft for the express purpose of taking advantage of Gert. I'm not going to waste my life defending myself against that."

God, she walked fast for someone with such short legs. They were very nice legs, it was true, but undeniably short. Her height, what there was of it, was in her torso. Boone double-stepped to catch up with her. "I explained to you how much she means to us."

"Yes, you did, and I explained to you that I wasn't going to bilk her of all her worldly goods. You act as though you believe me, then every time I turn around, you're throwing little verbal darts." She stopped and he almost ran over her. "Well, let me tell you this—" she faced him and poked his chest with one stubby-nailed finger, "—I bleed just like anyone else does and I'm tired of being picked at."

"You're right."

"Furthermore, if you and Crockett can't stand to be in the same room with each other, that's fine, but you worry your aunt to death. She says she expects to go up to the third floor and find a white line down the middle of the sitting room, dividing your half from his. You're adults, for God's sake, way up in your thirties. It's time you acted like it."

"You're right."

He'd heard that old aphorism where a guy told a woman, "You're beautiful when you're angry," and had always thought it was ridiculous. Lucy Dolan's ire did nothing to change that opinion. Her nose got red when she was mad. Not the slightly sunburned pink he found captivating, but honest-to-God-in-heaven Rudolph-red. Her cheeks were white in contrast, with a spray of freckles standing out like little beacons. Butterscotch-colored hair sprang loose from the French braid that was supposed to be confining it. Perspiration gathered in the hollow of her throat before rolling down into the scoop neck of her shirt and driving him crazy.

Crazy enough he lost track of where she was in her tirade. Playing it safe, he said, "You're right," again. Sims had always told him he couldn't go wrong by agreeing with a woman, even if she was wrong. Not that Sims had ever learned his own lesson—he argued with every word Gert said to him, but still…

"Stop saying that."

Boone gave Lucy an outraged sigh. "Saying what? I haven't said anything except that you're right." For good measure, he added, "You're pretty when you're mad." Because somehow she was, ridiculous old saying or no.

"Oh, sure, all I need is clown makeup to go with my Ronald McDonald nose," she scoffed, but laughter shimmered in her eyes.

"I like Ronald McDonald," he said. "He's one of the good guys. Will you go to the church supper with me? I'll even buy your ticket."

She hesitated, and he gave her his best smile, the one that had convinced Cassandra Whittenberger to… Oh, hell, back into puberty again.

"I'll behave," he promised. "I won't cast any aspersions on your character or the color of your nose. I won't break Crockett's pretty face. I'll even—" he stuck out his chest manfully, "—protect you from my sister. And I won't tell Aunt Gert you covet her Birkenstocks."

"That is something to consider. We wouldn't want her to know just how mercenary I am."

"That's what I thought."

"Okay," she agreed, "I'll go with you as long as we can walk over."

"You can't car date yet?" he said. "Aunt Gert's getting strict in her old age. You must be, what, twenty-eight?" He knew if he was stupid enough to guess a woman's age, he needed to err to the low side.

"Thirty-three." Her long-suffering sigh assured him the flattery had been wasted. "Old enough to know better than to get into a vehicle with you."

"You wound me," he protested. "I'll have you know I've never had an accident."

"Really?" The smile in her eyes belied the skepticism in her voice. "How many have you caused?"

"One, maybe, only the other driver took responsibility, so I—" He stopped. How could this conversation possibly come out well for him?

"Rescued her?"

"Yes, that was it. That's what I did." He had to touch her hair, to see if it really was as sun-hot and silk-soft as it appeared. He reached with a hesitant hand to stroke back one of the tendrils that had strayed from the braid, and didn't want to draw his hand away. It was just that hot and just that soft and he wanted to pull it loose from its plait and bury his face in it. What in the *hell* was wrong with him? "Six-thirty?"

She nodded. The movement of her head forced

his hand to cup her cheek. Really it did. Her skin was as silk-soft as her hair.

"I'll walk you home," he offered, and she nodded again, not drawing away from his hand on her face for a strange little space of time. When they started walking again, it was in silence, but she didn't move away then, either. They were close enough that their hands bumped occasionally, and he had to stifle an urge to grasp her fingers and swing their hands like they were kids making their first explorations into the world of touch.

She pulled open the door of the newspaper office. "I need to pay for the ad we put in every week."

"Hey, Lucy." A tall man in a University of Kentucky sweatshirt and jeans stepped out of the glass-walled office that had Editor on its door. "It's my day for receptionist duty. Would you like some coffee?"

Lucy shook her head. "No, thanks. I've had your coffee before. I just want to pay for the ad. Micah Walker, do you know Gert's nephew Boone? He's here for the summer to keep an eye on...things."

Micah grinned. "We were in the same high school yearbook, Lucy, just different years. Taft better batten down its hatches. I saw Crockett earlier today. I don't know if the town can hold both of you again."

Boone shook hands with him. "Hey, *you* came back after twenty years away and it's still standing. Shaken, but standing. Micah probably hasn't mentioned this," he said to Lucy, "but he, Tom Simcox, and Eli St. John were known as the Triangle of Terror. They left a reputation in their wake that the rest of us were powerless to equal."

"But God knows you and Crockett tried," Micah said dryly. His gaze behind his glasses became speculative. "Want to draw me some strips while you're here? Exclusive to the *Trib*? We can't pay your usual rate, but we'll run you up some nice business cards and advertise all your garage sales free of charge. As an added incentive, you know."

"I'd like that." Boone leaned his elbows on the counter. "I've got a new strip scrambling around in my mind called 'Eight Hours Work'. Want to be the guinea pig? And maybe write copy for it while you're at it? Didn't you used to do that with a cartoonist while you were in Lexington, pre-Pulitzer?"

Micah laughed. "Yeah, I did, though we never sold much. I'd like to do it again, though." He extended his right hand across the counter and the men shook hands again while Lucy observed in mild shock.

"Just like that?" she asked. They were both successful, handsome men—she might even go so far as to describe them as "hunky" if she were caught unawares. Surely forging a partnership would require a lot more noise and testosterone than what she'd just witnessed.

They looked at her, then at each other. "Yeah," they said in unison.

"This is Taft," Boone reminded her. "The home of no one special. He and Tom and Eli were kick-ass-and-take-names seniors when Crockett and I were freshmen with brand new backpacks. I had Micah's number in basketball. Crocket had Tom's. Everybody knew everybody else. Far as I can tell, they still do."

She knew that. It's what had made her give in to Crockett's urgings to come here. But it still surprised her that a prize-winning journalist and an internationally syndicated cartoonist conducted business in a way that seemed unconnected to the twenty-first century.

The receptionist—the real one—came to the counter, her brow furrowed with concern. "Gert just called." Her glance moved between Lucy and Boone. "She'd like for you two to come home. Sims has been hurt."

"Go," Micah said instantly. "You can pay for the ad later, Lucy. Take my car." He reached into his pocket for his keys. "And let Lucy drive," he called after them. "I think Gert needs for you to get there in one piece."

Chapter Four

Boone seemed to pay a lot more attention to the road if he wasn't actually driving on it. "The light was red," he commented, after she'd turned off Main Street.

"It's legal to turn right on red if no one's coming," she assured him. *And I used a turn signal and actually checked before I turned.*

"Go slow here. St. John always has a bunch of kids running around at the church. Most of them are his."

"I know." *I go to that church, I shake hands with Eli St. John every Sunday, the women's group meets at the tearoom, and I take my turn in the nursery. I'm the one that's here, not you.* Resentment nipped and flamed, and she had to bite down on her lower lip.

"Aren't you going to slow down before you turn? Mr. Morgan's crossing the street."

Mr. Morgan, walking his sheltie, was nowhere near the intersection in question. Only the tight lines of concern on Boone's face saved him. Lucy was not a proponent of violence, but she thought exceptions could be made. "Why don't you try to calm down?" she suggested. "Gert doesn't need anyone being hysterical."

It was the wrong thing to say.

"I told you Gert's everything to Kelly and me." His words were so terse they sounded as though they'd been snapped off like fresh green beans in nervous fingers. "That's not entirely accurate. Gert became our mother, but after Uncle Mike died, Sims was our father, too." He glared at her, then turned his eyes back toward the street. "The nosy old goat."

Gert, Crockett and Kelly were all standing on the porch when they got home, so Lucy stopped Micah's SUV at the curb. Boone was out of the vehicle before she had the key in the off position, loping up the brick path to the porch and taking the steps two at a time.

Gert raised her voice, so Lucy could hear as she approached. "He's going to be all right. I won't even consider the alternative." She had her hands on her hips, her purse hanging from one arm. When tears slipped down her cheek, she swiped them away with an impatient palm. "Martha Kline was bringing that big old Lincoln she drives in for maintenance when the brakes gave out completely. Sims was walking across the lot and the car bumped him. He hit his head on the pump island when he fell." Her voice wobbled dangerously, and Boone put an arm around her. "Damn fool should have retired years ago. Maybe now he will." She tucked her purse under her arm and moved purposefully away from Boone. "They've taken him to the hospital in Cincinnati. I'm going there now."

"Not by yourself, you're not." Boone's face was

white under his tan, his eyes dark again. The ring of keys he confiscated from his aunt rattled in his shaking hand.

Lucy wondered why he was trembling, but Crockett seemed to understand.

"I'll take her," he said easily, stepping forward.

Boone hesitated, then nodded, handing the keys to Crockett. "I'll go down and take care of the station. You'll call?"

"As soon as we know anything." Crockett took Gert's arm and started down the steps.

"I'm coming too." Kelly's chin jutted.

"Then step on it," Crockett said shortly, "and don't have any tantrums. No one has time for that now."

Lucy drove Boone to the service station before returning Micah's car to its parking spot. Having delivered the keys to their owner, she stood for a moment on the sidewalk outside the newspaper office, almost stepping foot-to-foot in indecision.

She didn't know what to do. The work was caught up at the tearoom as was the housekeeping in the private quarters. Even the laundry was done—the sheets dried on lines that stretched between T-posts in the backyard. Jack had mowed the lawn and helped her weed the garden. Free time was a commodity she hadn't had much of since arriving in Taft, and now that she had it, she didn't want it. She needed busyness to keep Sims's kind face from superimposing itself on her mind along with the memory of Boone's tortured expression when he'd taken Gert's keys.

He hadn't wanted to go to the hospital. Everyone else had known why—Lucy'd seen understanding in their features as Crockett took the responsibility of transporting Gert.

She wished she understood, too.

You're an outsider. You've been one all your life, so why is it all of a sudden a big deal?

Because she didn't want to be outside anymore. She wanted to be in Kelly's place as the comforter, holding Gert's hand against the fear that masked the older woman's face. Or she wanted to be Crockett, the rescuer, driving everyone where they needed to go. Even Jack had run to clean the windshield of Gert's car because she always parked it under the sycamore tree and the birds used its windows for a bathroom.

Lucy thought about Boone down at the service station and wondered what role he played. If this were a movie, he'd be the hero who managed to be both tortured and funny. But in real life, Boone was as alone as she was. He pumped gas and checked oil in the place of the man who'd been a father to him, probably praying and cursing in equal amounts.

Well.

Lucy could damn well pump gas too. She'd always done it for herself before coming to Taft, where there were only two stations and full service was a given. She could clean windshields too, as long as she had a step stool. Boone didn't have to be alone. Checking oil could be a problem—she wouldn't know a dipstick from a kitchen skewer—but she could learn.

And maybe, just maybe, Lucy didn't have to be on the outside. At least for right now.

She'd learned not to count on more than that.

"Everyone's just buying a few dollars' worth. They're really stopping to find out how Sims is doing," Boone said when she approached, staring with consternation at the cars lined up at the pumps.

"I can help."

"Go for it." He pulled a wad of bills out of his pocket and handed her some fives, tens, and ones, then brought a handful of coins out of another pocket. "There's your bank. Give me a holler if someone wants their oil checked."

She grimaced the first time she splattered gasoline on her shoes, grinned when a carload of teenagers asked for seventy-seven cents' worth and paid in pennies, and laughed when Eli St. John offered to trade a couple of children for a tank of regular.

"That's not very Christian of you," she chided the minister, pumping his gas while he used the squeegee on the windows of his van.

"Sure it is. I'll give you some of the good ones. They're housebroken and everything." Eli's features sobered. "I'm on my way to the hospital. Have you heard anything yet?"

She shook her head. "Crockett said he'd call."

Eli nodded in Boone's direction. "He doing all right?"

"I think so." But she didn't know, not really. Boone laughed and joked with the customers, but his eyes were dark and impenetrable.

"Call if either of you needs me." Eli raised a hand to wave at Boone. "Have cell phone, will travel." He patted Lucy's shoulder before getting into the car.

"Thanks. Is the church supper all set up?"

"Some of the ladies are taking care of it. I'll try to get back before it's over."

She watched Eli's aging minivan drive away, marveling anew at the closeness of the little community where she found herself.

Jack rode his bicycle onto the lot. "Is Mr. Sims okay?"

"We don't know yet, but I hate to think what Gert will do to him if he's not." Lucy smiled and ruffled his already messy hair with a tentative hand.

He didn't pull away, which showed her the extent of his concern. So did his words. "I'd like to help."

"You'll be able to," she promised, "and now you'd better move your bike. We're developing a line." She waved at the two cars waiting for service. "See you later, Jack."

During a lull, Boone approached her. "Full service still closes at five on Saturdays, right?"

She nodded. "But I don't know how to set the pumps up so credit card users can still get gas. Do you?"

"Yeah, I found the instructions. Can you take

care of this out here while I start shutting down the inside?" He squinted at the clock inside the station. "It's twenty after. I don't think anyone will say we closed too early."

The phone rang a few minutes later, its outside bell jangling. Lucy paused in sweeping the concrete-paved lot. Boone picked it up on the first ring. As he talked, he caught her gaze through the plate glass window and raised one hand in a familiar gesture, the thumb and index finger forming a circle. *Okay.*

Relief flowed through her, making her feel limp. She nearly dropped the broom. *Thank You, God.*

When he'd hung up, he leaned out the door. "Come on. We're going to have to hustle if we want to make that dinner not smelling like unleaded gas."

"Oh," she said, "I forgot."

"She forgot a date with me," he told the skies, lifting a hand in supplication. "I've lost my touch."

"Put this away." She shoved the broom at him. "It's not a date, you ninny. We're just going to the same place at the same time. Like now, when we're going home. What did Crockett say? Was he the one who called?"

He sobered. "Yeah. He says Sims has some broken bones and will be down for a while, but he'll be okay. Probably in a semi-permanent state of pissed-off, but that doesn't have to do with his injuries."

She watched as he locked the door and then fell into step beside him. "The inactivity will drive him crazy."

The comment made her think of her father, whose body hadn't failed him even as his mind had. In one of the lucid moments before Alzheimer's had gone into its later stages, he'd mentioned that. *"It's too bad I can't give this body to someone who still has the mind to use it. It seems like such a waste."*

A chill rippled down her spine with the memory.

"Where are you, Lucy John?" Boone's voice reached her, gentle and quiet. "You've gone away." He propped an arm around her, held in place by hooking a hand on her shoulder. It was a comforting thing. A warming thing that eradicated the chill.

And more. It made her aware of the strength of the man who walked at her side, of the depth of his caring. It made her think about being in his arms with nothing but moonlit darkness between them.

"Just remembering my father," she said, thinking she should move away from his touch.

"He's dead?" He steered her around a sycamore root that had created a small mountain range in the sidewalk. "What about your mother?"

"She died when I was five. An aneurysm. She came into the kitchen saying, 'Oh, Johnny, I have such a headache,' and just that quickly she was gone. I don't think he ever fully recovered from the shock of it."

A shudder ran through the arm around her. Even the side of his body quaked. The agony in his face was startling in its intensity.

"That's what...Maggie, my wife..." He stopped, regaining his composure. "We were dancing around the room when she said that, what your mother said about the headache, and then she left me. She never spoke again."

"Oh," she said. "Oh, Boone, I'm so sorry." Words failed her then.

She slipped her arm around his waist as they turned onto Twilight Park Avenue.

"But she didn't die." He went on as though Lucy hadn't spoken. It was her turn to steer him. His eyes were open, but he wasn't watching where he was going—rather, he was staring somewhere inside himself, somewhere deep and painful. His cheeks were pale, his mobile features carved and still. "I called 911 and they took her to the hospital. They kept her alive with machines for seven days. I knew she was gone, her parents knew she was gone, but we couldn't let her heart stop beating. There was nothing more that could be done, no hope she would recover, and I had to let her go. I had to." His voice was strained, sounding as though he were forcing the words out one by painful one.

Perhaps he was.

"Of course you did, but that didn't make it any easier, did it?"

He shuddered again as they stepped onto the porch of Tea on Twilight. She laced her fingers through his. She couldn't protect him from the pain, but maybe she could absorb some of it.

"No, and I've never forgiven myself for it. Neither has Crockett."

Lucy startled into motionlessness. "What do you mean?"

"I know there's a part of him that thinks if Maggie had married him, she'd still be alive and well—" he pushed the door open and nudged her inside before removing his arm from around her, "—and there's a part of me that agrees with him."

"Never?" Boone stared at Lucy in disbelief. "It's impossible to have lived over thirty years in the United States and never have been to a church supper."

"No, it's not," she said calmly, fluffing at the hair that framed her face in soft curls. "We didn't go to church as I was growing up, and even when I started going, I didn't get involved. It seemed like there was never enough time." She examined the sundress she wore, seeming to take offense to the sight of her suntanned knees and sandaled feet. "You're sure this is okay for it?"

He latched onto her arm and pulled her out the door. "If that dress was any more okay, Eli would be raffling you off to make money for the church. You know the man has no conscience."

She laughed, shrugging off his arm and running down the steps ahead of him. "He wouldn't get very much out of me. I'm generic, not a name brand."

"You have a skewed sense of self-worth," he commented, catching up and moving to the street side.

The smile she flashed at him was bright but brittle. "Life is skewed, Boone."

"So it is." He knew that, but he wished *she* didn't.

She wore an air of naiveté he didn't want to see diminished. It gave him an uncommon wish to protect, much like he felt with Kelly. But different. Way different. He reached for her hand as they approached the corner, liking the feel of her small fingers laced in his.

"But it's good," she added cheerfully, raising her free hand to wave to Micah Walker and his wife, Landy. "Not always, but sometimes. You need to hold onto the good things to get you through the bad."

Ah, there it was, the innocence that gleamed from her. Even if he wasn't sure he believed it entirely, he enjoyed it. Boone laughed aloud, feeling delivered.

The dinner was as all church dinners were—noisy and delicious. Boone and Lucy answered questions concerning Sims's condition so often, they took to offering the information before the query was made. Finally, using a ladle as a microphone, Eli announced to all and sundry that Sims would be fine, though all prayers would be appreciated.

Lucy was so delighted when her pie was the first one to be all gone that Boone delivered an impromptu lecture on humility that had their entire table laughing.

It was dark when they headed home, the air heavy with humidity and thick with awareness. They walked slowly, their hands together and their heads dipping close so that they could speak in low tones. The atmosphere felt so electric, Boone wondered if a storm was coming. The cloudless, moonless sky told him the electricity was personal and physical, conducted by leaf-green eyes and hands with nails bitten to the quick.

Lucy may not have considered the evening a date, but Boone had. His first since Maggie's death. Well, not exactly. It wasn't the first time he'd taken a woman out, bought her dinner, and taken her home. No, it was much more than that.

It was the first time he'd wanted to.

"Hot chocolate?" she asked when they walked into the silent house.

"Sure." He followed her to the kitchen, going to check the messages on the old-fashioned answering machine. There were no calls from Cincinnati, so he ignored the others and sat on a counter stool to wait.

He watched her move around the kitchen, her movements quick and sure as she poured the milk and measured the chocolate. Her hips had a subtle curve and sway under the bright sundress that held his attention. He wouldn't need whipped cream with this chocolate—she was delicious topping enough on her own.

But who was she?

She was from Richmond, she'd worked in a restaurant, her parents were dead and she knew Crockett. The description covered everyone in his family and many of his friends and it didn't narrow things down much.

She said she wanted a future, but exactly what

kind of future was she talking about and how did she intend to go about securing it? Had Crockett talked enough about his rich aunt that Lucy had set out to ingratiate herself? Crockett wasn't stupid by any means, but he wouldn't be the first man duped by false innocence.

That was what Kelly thought had happened, but it didn't quite ring true with Boone.

In the first place, Aunt Gert wasn't anybody's fool. Other than Crockett's, she'd never been taken in by a pretty face, and since he was her nephew—Crockett's mother was Gert's sister—Boone supposed that didn't count.

Secondly, in Boone's experience, which admittedly was confined to watching television and reading newspapers, people who set out to bilk others of their worldly goods did so because they weren't willing to work at making an honest living. Most of them didn't work in gas stations with no thought of being paid. They didn't stand on ladders to polish chandeliers, dismantle toilets to remove toys that had been flushed by small patrons, or help recalcitrant students study for chemistry exams.

Lucy had done all of those things this week. Jack had been reluctant to accept help with his homework, although he was happy with the cookies and milk Lucy offered. She'd nagged him until he sat at the island with his books and answered the questions she fired at him while she worked. When he'd wanted to give up, she bribed him with more cookies.

Gert'd asked if she'd ever considered teaching. Lucy said she hadn't.

Jack'd said that was a good thing, because she was godawful at chemistry.

Boone laughed, remembering Lucy's indignation and the cup of ice she'd dumped on the boy's head. Then Jack had taken out the trash without being asked, exchanging grins with Lucy when she opened the door for him.

"Where did Jack come from?" Boone took the cup of steaming chocolate Lucy handed him.

She sat beside him. "I don't know. He was already working here when I came." She smiled fondly. "He's a nice kid."

Boone nodded. "Seems to be."

They drank their chocolate, making desultory conversation, then Lucy stood, gathering their cups and putting them upside down in the dishwasher. "I enjoyed the dinner," she said. "Thank you."

"I did, too." He watched her disappear up the back stairs, then wandered through the house checking locks. He didn't want to think about the last reason he'd nearly decided to trust Lucy, although it was working its way around the edges of his mind. He started up the front steps at a sprint. If he could just get into his third-floor bedroom before the thought developed fully, he could escape it. He could shuck his jeans and crawl into bed and think about the strip or about an idea for the political cartoons he occasionally drew.

Then he'd fall asleep, having survived another day without…her.

But he didn't make it. By the time he reached the first landing, with its faceted round window displaying the light of the full moon, Maggie's face filled his mind and her laughter echoed softly through his heart. He could almost feel her hand on his face, nearly heard her voice as he remembered her saying, "Of course Elmer and Myrtle love each other, just like Sims and Gert do. What would ever make you think I can't see into your heart?"

He rounded the second landing of the staircase and lifted his head as a familiar scent touched his nose lightly, like a feather drifting past. Lilac. Maggie had always smelled of lilacs. Of spring. Of eternal hope.

"For our dreams," she used to say, dropping change from her purse into the crystal bowl that sat on her piano—the parlor grand he'd bought her when he'd signed the contract for the first collection book of "Elmer and Myrtle" cartoons.

By the time he closed his bedroom door, the pain had engulfed him. On auto-pilot, he opened the slatted blinds to let the moonlight and its shadows into the room before sinking onto the bed to lie on his back and stare at the angled ceiling. If he lay still and tried to force his mind to go blank and empty, sometimes the pain would ebb away to numbness and allow him to sleep.

Lucy kept her dreams in a glass pickle jar on Aunt Gert's counter. The fact that she kept them at all was the third reason he couldn't think she was less than honest.

He'd buried his own dreams in a cemetery outside of Taft under a stone that read, "Maggie Brennan. Beloved wife and daughter." He no longer believed in dreams or the future or hope.

Reaching into the wastebasket that sat between the bed and the desk, he took out the beer can he'd placed in it the night before. He crushed it slowly in one hand, working at it.

And realized that even though he didn't believe in any of those things, meeting Lucy Dolan had made him wish he did.

Chapter Five

"I never realized how hard Sims and Aunt Gert worked."

Crockett, Boone, Kelly and Lucy sat around the table in the sunroom off the kitchen. The weary remark had come from Kelly, but any of them could have said it. The three days since Sims's accident had been long and difficult.

"Why don't we close the tearoom, at least for the summer?" Boone suggested. "Aunt Gert's bound and determined she's going to take care of Sims when he comes home, and she can't do both. We can't close the gas station—I'm as scared of Sims now as I was when I was in high school."

"No." Lucy sipped sweet tea with a frown, thinking she'd added too much mint when she brewed it.

"No?" Kelly's voice rose and thinned with the word. "Need I remind you that this is still *our* aunt's home, and none of us has the time to run the tearoom *and* this house? Crockett will be going back to Virginia any day now. I have a practice that needs my attention. Even Boone has business he has to conduct."

"So do I," Lucy said evenly, setting her glass down so no one would see her hand shaking. "I know this is your aunt's house, but that doesn't alter the fact that I pay to live in it or that I own half the business. I need to make a living, and the tearoom is how I do it. You're welcome to keep an eye on the books to make sure I don't abscond with the funds or the china, but Tea on Twilight isn't closing, even temporarily."

"I hardly think a handshake and a contract written on a notepad from a campaigning politician are things I can't get around if I need to in order to protect Aunt Gert's interests," Kelly said evenly. "I don't want to put you out on the street, but I wouldn't hesitate to do so if I thought it was best for her."

"Kelly!" Fury vibrated through Boone's voice. "This isn't a time for threats, nor has Lucy done anything to earn them. If you don't have anything constructive to suggest, why don't you go home?"

"Oh, for heaven's sake, Boone, she's a perfect stranger, another stray of Crockett's. Don't tell me you're taking her side." Tears glittered in Kelly's eyes.

As angry as she was, Lucy felt the pain and exhaustion of those tears and was sorry for it. She was as tired as Kelly was, and the street of dislike definitely went both ways. "Maybe I should—"

"Let's stop before everyone says things they don't mean." Crockett's voice was calm and patient—Lucy didn't know how he did it. "Everybody's tired."

Kelly spoke stiffly. "I won't be here tomorrow

or the next day. I have to be in court." When she got up, she knocked her glass to the floor, flinching when it shattered against the hardwood. "I'll make sure not to count that one against you when we inventory the dishes, Lucy."

She didn't clean it up, either, just left the house without further comment. The silence between Boone and Crockett was even louder than usual after she left, and Lucy wished they would go home, too. This had been such a happy house before they'd descended on it, the easygoing atmosphere not affected even by Kelly's snippiness, but the anger between the two men hovered like a dark cloud.

She went for the broom and dustpan, and when she came back to the sunroom, Crockett was gone and Boone was picking up the larger shards of glass and laying them carefully on his plate.

"I apologize for my sister," he said, taking the dustpan and holding it for her to sweep the splintered glass into. "I really don't know what her problem is."

"Well." Lucy shook her head, hoping to somehow dislodge the weariness from her soul as well as her voice. "It seems to be me." She took the dustpan from him. "Thank you."

He helped her carry the dishes into the kitchen. "How did you meet Crockett?" he asked, double-bagging the broken glass.

She wanted to say it was none of his business, but that would have sounded as though she had something to hide. And she didn't. There was a difference between hiding something and not wanting to talk about it.

"I told you before, he came into the restaurant where I worked," she said. "Even in a city the size of Richmond, servers become familiar with regulars. You know, calling them by name, pouring their coffee before they order it. After a while, you remember if the customer hates tomatoes or wheat toast or whatever. It was that way with Crockett, although I never knew his full name until he gave me a business card and told me to come to Indiana and call Gert." She closed the door of the dishwasher and turned it on, then leaned wearily against it. "I just called him Father."

He forgot sometimes.

Boone changed into running shoes and left the house as quietly as he could. He stopped to warm up, pushing against the sycamore tree in the front yard, then took off, heading toward downtown. It felt good to stretch his muscles. He slowed to a walk long enough to make sure everything was okay at the gas station—it was closed for the night, but the pumps were still open for business—then speeded up again. After the bridge, he turned onto the River Walk. He hated running on the cobbles that paved the path, but he loved the Walk and the sounds and smells of the river.

He waved at Eli St. John, who was running the other way with a couple of his kids, and kept going. He passed the park bench where he'd proposed to

Maggie on a sunny summer day, another one where he'd sat and wept after he lost her. Crockett had sat with him that time, neither speaking nor touching him.

In the three years since Maggie died, Boone had often wondered if the man who'd sat on the bench with him had been doing his job or being a friend. Unless he was going to mass, Crockett seldom wore his collar when he visited Taft. He was just the guy who'd once been his best friend, who had a tattoo of a coonskin cap high on his thigh that matched the one on Boone's—the only lasting result of a hilarious and often drunken spring break spent on a Florida beach.

However, being reminded of his former friend's vocation lightened a load Boone hadn't realized he carried.

Father Crockett had met Lucy first, he'd invited her to come to Taft, and he was fond of her. But he wasn't in love with her—Boone would know if he was. It wasn't like fifteen years ago when Noah Crockett had come home from Notre Dame for the weekend, bringing beautiful Maggie Martino to meet Aunt Gert. Boone had been there too, home from art school for the weekend. That was when they all learned that there really was such a thing as love at first sight.

Sweat was pouring off Boone when he got back to Main Street, and his legs felt rubbery when he slowed to cool down. By the time he reached the house on Twilight Park Avenue, however, he felt energized. He'd be able to draw for a couple of hours before going to sleep.

Lights were on in the kitchen, and he went in to find Lucy working at the island, a row of piecrusts arranged in front of her. "Why are you still up?" He filled a glass with orange juice and lifted the carton in mute invitation. "You were exhausted at dinner, even before Kelly had her tantrum."

Lucy shook her head, pointing at her teacup. "I don't always sleep well," she said, "so sometimes I bake in the middle of the night." She smiled as she poured hot lemon filling into two of the crusts. "My guilty conscience, remember?"

He held up the hand that wasn't holding his juice, palm out. *"Mea culpa."*

"You're forgiven." She placed plastic wrap across the surface of the pies and turned to put them in the huge refrigerator.

"But, in all seriousness, why *can't* you sleep? Have you seen a doctor?"

"I was my father's primary caregiver." Her voice was devoid of emotion, but her eyes looked haunted and dark. "Long after he didn't know who I was, he could still cook. We lived above the restaurant, and he would go down during the wee hours and start serving up meals to clientele who weren't there. I'd have to come down and talk him back up to bed. It was nothing for it to happen three times a night."

"How long has he been gone?"

"He died a little over a year ago, but he was gone way before that. Whoever first called Alzheimer's 'the long goodbye' had it exactly right." She went to the stove, stirring the pan of cherry pie filling that simmered there. "Even then, you're not really prepared. My life had been on hold for five years before Dad died. Everything I did revolved around him. I had no idea what to do with myself when he was gone and all the legal stuff was over, and I still wanted him back." Tears shone in her eyes, darkening them still further. "I still wanted my daddy, just like a little kid."

"I know." Boone finished his juice. "Our parents were killed in a car wreck when I was twelve and Kelly was ten. Twenty-some years later, I still want them sometimes. I just want to be able to tell them things." He went to refill the glass. "When Maggie and I got married, she set a picture of Mom and Dad on the altar with the candles, 'so they could see the whole thing,' she said." He couldn't help it—his voice grew thick with the memory. "My faith is iffy at the best of times, but I hope she's with them now, that they're taking care of each other. Maggie's mother says she believes they're together. It's helped her to cope."

"I hope so, too." Her gaze met his, and the tears spilled over, trailing starlike down her cheeks. "And I hope Dad's cooking for them."

Boone supposed as romantic moments went, this particular one was a failure, but he felt closer to Lucy than he had to anyone since Maggie. Not only emotionally close, but something else, too. He just wasn't ready to identify what it was, much less do anything about it.

"Well." He cleared his throat. "I'm going to bed. Anything I can help you with?"

She shook her head. "Good night."

He walked behind her to the back stairs, then stepped back to put a hand on her shoulder and massage lightly. "Don't let Kelly bother you, okay? I'm not close to her anymore, so I can't begin to explain what's wrong with her, but—I don't know—just give her a break, I guess. I'm not sure she deserves it, but I think she needs it."

"I'm all right." She turned far enough to meet his gaze. "I don't really think it's me she's mad at, just circumstances. We've all been there."

So they had. He grabbed his clean clothes from the table in the laundry room and went up to his room. He paused in the sitting area on the third floor landing. The door to Crockett's room was closed. Maggie had been the "circumstances" that had driven a wedge between them, and even though they were at least polite these days, they'd never become close again.

Boone missed his best friend.

"Come see what I found." Crockett's voice rang through the first floor, and Lucy came out of the kitchen, tossing a dish towel over her shoulder.

"Gert!" She embraced the older woman who stood in the parlor casting a critical eye on the tables already set for tomorrow's lunch. "You've lost weight. Come on in here and have something to eat while you tell me about Sims. I saved a piece of pie for Crockett, but you can have that, too. It's a nice big one."

"Thanks a lot, friend," Crockett said dryly. "I'm going down to take over for Boone at the station. One of us will take you back to Cincinnati in the morning, Aunt Gert," he promised, kissing his aunt's cheek.

"Nonsense." She batted his shoulder. "I can drive myself."

"Yeah, right. You taught Boone to drive. I can't in good conscience turn you loose on the interstate, much less on the city of Cincinnati. Just think how many people that would endanger. Lucy, you got anything you need me to deliver?"

"Four pies to Nancy Walker if you have time. She's hosting a retired teachers' meeting tonight. Ethan—you remember she's married to Micah Walker's father?—is going to work at the station, too, since he says he'll be in the way if he stays home, so you'll only have to be there a few hours, Crockett."

"Oh, good, I can see you all at once," Gert said. "I'll call Kelly and invite her over for dinner. I can let everyone in on what will happen when Sims comes home." Her gaze was apologetic when she met Lucy's eyes. "I plan on bringing him here. He's healing well for an old buzzard, but he can't handle the stairs at his house."

Lucy wanted to protest. Bringing Sims to Tea on

Twilight to convalesce would necessitate closing at least one of the serving rooms—the only bedroom downstairs was Gert's. Would the older woman want to close the tearoom while Sims healed? If she did, how would Lucy live during the down time? *I'll find a way. Jenny might hire me or maybe Sims would put me on the payroll. I've figured out what a dipstick is, at least.* The thought made her grin despite her concern. "Come have some lunch," she said. "It was that new quiche recipe. You can tell me what you think."

She emptied the dishwasher while her landlady ate and called Kelly at her office to issue an invitation to dinner. Lucy pondered the big room with its wide windows and open shelving. She could spend her whole life in this kitchen, with old and new so beautifully and comfortably mixed in its décor.

"Seven o'clock." Gert hung up the phone and rubbed her hands together. "Kelly works until six today. I'm cooking," she added decisively, "so you, my dear, have the rest of the afternoon off."

Lucy scanned the older woman's face, certain more lines had appeared over the past five days. "Don't you want to rest, Gert? I don't mind cooking."

"All I do at the hospital is rest. The nurses take wonderful care of Sims—I'm just there for him to complain at, which he's got down to a fine science. Now, be off with you."

"Okay, okay." Lucy put the last of the dishes away and took her apron into the laundry room. She loaded the day's tablecloths into the washer while she was in there, and when she came out, Boone was hugging Gert.

Lucy wished he was hugging her—that his hands were splayed over her ribs, his chin against her temple. Girl-type muscles she tried not to think about tightened in response to the idea of being in his arms, and she leaned against the counter. Weakness crept warmly down her legs, and she took a moment just to enjoy it.

"You've got close to three hours free." He met her eyes over his aunt's head. "What do you say we drive down to Rising Sun and hit the gambling boat there? We can probably win enough to buy red velvet wallpaper for when you turn the place into a brothel."

Lucy widened her eyes in mock outrage. "You told him we were going ahead with the bordello this year? I thought it was a secret."

"He pried it out of me." Gert flapped a hand at them. "Now, go on, you two, I'm going to make lasagna."

"Do I need to change?" Lucy took stock of her peach T-shirt and brown capris. At least she wasn't wearing the ingredients to anything. One thing growing up in a restaurant did for you was teach you to wear an apron.

"Nope. You'll be fine. Come on." Boone kissed the top of his aunt's head and reached for Lucy's hand.

"Wait." She pulled away and went over to her

pickle jar, rummaging among the coins, bills and pieces of paper until she came up with two twenties. "This is it," she said, waving the cash. "If I can't win enough with this, we're going to have to forget the wallpaper and make do with pasting up comics from the Sunday paper. We could make 'Elmer and Myrtle' a focal point and work from there."

In Boone's Jeep, Lucy buckled her seatbelt and settled into relaxation mode to enjoy the twenty-minute drive. Maybe if she closed her eyes, she could ride with Boone without panicking. Not likely, but anything was possible. "This was a good idea," she said, wondering if she had an allergy pill in her purse. Not that she was allergic to his driving—specifically—but one of the little pink caplets would help her relax. "I haven't been outside the city limits in a week." She closed her eyes—at least that way, she couldn't see whatever was coming. Besides, riding along with her eyes shut and the sun shining warm through the windows felt good. She tucked her knees up into the seat and pillowed her cheek on a soft sweatshirt he'd reached into the back for and handed her.

"The sign hasn't changed. No one was born or died this week." He said something else then, but she didn't quite catch what it was.

He woke her when he parked outside the casino. "Were you really that tired," he asked, "or should I take all that snoring personally?"

She grinned at him. "You forget that I've ridden with you before, so you can take it as personally as you like."

He laughed, reaching to tug at a curl that had sprung loose from her ponytail. "Come on. Let's go win your wallpaper."

Lucy hadn't been in a casino since a weekend restaurateur seminar in Atlantic City many years ago. She'd lost a week's worth of tips in her first hour on the glittering premises and sworn never to gamble again. This one was as bright and noisy as she remembered. However, there had been something added since her last venture. "They have penny slot machines," she said, pointing. "I want to play those."

He gestured. "Lead the way."

"Oh, look!" She charged ahead, assuming he would follow, and sat on the stool in front of the machine. "*Star Wars*. Jack and I have a running competition on who remembers the most from the movies and who should play Luke Skywalker in a remake. My bet's on Whatshisname from that soap opera, but Jack thinks he should do it."

"He who?"

"Jack." She smirked. "And I get to be Princess Leia. He promised."

"Ah." He sat at the machine beside her *Star Wars* one and stared with consternation at the Transformers. "Did he promise before or after you dumped the ice over his head?"

She fed her first twenty into the machine. "After,

but I'd just helped him with his history homework. Sort of."

"Wow, the kid has faith in you."

"Well, there was a little thing about me not baking any more of the cookies he likes and taking back the amount I pledged him for the football team fundraiser. Which I must admit I couldn't afford anyway. They're lifting weights, you know, and I had no idea Jack would be able to lift nearly as much as he can. We had to do a little bargaining or I'd be put in the clink for welching on my debts."

He'd lost his twenty dollars in half as many minutes. "I'm going over there," he said, gesturing vaguely. "I can't afford these damn pennies."

She stepped away from the machine fifteen minutes later and went to where Boone played blackjack. "Fifty-seven dollars!" she crowed, waving her receipt. "I'm quitting while I'm ahead."

Wearing a disgruntled expression, Boone cashed out too. "I'll quit while I'm behind—after losing the mortgage payment and grocery money but prior to bankruptcy. Want to walk around downtown?"

They parked in an angled parking spot on the little river town's main drag and meandered around, visiting an art gallery, a music store and the historical society. They went into a cozy bar in the basement of a restaurant across a narrow street from the Ohio River where they were the only patrons. At every business they entered, Lucy picked up a business card and tucked it away with her fifty-seven dollars. From the bar, she took a napkin. When the bartender offered her a book of matches, she shook her head. "Thanks, anyway."

"Tell me about the pickle jar," Boone requested as they walked along the river on the scenic path. "I've seen tip jars before—my wife even kept a big brandy snifter on top of her piano and I used to put money in it to tease her. But yours has more business cards and pieces of paper in it than it does money." When their hands bumped between them, he took hers. She thought about pulling away, but only for a moment. The truth was, she liked it when Boone Brennan touched her and so did those girl muscles that were already tightening and loosening in reaction.

This was, she decided, a truth she didn't want to examine too closely. The question he asked, though, was one that was fun to respond to because the answer was fun to remember.

"When I started waiting tables at Dolan's—that was Dad's restaurant—I wanted things, normal things like a car and cool clothes, but Dad said the only way I could get them was to help pay for them. Whatever I saved, he said, he'd match. While he was telling me this, standing there in the kitchen with the whole restaurant staff as witnesses, he rinsed out the pickle jar—the same one I still have back at the tearoom—and handed it to me. 'Here you go, kid,' he said, and I've been saving tips and wishes and dreams in it ever since." It was one of her best memories of her father, and she smiled with the telling of it. "Only problem is, no one gives me matching funds anymore."

"Business cards?" He reminded her of his original question. "Slips of paper?" He sat on a park bench and drew her down beside him. "Is that where the wishes and dreams come in?"

She left her hand in his. "A busboy named Andy started it. When I started scoping out cars when I was sixteen, he cut a picture of a used Camaro out of the paper and dropped it in the jar. Before the prom, I was waxing dramatic about what kind of dress I wanted and one of the waitresses put a magazine picture of this gorgeous black and white dress in there. My guidance counselor from high school, Mrs. Seaforth, came in one day and talked to Dad about me going to college and she left her business card." Lucy's smile faded. All these years later, the loss of that particular dream still hurt. "I put it in the jar."

"Did you go?" he asked. "To college, I mean."

"No. Every time it started to seem possible, something would happen to prove it wasn't. A few times, I even signed up." She brightened. "I've taken tons of classes, though. I *almost* have an associate's degree in the most extremely general of general studies you've ever seen."

He laughed. "So, what do you want to be when you grow up?"

"That's the nice part." She beamed at him. "Just what I am. I love restaurants, cooking, being with people. I want the education because I like knowing things. Some of the pieces of paper are about things like that. A lady came in one time and we got to talking about the dreams in the jar and she asked for an empty one of her own. I taught her to make foolproof piecrust and she taught me to decorate cakes. We each got to cross off one of our wishes, but the paper's still in the jar so I don't forget her."

As she warmed to what she was saying, heat from his arm sent tingles of awareness up the length of her. "A man from Italy who had immigrated here to be with his family taught me about pasta and I gave him English lessons," she went on a little breathlessly. *It's hot out here—that's all. And muggy. Sheesh, yeah, muggy.* "I got to be in the courtroom with him the day he became an American citizen. I never want to forget that, so I still have his business card with all the details of that day written on the back." She smiled with the sweetness of the memory, then felt herself blush. "Like the napkin from the bar today. That was fun, and I don't want to forget that, either."

He'd wanted to kiss her while they were sipping beer and talking. He hadn't said so, but she'd known. Another memory for the cache she kept behind her heart. Another wish for the jar. That was something she hadn't told him—or anyone else—that some dreams were both unspoken and unwritten. She just kept them close and didn't forget.

"I'll remember it." Although his smile was easy, like it always was, the message in his chocolate-brown eyes was not.

"Living with someone with Alzheimer's makes you paranoid about forgetting, I think," she said. "For a long time, I'd write things down for Dad and it would help, but we couldn't ever anticipate what would be the next thing." She blinked impatiently at the tears pushing in where they weren't wanted. Where they never did any good. "I was one of the lucky ones. Even though he eventually didn't know who I was, he still liked me. Every day required an introduction, but then he'd set out to charm me just like I was a customer." She sniffed. "It worked every time, too."

"How did that make you one of the lucky ones?"

"I knew people whose parents or even spouses couldn't stand them after they didn't remember who they were. That's extra hard."

He nodded. "I'll bet it is." He gazed across the river, and she wondered what was going on behind the unsmiling brown eyes.

"What are you thinking?"

"I was trying to imagine how it would have been if Maggie had survived the bursting of the aneurysm but been damaged to the extent she wouldn't have been herself anymore. I think maybe it would have been even worse than it's been learning to live without her." He chuckled, a dry and humorless sound. "I can say this—I know *she* would have said it was worse." He squeezed Lucy's fingers. "Strange, isn't it? You had to say goodbye way too many times, and I'd give ten years of my life to be able to say goodbye just once."

"What would she...Maggie say to that?"

He sat silent for a moment, and she was afraid she'd offended him with the question, but then he laughed. Not the ghostly chuckle she'd just heard, but a real hoot. "She would say—and this is without so much as a 'Gee, I'm sorry you're sad, Boone,'—she would tell me to get off my ass and stop trying to make people feel sorry for me."

The unexpected answer startled a laugh from Lucy, too. "You think?"

"No, I don't think. I *know.* Maggie's life was cut way too short, but she lived every minute of it. She wouldn't have a whole lot of patience with someone who didn't."

Lucy felt something lift away, a weight she hadn't realized she carried. "You know, Dad wouldn't either. Whether he was sick or well, he had a huge appreciation of life. When he talked about my mother, it was with complete joy, as though they'd had their whole lives together and she wasn't really gone at all. Just out for a while. If I don't have that same appreciation, if I let being scared of things rule how I live, it will be an insult to how he raised me."

"And if I don't start living again, it will be an insult to the life Maggie and I had together." He lifted their hands between them. "Shall we pretend we have glasses and drink to our decisions to appreciate and go forward?"

"Absolutely." She clicked imaginary glasses with him, then cupped his face. "Thank you. It was nice to talk about Dad without swimming around in a pool of regret."

"Thank you, too." He turned his face into her hand, kissing her palm. "I haven't felt this...alive for a long time."

When she took her hand away, he checked her watch—he never wore one. "I hate to say it, but we should probably head for home. If we're late for dinner, Aunt Gert will blame me and I'll be peeling potatoes for a week or something."

"I've enjoyed this afternoon," she said, getting up and falling into step beside him.

"Me, too." He brought them to a stop before they walked up the bank from the riverside path, sliding an arm around her waist. "There's something I have to do before we go home."

He tilted her face to his and drew her into his arms. "Maybe if we do this," he murmured, his lips just grazing hers, "it will be out of the way and you won't drive me crazy anymore." He nibbled, coaxing, and then his mouth wasn't grazing at all—what had been soft and gentle and sweet became something not soft and not gentle at all. But still sweet. Very, very sweet.

She wondered, as they got in the car a few minutes later, if his road to crazy had been curtailed.

Because hers certainly had not.

Chapter Six

"Chianti." Gert spoke firmly, shaking her head at the bottle of merlot in Boone's hand.

"But this is the right color," Boone argued, knowing it was useless—he would have to go back to the basement for another bottle.

"You're a doofus," Kelly said. "It's why Aunt Gert never really liked you." For the first time in a few days, she didn't sound angry.

"That's not why." Crockett headed toward the sunroom with a stack of plates. "It's because of the earring."

The comment surprised a laugh out of Boone and a query from Lucy. "Earring?" She looked from one of Boone's naked ears to the other.

"It happened one night after partaking of veritable buckets of something much cheaper and a whole lot more domestic than this." Boone held up the bottle of merlot. "As a matter of fact, I think Eli St. John and Micah Walker fermented it in somebody's garage. Eli wasn't a minister then and the good father—" he gestured toward Crockett as he came back into the kitchen, "—was still living real precariously on the other side of the confession box."

"Drunk," Crockett supplied. "We were drunk."

Gert tsked. "You were rotten is what you were, both of you. And Micah and Eli were even worse because they were older. They should have known better." She straightened with a little frown. "One of you lift this pan out of the oven for me. Sleeping on that cot in the hospital has made my back a bit sore."

"Well?" Lucy tossed hot pads to Crockett. "What happened with the earring?"

"We—the 'we' being most of the basketball team—wanted to pierce our ears," Boone said, "but none of our folks would let us. Except Aunt Gert, that is. The way we figured, she didn't mind because she'd never told us she did."

"Nor did we ask," Crockett interceded, setting the lasagna on the island. "Of course, we *couldn't* ask, because then she would have known we were… impaired. And she might have said 'no.'"

Boone huffed. "I think 'impaired' is too strong of a term. Anyway, Micah found a big-ass darning needle and we snuck in and swiped earrings from Aunt Gert's jewelry box. We just took little ones, figuring that would cause less trouble, and we were very clean about it. We washed both the needle and our ears in the junk we were drinking. Since I was the youngest—"

"Not to mention dumber than a box of rocks and twice as clumsy. He couldn't walk and chew gum at the same time even stone cold sober. Which he wasn't," Kelly supplied lovingly.

Boone went on as though she hadn't interrupted, although he did think maybe he liked her better when she was mad. "—I was elected to go first." He arrowed a gaze at Crockett. "And last."

His former best friend's eyes, what Gert always called shanty-Irish blue, brimmed with laughter. "It seemed sagacious to me," Crockett said pompously, "in light of the ruckus Boone raised, not to mention the whimpers and sobs, to just say I thought ear-piercing was immature and not nearly as cool as, say, sneaking into the movies or whacking mailboxes with baseball bats."

"Rotten," Gert repeated, "right to the core. Dinner's ready. Lucy, go get a bottle of Chianti, and we can eat—Boone will never be able to find the right thing. Kelly, do you have the salad on the table?"

"Yes, ma'am."

"So," Lucy said, when they were seated. Gert had slapped her grabby nephews' hands and grace had been said. "What happened next with the earring?"

"Oh." Boone scowled at her. "I thought we'd gotten past that."

She smiled brightly. "I didn't think so. Did you?" she appealed to the rest of the table.

"No, I didn't," Kelly said. "I was even there, but I'd love hearing it again. Without the whimpers and sobs, I mean. Or, on second thought, go ahead and include them. Sometimes a little drama can be a good thing."

"Well, come to find out," Boone said in a long-suffering voice, "the little earrings we appropriated—you notice I said *we*, not *I*—were a present from Uncle Mike for their something-or-other wedding anniversary."

"Nothing important." Gert patted her mouth with her napkin. "Just our twenty-fifth. They were diamonds."

"Real ones," Crockett added helpfully. "I put back the one I was going to use. Boone, on the other hand…" His voice trailed away on a mournful note and he shook his head in resignation.

Boone sighed. "…lost the one from his ear."

"In his defense—" Crockett began.

"There can be no defense," Kelly interjected.

"Actually, in *our* defense," Crockett persisted, "Sims let us work extra hours at the station so we could replace the earring. Uncle Mike ordered it to make sure it was the right one, and she's still wearing them. Right, Aunt Gert?"

"Yes, dear, that's right."

Lucy held up her glass for a refill. "So there must be some other reason."

"Reason for what?" Boone asked.

Her eyes twinkled at him, and he thought he could bask happily in that expression forever. "For your aunt not liking you."

Boone thought a moment. "Not that I can think of. Is there, Aunt Gert?"

She smiled and drew him close enough to give him a smacking kiss on the cheek. "Only that you're a doofus, sweetheart."

"Speaking of Sims." It was Kelly's lawyer voice. Her good mood time had evidently run out, but things were improving—it had been a good hour or more since she'd had anything truly snide to say about anyone, particularly Lucy.

Boone met Crockett's eyes across the table and they shared a shrug and a lopsided grin. It felt good, Boone thought. Even if they were never close again, if they were never Crockett-and-Boone, spoken as one word because they were always together, he could live with just being in the same room without anger.

"He'll be coming home in a few days," Gert said, "and I'm bringing him here. He'll stay in my room and—I'm sorry, Lucy—we'll have to stop serving in the den so I can move some of my things in there and sleep. I know we normally have private parties in there and it will mean giving up revenue, but it's the best alternative for right now."

Boone waited for Lucy to suggest a convalescent home for Sims. There was a perfectly nice one less than ten miles away, with professionals much more suited to the old man's care than Gert was.

"That'll be fine," Lucy said. "We can use the front parlor for the private parties we already have scheduled and just not book any more until Sims has recovered. We'll survive."

"Aunt Gert would probably be willing to buy out your part of the business," Kelly suggested, "or close it altogether. She's not able to give you the help you need. I'm sure you could find a building more suited to a tearoom than this one. I'd be glad to help in the search."

Even though Kelly's voice was quiet and calm,

almost conciliatory, the words fell hard and splintery into startled silence. When Lucy spoke, it was in a voice that didn't sound like her at all. "If that's what Gert wants, I'll move on. She doesn't owe me anything." She folded her napkin carefully, giving it a little pat to secure that it lay flat, and gathered her dishes and flatware. "If you'll excuse me, I need to bake for tomorrow."

She went into the kitchen, closing the connecting French doors behind her, and Boone stared across the table at Kelly, wondering what had happened to his little sister in the years since life and adulthood had caused them to drift apart. He'd spent their adolescence protecting her against outside forces, and now he wanted to protect someone *from* her. What was wrong with this picture?

"Whatever possesses you, Kelly?" Gert asked calmly. "I don't think I've ever been ashamed of you, but I am now."

"Why are you so sure it's me?" Kelly demanded. "You've all taken this girl to your hearts as though she's a cross between *Pollyanna* and *Anne of Green Gables* with a little bit of *Rebecca of Sunnybrook Farm* thrown in for good, saccharine measure. You're so impressed with how much she knows about running a restaurant and how she cared for her poor, ailing father. I keep expecting one of you to ask me to draw up papers to adopt her into the family."

Boone sighed—good God, he sounded like an ailing old man. "What are you getting at? Why don't you cut the whole drama-queen-lawyer act and just say what you want to say?"

Kelly's eyes flashed as she glowered at Crockett. "Aunt Gert, haven't you and Boone ever wondered what happened to the restaurant where she worked? Or even worse, to her father? Exactly who did Crockett fob off on you? And why?"

Lucy turned on the CD player that sat beside her dream jar so she couldn't hear the conversation taking place in the sunroom. Not so much to give them privacy—she wasn't anywhere near that noble—as to protect herself from hearing whatever Kelly Brennan was saying.

After getting two orange cake mixes and a bottle of canola oil from the pantry, Lucy set the stand mixer on the island and positioned herself with her back to the French doors. She poured the ingredients into the large stainless steel bowl, added eggs and water, and let the mixture blend while she sprayed a sheet cake pan and made sure the oven rack was in the right place.

Kelly had been aghast when she learned Lucy didn't bake cake from scratch. She'd suggested Tea on Twilight order their pastries from a bakery rather than serve dessert that was little better than fast food. Trembling with anger, Lucy had walked around the block for a half hour, not returning to the house until Kelly's Volvo pulled away.

Gert's niece and nephews were all so different it was hard to believe they'd grown up in the same house, under the same benevolent rule. Boone was laid back and funny, wearing his pain somewhere just under the surface and stashing anger somewhere it could do no harm. He was absentminded and clumsy and more than anything else, Lucy wondered what it would be like to be loved by him.

Kelly was almost manic, never still and seldom quiet. She loved as energetically as she did everything else. It would be nice if she'd stash *her* anger somewhere, too, or at least find another direction for it. But Lucy had seen Kelly's interaction with children—she loved them. Sometimes she watched Jack as he worked, and it was as though there was an ache in her eyes, but she never went beyond saying "hello" to the boy in passing. Lucy knew how much work she did *pro bono* as an advocate for children. It was hard to stay mad at someone that generous. At least, sometimes it was.

Crockett had come to Taft when he was thirteen and his parents had gotten a divorce. "They couldn't figure out how to divide me," he'd said, laughing. "I think Aunt Gert and Uncle Mike kept them from slicing me down the middle, Solomon-style."

His mother lived in St. Louis and his father in Charleston. Crockett saw them a few times a year and as far as Lucy knew, seldom talked about them. Gert mentioned his mother, her younger sister, sometimes, but only in the context of their shared childhood, never in connection with Crockett.

Lucy was sure there was pain in him, too, but he kept it buried, hidden behind the dark blue eyes. It was only Father Crockett he allowed out into the open, a loving and giving man unless what one wanted from him was a part of himself.

She remembered a day in Dolan's when he'd sat still and silent for at least an hour, letting his coffee get cold—which he hadn't done in all the times she'd waited on him. When she slid into the booth across from him, his gaze was startled, as though he didn't even know her. His eyes cleared quickly, and he smiled a welcome, but not quickly enough. "Are you all right, Father?" she asked.

"Of course. And how are you today, Miss Dolan?"

"I'm fine, but it's not my coffee that's gone cold." She got up, taking his cup away and coming back with a fresh one. "Are you okay?" she asked again. "From what the customers and the television news say, the flu's taking Richmond by storm."

"No, I'm not sick." He sipped the coffee, sighing appreciation. "Before I was Father Crockett, Lucy, I was Noah, or just Crockett to people I was closest to, and sometimes…sometimes, I miss that. Miss being him. In a lot of ways, he was a better person than Father Crockett is. A more real person."

She'd never thought much about that conversation—it made sense that a priest would sometimes want to be just a person like anyone else. But now, in this house with this tangle of people who loved each other but whose connections sometimes jammed, she wondered if there was more to Crockett's sadness than she'd realized.

The cake was in the oven and Lucy was rolling out piecrusts when the door into the sunroom opened. The others streamed into the kitchen, carrying their dishes. Kelly came to where Lucy stood.

"I apologize for my rudeness," she said stiffly. "I don't think you understand the depth of my concern for Aunt Gert—I owe her everything—but I have no right to condemn you without being in full possession of the facts, which my brother took great pains to tell me. I also wanted to apologize for leaving the mess with the glass I broke the other day. There's no excuse for that kind of behavior." Tears filled her eyes in a rush, and she grabbed a paper towel to mop them away. "I hope you'll forgive me."

Lucy was a pleaser. A counter-apology— "I'm sorry I upset you"—came right to the tip of her tongue, but she bit it back. She nodded, meeting the other woman's turbulent gaze with what she hoped was a noncommittal smile. "I care for her too."

Within a few minutes, the dishwasher was loaded, the leftovers put away, and Kelly was headed out the door. "I have a briefcase in the car just waiting for me," she said, kissing her aunt and her brother and nodding at Lucy and Crockett.

"I'll run over and check the station." Crockett checked the time. "Ethan's fully capable of closing it, but he hasn't done it in a long time. Wanna come along, Aunt Gert? I'll buy you an ice cream. At least, I will if Boone loans me a couple of bucks. I'm broke until I find a friendly ATM."

"Any chance I'll get it back?" Boone asked, reaching into his pocket.

"Nary a one," Crockett said cheerfully. "I took a vow of poverty. I'll take that twenty. If I'm bumming anyway, a big bill's as good as a small one."

"Did you really?" Lucy crimped piecrusts, her tongue between her teeth.

"Did I what?" Crockett asked. "Oh, the poverty vow? Well, no—I'm a diocesan priest and I didn't have to—but it sounded nobler than admitting I'd never remember to pay him back."

When Boone and Lucy were alone in the kitchen, he came over to her, cupping her chin and smiling down into her eyes. "I keep apologizing for Kelly, don't I? But I don't do anything about her."

"She's an adult, Boone. You don't have to apologize for her, much less 'do anything.' We're big girls. We can take care of our own issues." She thought of the apology. It had cost Kelly something to make it, but she hadn't backed away—it had been a classy show of reconciliation. But the "issues" were still there, Lucy was sure. She smiled at Boone. "It'll work out."

Lord, she loved his eyes and the way they looked at her, as though she was the only person in the world. She loved the way his lean cheeks curved when he smiled, with a dimple slashing into one side. And his mouth. She particularly loved his mouth. Especially since the kiss that afternoon on the walkway in Rising Sun.

"I imagine," he said, "you've been a 'big girl' your whole life, haven't you?"

"I guess," she admitted. "You are when you grow

up in a restaurant. I had a place in the kitchen where I had toys and books, but it was more fun helping the chef and the pastry chef. I was a whiz at making salads by the time I was five. That was good for the wait-staff, because I liked doing it and they didn't." She gazed off into a sweet memory. "They ordered aprons just for me and had my name embroidered on them. Gladys, one of the waitresses, took them home with her to launder because she didn't think little girls should have to wear things with starch in them."

Boone sat on a stool and watched her work. He didn't have his omnipresent sketch pad close by, and she wondered if he was memorizing her appearance, with her messy ponytail and her apron with cherry pie filling smeared across it. Would someone show up baking pies for Elmer and Myrtle in a comic strip somewhere down the road?

"Coffee?" He took mugs from the hooks above the coffee pot.

"Please."

He brought her a cup, finding himself a pencil and a pad of drawing paper in the process, and returned to his seat.

"Your aunt seems okay," she said. "I was afraid she was wearing herself out, but she doesn't seem to be. She still has the energy to come in and whip us all into line."

"Will it put a serious damper on tearoom business, not having the den for a while?"

"I don't think so, and if it does, that's too bad.

This is Gert's home first. I remember that when we were making the business plans, I wanted her to keep one parlor as part of the living quarters. She just laughed at me. 'There's room in there for four tables, girl, and if they're part of the tearoom, I won't have to clean them!' she said."

His hand moved with broad, firm strokes over the pad. "Do you get lonely here?" he asked. "Richmond's a lot bigger than Taft, and you must have left behind everybody you cared about when you came here."

She'd left them before that—scandal takes prisoners, so she'd distanced herself from the chefs and the wait-staff who'd been like family. She missed them, but they'd all gotten good jobs in upscale restaurants in other neighborhoods—some even went to other cities. She wrote references that should have guaranteed them employment anywhere they wanted to go. She made congratulatory phone calls and sent cards with her plans to leave Richmond mentioned as an afterthought. "I don't know where I'm going," she'd told them all. "Don't worry about me. Things will be all right."

And things were. She'd landed on both feet in a town she liked, in a kitchen that matched her personality and culinary needs, with people she… liked being with. More than "all right," things were really good. Life was in balance.

She took the cake out of the oven, replacing it with pies. "I feel out of place sometimes, as though I was on a bus and got off at the wrong stop. I miss delicatessens and specialty stores and public transportation, but I like it here." She went to stand at the window, her back to him.

Jack was working in the garden. He turned as though he felt her gaze, and she waved to him. He lifted a desultory hand, not smiling, and she wondered if something was bothering him. He was a nice kid, could eat a dozen cookies without taking time to inhale, and worked harder and more efficiently than many adults she'd known. In only a few months, he'd become part of the new family she was making her own. She frowned, watching him, and went to open the door. "Hey!"

He lifted his head. "What?"

"You all right? Do you need homework help?"

"Nah, it's going okay." He raised his hands in a shoulderless shrug. "Just stuff."

"You'll let me know if you need anything?"

"Yes, ma'am."

"Don't call me ma'am. I'm Princess Leia in training."

He grinned then, and made a shooing motion. "Princess Leia probably needs to work at making cookies."

She laughed and stepped back inside.

Jack was the little brother in Lucy's family circle, becoming dearer to her on a daily basis. She wondered how Kelly would feel about being placed in the "bratty sister" spot.

Even building a new life in Taft, she still missed the one in Richmond, missed Dolan's and the staff that had been her family, missed her father. But lonely wasn't the right word. At least, not exactly.

Now, if I could only sleep through the night. Or wake up without smelling smoke. Or tell Dad I'm sorry.

I'm so sorry.

Why didn't she just tell him? Boone was certain the story Kelly hinted at so darkly and caused Crockett to maintain a priestly silence was nothing he couldn't deal with hearing. He'd lost his parents and the woman he loved more than life. What could be worse than that?

He drew and Lucy baked as twilight became darkness and soft cool air came through the kitchen windows. He nodded thanks when she refilled his cup and offered him a piece of pie. They didn't talk much, even though Kelly's cryptic remarks were an elephant in the room, and he was surprised at how comfortable it was being quiet with Lucy Dolan.

When Gert and Crockett came in, Gert went straight to bed. She was nearly gray with exhaustion. "I'm getting so damn old," she mumbled, kissing everyone good night. "I'll want to leave early, whoever's taking me to Cincinnati in the morning."

Crockett poured himself some coffee and brought the cookie jar to the island. He sat on a stool at the end and offered up the cookies before speaking to Lucy. "You were right, weren't you?"

"Yes."

Her smile was so bright that Boone knew instant

and unreasonable jealousy that it hadn't been aimed at him. Crockett was a priest, for God's sake—it was probably time Boone stopped thinking they were always going to love the same woman.

Not that he loved Lucy Dolan. He didn't. But he had to admit to wanting her, to thinking of leaf-green eyes and butterscotch-colored hair at unexpected moments. It was the first time he'd noticed a woman—*really* noticed her—that he hadn't seen Maggie instead.

He knew a moment's fear that he would forget his wife's face. He had trouble recalling the sound of her voice sometimes, although answering the phone when her sister called could still bring tears to his eyes. In that first heartbreaking moment of familiarity, he forgot every time that it couldn't be Maggie calling. Couldn't ever be Maggie again.

"Right about what?" he asked, when neither of the others seemed inclined to tell him what they were talking about, which he thought was a little bit rude on their parts. He sounded grouchy, and nearly apologized, but didn't—he *was* grouchy. Their closeness annoyed the hell out of him, and he wasn't going to spend a lot of damn time examining why. Not now, at least.

Crockett's face registered chagrin. "When I suggested Lucy come here, it was partly because I know as well as anyone that Aunt Gert's is a soft place to fall. You do, too, Boone." He laid a twenty-dollar bill beside Boone's plate with a pathetic sigh and heavenward gaze. "It was also because I was worried about her. She's always been so sharp, and it seemed to me she was forgetting things. Leaving us by little bits and pieces." His eyes were gentle when they rested on Lucy. "Unfortunately, Lucy's very experienced with the ravages of Alzheimer's. She's not qualified to diagnose, but she's well able to see the signs."

Lucy took the canola oil to the pantry. "When we were preparing to open the tearoom, we both had physicals. We were going to be working with people's food, so it seemed a good idea to rule out anything infectious. But we checked for other things, too. Maria Simcox, her doctor and mine, almost laughed at the idea of Alzheimer's." She slid the pies onto the shallow shelves in the commercial refrigerator, covered the cake and sat down. She took a cookie off Boone's plate. "However, Father Crockett didn't believe either of us."

"I did," Crockett protested. "Mostly. I just needed a little extra convincing. I got it today when we were coming home from the hospital. When she was giving me hell precisely as she did twenty years ago, she wasn't living in the past, she was absolutely up to the minute in her…uh…observations. And believe me when I tell you she didn't forget one little thing."

"Uh oh." Boone shook his head sadly. "When Aunt Gert makes observations," he told Lucy, "we never come out well. Was there any indication my turn was next?"

"No," Crockett said, "and believe me, I tried to

steer her that way. If I'd known you were going to really take back that money you loaned me, I'd have tried harder."

Lucy laughed. "She's not even my aunt, but she's 'observed' about me too. She's always right, but I usually don't like it."

"Do you have any sisters or brothers?" Boone asked. She acted like a sister to Jack, and even to Kelly, if sisters didn't get along that was.

Come to think of it, she pretty much acted like a sister to Crockett, too. Boone smiled with that thought. It went well with the cookies.

"No. My parents had been married for years and years when Mom got pregnant with me, and then it never happened again. Dad used to say that as oopses went, I wasn't too bad."

The loneliness of being without Maggie was excruciating, even though time had dulled the razor edge of new sorrow, but Boone couldn't imagine how awful it would have been if he'd been alone as well as lonely all this time. How awful it would still be. Kelly might be a pain in his ass, and they'd lost the closeness they'd shared as kids, but she was always there, as was Gert. Even Crockett, despite the coolness of their relationship, would have come if called. Probably.

"You can borrow Aunt Gert any time you like," Boone offered. *And me, too. But tell me the truth, Lucy. Trust me.*

Chapter Seven

"I am not going to sit in this room like some decrepit old man." Sims glowered at Gert and Lucy, his white brows beetling threateningly above blue eyes that were usually full of laughter and kindness.

Usually being the operative word here.

"Listen here." Gert glared back. "You *are* a decrepit old man. Everyone has bent over backwards to help you. The girls have done all my work so I could spend time with you—which you haven't appreciated a damn bit, I might add. The boys have run the station and Jack's mowed your yard and taken care of your garden. The least you can do is behave yourself while the tearoom is open."

"He may as well behave himself at the station." Boone stood in the doorway between the kitchen and the dining room. "He can enter the numbers while we count inventory. That work for you, you grouchy old goat?"

"Keep a civil tongue in your head," Sims grumbled. He nodded at Lucy. "That broccoli and cauliflower soup needs to cook longer. The vegetables almost bite back and the cream part is too thin."

She smiled at him, trying to keep the expression sweet while gritting her teeth. "You won't notice that a bit when I dump the whole pot over your head. I'll do it, too. Just ask Jack."

Sims's mouth opened, closed, and opened again. "I may as well go with you," he told Boone grumpily. "Sure can't get any respect around here. But don't be driving over curbs and parking meters. Tom Simcox will arrest me as an accessory."

Gert, sliding meat loaf into the oven, scowled at him. "That might not be all bad. He could take you to jail. See how long they put up with your shenanigans over there."

When the men had gone—a painstaking process involving the handicapped ramp at the side of the house, a wheelchair and a very grumpy old man—Lucy pushed Gert into a chair at the little table by the windows. "I can finish the cooking." She poured a cup of tea and placed it in front of the older woman. "You have to stop doing this. Every time you get upset with Sims, I see your blood pressure rising with every heartbeat."

"It's hell getting old." Gert sipped the apple-cinnamon tea and stared out the window. She seemed morose and exhausted, as she had most of the time since Sims's accident. The expression sat out of place on her features.

Lucy refilled her coffee cup and sat across the table from Gert. "So tell me," she said gently, "do you remember being young as a walk in the park?"

Gert glanced at her, then returned her gaze to the window. "There are days when I don't remember being young at all."

Before he'd slipped away entirely, Johnny Dolan lived for hours at a time in his youth. When he looked at his daughter, he saw her mother. For a time, Lucy had felt an unexpected and treasured closeness to the woman she scarcely remembered. All too soon, however, her father had forgotten his wife too. When he was out of the kitchen, he was confused and—more often than Lucy could bear to remember—sad.

She drained her cup, closing her eyes in a conscious effort to push back painful memories. "Memorial Day is Monday. I'm going today to order flowers for my parents' graves in Richmond," she said. "Do you want me to send or get any for you?"

"No, thank you, dear. I've already taken care of it." Gert gave her a weary smile. "I'll be all right. Don't worry." Something sparked in her eyes, a ghost of the twinkle that was usually there. "Of course, you might want to worry about Sims. I may have to hurt him more than he already is."

"Want to pour my soup over his head? We can let it cool some first."

"Heavens, no. Your soup is far too popular to waste."

The phone rang while Lucy was making lemonade, and she tucked the receiver between her ear and her shoulder. "Tea on Twilight. Meat loaf and mashed potatoes today. May I help you?"

"Only if you have spare pies." Jenny Sawyer, the proprietor of Down at Jenny's, Taft's most popular café, sounded desperate. "My ovens are down—

damn technology anyway—and the only thing I have for dessert is ice cream and a cake made from a new recipe I never should have tried. The bakery's cleaned out for the day."

Lucy sketched numbers in the air. "We can let you have six, and half of them will be frozen. That work?"

"Oh, yes, you're a godsend. I'll run right over and get them. Just let me close up for a few minutes. Wanda called in today—her daughter's in labor."

"I can bring them to the café. We're all set for lunch here and I need to pick up some half and half anyway. You have an extra quart?"

"Sure do."

Lucy delivered the pies to the back door of the café, accepting a quart bottle of half and half in trade. She was getting into the van when she smelled something familiar.

Familiar and awful.

She backed out of the vehicle and closed its door. Nothing seemed untoward in the alley where she was parked. There were no plumes of smoke or angry tongues of flame shooting from anywhere. Abby, the head librarian, waved at her as she rode away from the back of the library on her bicycle. She was on her way to the tearoom for lunch—she always ate there on Fridays. Lucas Trent, the mostly retired senior partner in the law firm where Kelly worked, walked into the pharmacy at the end of the block. He'd be at the tearoom today, too, but not until one o'clock. Hummingbirds whirred around the feeders suction-cupped to the side windows of the café.

Nothing.

Lucy opened the car door again, setting the bottle of half and half on the passenger seat. After a few seconds of dithering, she got in and started the car. And smelled *it* again.

Oh, Lord. The van had twelve years and nearly three hundred thousand miles to its credit—it could be anything. She turned off the engine and got out, going around to open the hood and peer at what was under it. Like she would know if there was something wrong. The car either ran or it didn't, and it had been running like an antique charm since Sims went over it after it died on Lucy's first day in Taft.

Boone. He'd know what to do. He'd know if it was safe to start the car again. She wouldn't let him drive it, but she was certain he was mechanically superior to her. She reached for her cell phone. And stopped. It was all her imagination. Surely it was.

Jack rode his bicycle past the alley at the end of the block and Lucy waved frantically. He was a teenager—he'd know, wouldn't he? But he didn't see her and kept going, disappearing when he'd passed the alley.

She smelled it again and this time she dialed Boone's number. "I hate to sound like an idiot," she said when he answered, "but I'm over here behind Down at Jenny's and I smell something funny."

He laughed. "Well, don't tell Jenny."

"No, really." She was close to tears. "I don't know if it's my car or what, but it smells like something's burning and I can't find it." Her voice rose and she heard hysteria in it when she repeated, "I can't find it, Boone."

She must not have been the only one to hear the sound of panic, because he said, "I'll be right there," and hung up.

Lucy stood in the middle of the alley, undecided on what to do. She could wait for Boone, but she was blocking the alley. If someone wanted to come through, she'd need to move her car and she was afraid to start it.

Then she saw it. The thin curl of smoke came from under the crooked lid of a galvanized trash can. The rack of cans sat near the small storage building behind Down at Jenny's.

"Oh," she said. "Oh, God."

She fumbled with the phone as tendrils of flame began to lick from under the lid, reaching for the wood trim around the window on the building. What was in there? What if it was cooking oil or aerosol cans? *Oh, please, oh, please...* She dialed 911. Was that right? Was that where you called on a cell phone or was it another number? She couldn't remember. "Oh, God," she said again. "Please." Oh, she hated the smell of smoke. Hated it. Nausea pushed at her throat and she swallowed hard once. And again.

She headed toward the building. "There's a trash

fire behind Down at Jenny's," she said when the dispatcher answered the phone. "The flames are in a can but they're getting out. They're getting out. What if—"

"Don't approach it," warned the dispatcher, her voice soothing. "Someone will be there in a few minutes—they're already out. Is the way blocked?"

"Yes, but I can—" Boone was coming up the alley at a dead run with Crockett on his heels, and she felt the blood rushing around in her veins—it was as though she could actually hear it. "I'll unblock it," she said, although she was pretty sure she couldn't move at all. "Do I need to stay…"

She saw Boone and Crockett pull the garbage can rack away from the building, and she heard noise, lots of noise, but darkness was coming in from somewhere. Darkness and cold and the damn nausea, and she tried to fight all three sensations. Something would happen if she gave in to them. Oh, God, something would happen to Boone.

"Boone?" She tried to shout, because he might get burned—he might die, for God's sake—but she couldn't make her voice work. "Boone?"

"Hush." It was his voice close to her ear, his arms drawing her close. "It's okay. Don't cry, Lucy. It's okay."

"Whisht, Lucy John, whisht, 'tis all right."

Johnny Dolan's voice mingled with Boone's in her fading consciousness. "Boone?" she said faintly. "I didn't—"

And then the darkness won.

* * *

"It's *Cats* and Micah gave me the tickets—another one of those perks I get for letting him try out the new strip in the *Trib*. I hope he doesn't figure out he's the one doing the favor, not me. It'll be a real date, so I'm expecting you to comb your hair and wear one of those sundresses that show your knees." Boone did his best to keep his features innocent. "I don't know what it is about your knees, but I really like them. If you wear makeup, I'll spring for dessert when we have dinner before the play."

"Do they serve dessert at McDonald's?" Lucy asked.

"They certainly do. Ice cream sundaes and turnovers. But we're going to the restaurant next door to the theater. Will you go?" He smiled at her. "I was kidding, Lucy. You can wear anything you want and I don't care at all if you comb your hair or wear makeup and you can have all the dessert you want."

"What if I faint on you again?" Her cheeks were pink with embarrassment, and he had to stop himself from putting his arms around her. Kelly was in the sunroom talking to Gert and Crockett, and she'd undoubtedly have some remark to make that he didn't want to hear.

"It's okay with me," he assured Lucy. "I get to be the hero when I catch you. It's just way cool. Plus, there's the part where I've probably already spilled something on you, so I'd appreciate the opportunity to gain good guy points."

"Okay." She sounded uncertain, but her eyes smiled at him. "I'd like to go."

"Good. I'll pick you up at six."

Her eyebrows rose, disappearing into a froth of sun-streaked bangs. "Pick me up? As in, you're going to stop by the second floor on your way downstairs?"

"Well, hey, at least I'll be on time. I've heard punctuality is an admirable quality." Unfortunately, it had never been one of his. It ranked right up there with his driving, but there was no need to admit that to her. At least, not until he was too late to talk his way out of something.

"Then I should probably shower. And you'd rather I didn't wear an apron, right?"

"Nah, an apron would be good."

Even after she'd disappeared around the landing going upstairs, that little comment gave him all kinds of visions and thoughts, most of which would get his mind washed out with soap if Gert knew about them and could find a way to do it.

When Boone had changed into slacks and a shirt with the sleeves rolled to the elbows, he went into the sunroom. "Lucy and I are going to a play at the community theater over at Lawrenceburg," he told his aunt. "Will you and Sims be okay here?"

"Of course. Noah will help me get him to bed." Gert sighed.

"Sure." Crockett grinned. "If he gets mouthy, I'll threaten to pray over him for a long time. He thinks that's a real failing of clergy, especially Catholics—that we don't know when to shut up."

"He has a point," Kelly said acidly, coming into the kitchen with a stack of tablecloths. She ignored Crockett's frown. "You might want to call ahead, Boone," she added. "Warn them that Pyro Lucy's going to be in the theater."

"And you might want to find a new song to sing, because I'm getting really sick of hearing that one," Boone said evenly. "As far as I can recall, I haven't interfered with your life since we were in high school. It's time for you to return that favor."

"You must admit it was odd the fire chose the very moment she was in the alley to start, especially since we know it was arson. There was no spontaneous combustion involved." She met his gaze defiantly. "I'm afraid you'll get hurt."

"That's not really a concern anymore," he said quietly. "You have to feel things before they can hurt you. So leave it alone, Kelly, and leave Lucy alone, too. And, while you're at it, maybe you should leave me alone too." He avoided her gaze, not wanting to see the hurt he knew would be in her eyes. Even if she deserved it, he didn't like causing it.

He thought of Maggie, closing his eyes so he could see her face in his mind. *Boone, honey, I have such a headache.* The pain nearly brought him to his knees. He breathed slow and deep so he wouldn't sound as though he was gasping for air. So much for not feeling things. But that was how the grief process went, wasn't it? One step forward and two steps back. Damn it. Maybe it was four steps back.

He met Crockett's eyes. The other man's gaze was inscrutable, and Boone wished for the hundredth time since he'd been home that their friendship could find its old easy footing.

"You kids have fun." Crockett turned his attention to the newspaper on the table. "I'll sneak down and let you in if Aunt Gert locks you out."

Lucy came down the stairs in a black and white dress, her butterscotch hair flat-ironed into sleek submission and her freckles semi-covered with a dusting of something a little sparkly. She wore strappy high-heeled sandals and her toenails were polished. Her fingernails were, too, but they were bitten down so short the shiny varnish was almost invisible.

Boone smiled. Her knees were showing, and he hadn't been kidding—he really did like them a lot. "Wow."

"Thank you. Why don't you let me drive?"

A snort of laughter came from the sunroom, and Boone scowled in that direction before handing her his keys. "I feel like an alcoholic. Do you know where we're going?"

"Uh-huh." She waved at the others and followed Boone through the house.

"I can't believe I'm letting a girl drive on a date," he complained, opening the door for her.

"If you let the girl drive," she suggested brightly, "it gives you a better chance at a second date. She's much more likely to say yes if she hasn't actually ridden with you."

"You've ridden with me before, although I don't recall you opening your eyes. And this is our *third* date," he reminded her, "and that's only if you don't count working together at the gas station, delivering pies, and walking to church. If you count those as dates, we've had lots of them."

"We need to be careful about that, too," she said, getting into the Jeep on the driver's side. The maneuver showed enough of her right leg that Boone enjoyed a little pulse quickening as he settled into the passenger seat. "Landy Walker says if you go to church together in Taft, it's no time till the whole town has you engaged."

He grinned. "That's about the truth of it too."

Lucy blushed. "I'm sorry. I wasn't trying to suggest—"

"Lighten up, Lucy. We're grownups. We don't have to worry about being engaged until we've gone out four or five times. Unless we've gone out that many times *and* gone to church together. Then it becomes a concern. We might have to schedule counseling with Eli, although how a man with nine kids can counsel anyone is beyond me."

She laughed. "Okay. I'll hold you to that."

In the restaurant, they talked through the first two courses, and Boone was once again amazed at how comfortable he was with her. He even talked about his parents, which he hardly ever did with anyone other than family. None of his friends had known them, and though most were sympathetic, they couldn't relate to the devastation of losing your parents when you're twelve.

"I'm like my dad," he said. "Sometimes Kelly will give a little gasp, and I'll know I've said or done something that's like what she remembers. She, on the other hand, has my mom's face, figure, even her hands. Her voice sounds like Mom's did, and I like to hear it. That's when she's not mad at anyone, which I'll admit doesn't happen often."

"How did you find out what had happened to them?" Sympathy softened Lucy's voice.

"It was so strange. Dad and Mom had date nights every Saturday night. Usually it was nothing big. They went to movies or bowled or just ate somewhere that didn't have a drive-through. The next-door neighbors were always on call, but Kelly and I had stayed by ourselves on those nights for at least a year. That week—it was in February and cold—Mom was antsy about leaving us, so they drove us all the way to Taft, a couple of hours away, and left us with Uncle Mike and Aunt Gert. Then they spent Saturday night in a bed and breakfast. They called to tell us good-night. They were having such a good time." He stopped, turning his water glass round and round on the table. "The phone rang the next morning while we were getting ready for church. The car in the opposite lane had lost control on black ice and hit them head-on. They died instantly."

"Oh." She touched his hand. "I'm so sorry."

"It was almost like they knew something would be different. Dad had kissed me goodbye, for one thing, and I was twelve—I didn't want anyone kissing me, much less my father. What if my friends saw it? I remember Kelly started screaming before Uncle Mike even got the words out to tell us. She screamed and screamed until she didn't have any voice left, and Aunt Gert sat and rocked her all that day. A doctor came and gave her a sedative—I think he gave me one, too—but Aunt Gert wouldn't let her go. She just stayed in that chair that's still in the kitchen and rocked her."

Lucy's eyes glistened, dampness clinging to her lower lashes. "It must have been so awful for all of you. It changed my childhood that Mama died when I was so little, but it didn't end it. I doubt Kelly was ever really a little girl again. And you weren't really twelve, either, were you?"

"We grew up faster in some ways, that's for sure. What about you?" Boone smiled at her, trying to dispel the lingering sadness. "Tell me about your dad."

"He came straight from Ireland when he was eighteen." Lucy's green eyes were dreamy. "And he never lost the brogue—even a little bit. When I hear someone from Ireland talk, I still listen for the same inflections I remember."

"So, was your restaurant Irish food?"

She laughed. "No, pure American diner, except for a dessert, sticky toffee pudding, which I guess is English, but Dad swore was Irish. We have it in the tearoom every few weeks. Oh, and Guinness stew. Dad said it was different here because the Guinness is different, but it's still good. I should make that one of these days."

The waiter refilled their coffee cups, and even though Boone had told himself he'd mind his own business, the question slipped out both unexpected and unintended. "What happened to the restaurant, Lucy?" He wished the words back immediately. "I'm sorry. You don't have to answer that."

She picked up her cup, then set it down with the coffee untasted and stared at a point somewhere past him. "We lived above it, and, like I told you before, sometimes Dad went down at night and cooked. I always woke up, and could get him to go back to bed. He was a very safe cook, even after he got sick. We had more fire extinguishers than was required, an up-to-date sprinkler system, and state of the art ovens, grill, and cook top. Our smoke alarm system was hard-wired and monitored by the company that had installed it. Plus Dad was just so damn careful."

Her eyes were dry, but her face was pasty white underneath the dusting of freckles and glittery powder. Boone reached for her hand. "You don't have to talk about this. It's not my business."

"Well, you know," she said, "in a way it is. I know you love Gert, and that whole thing with the trash fire today makes me seem like a complete idiot in addition to a probable arsonist, so I think maybe you and your sister *do* have a right to know."

She took a drink of coffee and a deep breath and went on, “That particular night, I heard Dad go downstairs, and I lay there for a few minutes—actually it was four minutes—it’s amazing how digital clocks can make expert witnesses out of people, isn’t it? I was so tired that I didn’t want to get up, but I did. I smelled the smoke and heard the alarm on the way down the stairs.” She shook her head. “The fire had started in the dining room, not the kitchen, and Dad had walked right into it. He was just inside the door, and I dragged him outside before I even called 911, but it was already too late.”

“Oh, God.” He held onto her hand, and her gaze. “What happened?”

“The restaurant was non-smoking by then, but there were still a few who remembered the old days and would light up if they thought no one would notice—especially if it was nearly closing time and there weren’t a lot of customers. Only thing was, there weren’t any ashtrays, so they’d put their cigarettes out on the floor under the tables if they saw someone coming. This time, as nearly as the investigators could figure, someone hadn’t put his or hers out at all, just kicked it back against the banquette.”

“How long did it take for them to figure out what happened?”

Her expression was tortured and her voice sounded strangled when she continued, “They thought it was me at first, you know? They thought I’d become so frustrated trying to take care of Dad and the business that I’d snapped and set the whole thing up. They had it all figured out how I'd done it, right down to sabotaging the smoke alarms and the sprinklers in the dining room not containing the smoke. After his funeral, they came to the motel where I was staying and told me not to go anywhere because I was a 'person of interest' in the investigation."

Boone felt as though he'd been kicked in the stomach. He remembered telling Kelly today, *You have to feel things before they can hurt you.* What a pompous-assed remark to make, because he'd felt a lot of things within the last couple of hours.

"It didn't last long. They knew within a few weeks what had happened, but I still felt as though everyone thought I'd started the fire and killed my father. The press had written investigative stories that, while they didn't actually point fingers, made people wonder what had *really* happened that night in Dolan's." She shrugged. "There was enough insurance to cover most debt, but not to rebuild, though I still own the property. The staff all got jobs—they were excellent at what they did—so when Crockett suggested I take a few weeks and visit his Aunt Gert, I did."

She smiled at Boone, the expression animated by the starlike tears on her face. "They saved my life, I think, Crockett and Gert, because even now with that twenty-twenty retrospect we're all blessed with, I don't know what I would have done. Dad was the one who died, but my life as I knew it ended too."

Crockett. Damn, even wearing a sworn-to-celibacy collar, Crockett had trumped him. Boone pushed back the thought, knowing it was both inaccurate and immature.

"I'm glad you're here," he said, lacing her fingers with his. "I'm sorry for the reasons, but still glad you're here."

The tears had dried, leaving only dusty little tracks in the sparkly powder on her cheeks, and he thought her smile brightened at his words. "I am too."

Chapter Eight

Lucy loved *Cats*, though it made her cry. She'd forgotten how much fun it was sitting in a theater seat beside a guy you liked. *Really* liked. They played dueling elbows for the common arm rest until he captured her hand sometime after intermission and held it until the lights came up. Even through the fabric of his pants, she felt the warmth of his leg against hers.

"That was so much fun," she said, when they stood for the ovation following the performance. "I think I like dating."

"Me too." His smile was warm, and right in front of her eyes she saw the twinkle happen. She wasn't sure how a six-feet-plus-some man with big feet managed to appear impish, but he did. "Does this mean you're going to sleep with me?"

Probably sometime. She barely stopped herself from saying the words. "No, but I'll buy you a cup of coffee."

When they sat in a vinyl booth with their knees touching, thick mugs of coffee and plates of strawberry shortcake between them, Boone said, "Tom Simcox said someone set the fire in the trash can."

"I know." Lucy had been interviewed by the

burly sheriff. Easily twice the size of the pretty physician who was his wife and with a military past he never talked about, he was more calming than intimidating. Landy Walker said he'd gotten that way in high school when he spent all his time keeping Eli and Micah out of trouble. Eli and Micah, on the other hand, insisted Tom was the one who *caused* most of the trouble.

"He acted as though it was just some random vandalism," Lucy said doubtfully, "but he had to wonder. This is Taft, for heaven's sake. There *isn't* much real vandalism. I asked Jack if there was gang activity here and he gave me a blank stare and asked why anyone would want to mess with that. This is a kid who's sixteen and even though I don't know much about him, I'm pretty sure his life isn't like an episode of *Happy Days.* He spends too much time away from home for that. I know his dad isn't around, but his mom never seems to check on him, either. He would *know* if gang activity was going on."

Boone shook his head at her. "Don't borrow trouble. Even in cozy little towns, people do bad things. No one knows that any better than Tom. Landy Walker's first husband was the quarterback when they were all in high school. He beat the hell out of her off and on for years, one of those things people suspected but no one really knew. When he came after her and his *next* wife with a gun, Landy shot and killed him by accident and ended up on trial for murder. It was a grisly time."

"I didn't know that." Landy was one of her favorite people in Taft. She hated the idea of her having been hurt.

He took a bite of shortcake. "Yours is better than this."

"I should hope so," she said indignantly. "This cake came right out of a cellophane package. I use sweetened biscuit dough."

He laughed at her, and she set her fork down to enjoy the sound of it slipping along her nerve endings, sending warmth and heaviness directly to the area between her legs she tried her best not to think about. Usually.

But not always. Sometimes she thought herself into a frenzy of need and frustration. However, just occasionally, the thinking was…pleasant. The sound of his laughter, the long touch of his leg against hers in the theater, the way his knees bumped hers under the table—those were pleasant too.

The warmth between her thighs was developing a distinctive tingle. She'd really like it if he kissed her. And held her. She absolutely knew there'd be no safer, better feeling than being held by Boone Brennan. Well, maybe not safer. Boone being Boone, he might very well drop her. Even that would be all right, though, because he'd stick around to help her up.

Oh, he was talking.

"Are you missing Richmond and those conveniences you mentioned the other day? I've heard they have more than one gas station there."

Heat climbed her cheeks. She wondered exactly how much she'd missed. "I'm sorry. My mind was out there somewhere." She didn't think she'd tell him exactly where. "Oh, Richmond? No, I really don't miss it very much. I miss everyone who worked at Dolan's. The last few years I was there, they were the only people I really talked to. I always worked at the restaurant, but I'd had my own apartment for eight years or so when Dad was diagnosed. I didn't move back home until it became necessary, about five years ago, but then there was no life other than Dad." She smiled sheepishly. "I started going to church so I could have a couple of hours on Sunday that were all my own. I gained faith as I went along, but in the beginning it was just so I could have that two hours."

"Never married?"

"No. Went steady in high school. Engaged once later on."

He raised an eyebrow. "Cold feet?" He moved his knees so that they bumped the sides of hers and the crisp cotton of his slacks caressed her bare legs.

"Not mine. My high school boyfriend went away to college and met a cheerleader with great legs and a black Corvette. My fiancé—" she hesitated, surprised that it still hurt when she thought of Scott Knight's defection, "—forced the choice between him and my father. Dad was already sick, and I was all he had. I couldn't leave him."

"Hard to call that a choice. You really didn't have one."

She shrugged. "Made the decision easy." And lonely.

It was just after midnight when she parked his Jeep behind Crockett's car. Boone walked around and opened her door. "I'll walk you home."

"All that way?" She met his eyes in the moonlight. "Do you mind that I consider this my home?"

"I'd mind if you didn't." His lips were close to hers. "Do you mind if I do this?"

He didn't wait for her answer, just captured her mouth. He tasted of coffee and strawberries and longing. Response flowed warm and liquid through her. Oh, dear Lord, nothing had ever felt this good. It wasn't as though she was completely inexperienced—she was nearly thirty-three and had left her virginity with the high school boyfriend on prom night—but she was positive nothing had ever been this right.

"Good," he murmured, breaking away just long enough to catch her bottom lip in a nibble before kissing her again. Longer and deeper, his embrace fitting her body to his.

Her arms went up around his neck, her right hand tunneling into his streaky brown hair. The night air was deliciously cool against her skin, contrasting sensuously with the heat where their bodies touched. And where they wanted to. She imagined steam rising and stifled a giggle against his mouth.

"Funny?" he murmured, breaking contact. "I'm doing my very best 'come and see my etchings' act and you think it's funny?"

"Huh-uh." She framed his face, relishing the feel of his skin against her fingers, smiling into his eyes. "Just fun."

"Ah."

From somewhere came the faint sound of music. "Hear that?" he whispered. "I ordered it so I wouldn't have to let you go." His arm went around her waist and he took her hand in his other one. "I have to count," he said, leading her into a two-step, "but it's really very romantic if you can ignore me saying one two, one-two over and over again."

She tilted her head into his shoulder, laughing. He smelled so good. "I can ignore the counting if you don't dance us into the rose bushes."

"I wouldn't think of it. Aunt Gert would—one two, one-two. No, left foot—be out here in a heartbeat telling me to cut a switch so she could—one two, one-two—whale the tar out of me."

They danced the length and breadth of the driveway, swooping between cars and around bicycles. When they got close to the bench that sat in the flower bed, Boone lifted a foot to its seat and draped her dramatically across his leg. "Beautiful," he said. "You're beautiful." He kissed her. Not an especially sexy kiss—his lips were barely open, hers even less so—but appealing and arousing all the same. It made her feel everything with startling intensity. The soft cotton fabric of her dress against her legs, his hand warm on her arm, the strength of him. As precarious as their positions were, she had no fear he would drop her.

The dance ended after the song did, but she didn't notice when the music stopped and she didn't think he had, either. They stood at the back door of the house and he released her hand to lay his on the upper curve of her breast. "Your heart's beating fast," he observed, slipping his fingers inside the vee neck of her dress. "You feel like warm silk."

His kiss was deep this time, his tongue exploring, doing an erotic little tangle with hers before withdrawing. His fingers mirrored the movement, teasing her nipple to a pebbled crest then pulling away just enough to weigh the curve of her breast with his palm.

"We need to go in," she said, when she could get her breath.

"I know." He kissed her some more, his hands sliding up and down her bare arms. Up and down, chasing gooseflesh in their wake. He held her, swaying a little to music only they heard. "Really," he murmured, "we should go in."

A few minutes later, they did. She straightened her dress and he re-fastened his shirt where the buttons had mysteriously come undone.

"Thanks for the evening," she said inside the kitchen. "It was fun."

He backed her up to the island and kissed her once more. Long and leisurely and deep. Way deep. She'd never drunk brandy, but his kisses reminded her of how she'd read it described. Dark and sweet and hot. Oh, God, hot.

"It was. What do you say we do it again soon?"

Easy question. Her answer was instant, whispered against his mouth. "Okay."

"I'm going to check on Sims before I go to bed."

"Good night."

She took off her shoes and went up the back stairs, humming almost silently. She felt like a Rodgers and Hammerstein movie. All that was lacking was a swirly skirt and a little more cleavage. The thought made her breathe soft laughter as she slipped inside her room.

For the first time in longer than she could remember, she slept through the night, not waking until the sun made its presence known at the east windows of her room.

"I have to get back to Richmond," Crockett said. "I've already been gone longer than I intended. They get along fine without me, but there are things I need to attend to. Programs that involve kids like you and I were, like Jack is. "

Boone stood at the door of Crockett's room, watching him pack his things neatly into a black leather duffel bag. "When will you be home again? Aunt Gert likes having you here." *I do too.*

"When I can, or when she really needs me to be." Crockett's eyes met his, and something light glimmered past the sadness that seemed to have settled there. "So. You and Lucy, huh?"

"I don't know." Boone shrugged. "She's a nice girl. Fun." The room was motel neat, the bed made, the dresser without so much as a handful of change on its top. He remembered when Crockett's room was as messy as his own—they used to bribe Kelly to clean for them. Forcing them to pay up on the bribes was probably why she'd become a litigator. He guessed that meant both he and Crockett had something to answer for in the hereafter, because he didn't think Kelly Brennan as an assistant prosecutor was a whole lot of fun.

Crockett frowned. "Fun? Is that all?"

"I feel something for Lucy, something I hadn't expected to ever feel again," Boone admitted, "and I feel guilty as all hell."

"Don't."

The terse reply stung. And irritated. "Oh, come on, Crockett. I know you're still mad at me, but surely we can talk about it after all these years."

Crockett glanced up, his expression startled. "Mad at you?"

"Yes, mad. Over Maggie. Because I loved her when you did, but not enough. I lost her when you wouldn't have, and I don't think even you have enough faith to forgive that." There, he'd said it aloud, and the pain was as sharp and ragged as he'd feared. "If I'd stayed out of the way, she'd have married you and she'd still be alive and you'd both be happy. You'd probably even have a bunch of little Crocketts running around. I knew you cared for her that first weekend when you brought her home. I knew it and, God help me, I didn't care."

"Boone." Crockett just stared at him, then walked around the room shaking his head. "Gentle Jesus, where do I start?" He stood still, apparently listening. "Why can't I be one of those who hears the voice of God when I want to rather than when He wants me to?" He paced more, then faced Boone over the space between them.

Facing him over fifteen years of…no, not silence—they'd stayed stiltedly, steadily polite—but stormy quiet.

Boone braced himself. What if the quiet was better? Sometimes it was. Grief had become more bearable when he'd stopped feeling like screaming. Work had even become easier when he'd learned to draw with less volume in the music filling his studio.

Crockett sighed, sounding uncannily like Aunt Gert when she was about to cut loose on one or more of them. "You're completely nuts."

Oh, for God's sake. "That's beside the point."

"No, *usually* it's beside the point. Right now, it *is* the point." Crockett seemed to be trying to gather his thoughts. "I was in love with Maggie from the moment I met her," he admitted. "Something you can identify with. But that didn't mean she was in love with me. Not for one minute. Even before you and she met, that ship had already sailed and I was getting over it. Besides," he added wryly, "I already had a pretty good idea that my particular ship was taking me in another direction altogether. You don't enter the priesthood because of a broken heart, Boone. At least, you shouldn't. Maggie probably had a little more to do with it for me than she should have, but that's not your fault or hers—it's mine."

"But she would still—"

"No, she wouldn't. She had an aneurysm. You didn't give her that. No one even knew she had it. Had I been with her, *I* wouldn't have known."

Boone hadn't cried over Maggie in a long time. He'd cursed and shouted out his anger and mourned in long and mostly silent pain, but he thought he'd come a long way. He spent time with her family without falling apart. He enjoyed seeing pictures of her in Aunt Gert's photo albums. He was able to talk about her without losing his voice to grief. He'd found pleasure with other women and was pretty sure he was finding something more than just pleasure with Lucy. But he'd always felt guilty. Still felt guilty.

Tears pushed at the backs of his eyes and he lifted his hand to his face, trying to keep them back with his fingers. He hadn't been raised with the old archetype that said men didn't cry, but he'd never gotten comfortable with the fact that sometimes they did.

"How could I not have known?" he asked, although he understood that even Crockett's God-endowed wisdom probably didn't have an answer for him. "How could we have been together damn near every minute for ten years without me knowing she had a time bomb inside her?"

"You weren't given that power," Crockett said. "I don't know why. I don't even *begin* to know why. God wanted Maggie in a different place, and I don't know the why on that, either. But there's one thing I *do* know."

"What's that?" The tears were there, moving past his fingers and down his cheeks. He turned his face away.

"I see lots of people, even elderly people, who never, ever have what you and Maggie had. Who have never loved anyone the way you did her and who've never *been* loved the way she did you. For ten years, you both started and ended every day fully aware you were somebody's heart and soul. That was an unparalleled gift, Boone. It ended too soon—I know that, and I can't tell you the reason for it, but that doesn't take away from what it was."

Boone nodded. He knew that too, but knowing it didn't make the ending any more bearable.

"And I know something else."

Crockett wasn't going to go on unless he turned to face him. Boone finally did, after wiping his face with his palms. "What?"

"That it's time."

Boone didn't have to ask, "Time for what?" It was time to let Maggie rest, to accept memories as just what they were: memories. He thought he'd done that in Rising Sun with Lucy, but it had only been one of the intricate steps in the grieving process. He still wasn't sure he was ready for that dance to be over. "I don't know if I can do it," he said aloud.

"I don't know either," Crockett admitted, "but I know you should."

"It wasn't just Maggie I lost," Boone said. "I lost my best friend too."

Crockett met his gaze again before stepping into the bathroom between their rooms and coming out with a tissue and handing it to him. "I've been here the whole time," he said, unsmiling, "and the truth is so have you. We don't talk a lot, but I never doubted that if I needed a friend, I always had one."

Boone realized he'd always known that, too, though it wasn't the same as it had been when they were young. Maybe it wasn't supposed to be. "I kept thinking you were the one who was angry and blaming you for it," he said. "Maybe it was me."

"Maybe. And maybe—" Crockett hesitated, "—maybe the only way I could do the priesthood thing was by giving up who I'd been, including being your best friend. Being whatever I was to Kelly. I think I was wrong."

Boone drew in a wavering breath. "Wanna kiss and make up?"

Crockett grinned. "I think I'll pass."

They'd known each other their whole lives, but they'd never, ever hugged. Not that they *minded* men hugging, but they'd always been more the shake hands and say rude things and slap shoulders type.

Boone didn't know who stepped first, but for a moment, they *were* the hugging type, holding hard and close. "Be careful going back," he said gruffly.

"Will do. You and Lucy—take care of each other."

"Okay."

Back in his room, Boone sat on the bed and held

the picture of Maggie for a long, aching time. "If I let you go," he said aloud, "it doesn't mean forgetting, does it?"

There was no thunder or lightning, no epiphanic understanding that life would go on from this day forward unfettered by memories or grief. It would have been nice if he could have heard Maggie's voice urging him to freedom. *"Oh, for heaven's sake, Boone,"* he wanted to hear, *"what's taken you so long?"*

But when he kissed his fingertips and pressed them to the glass in the picture frame, as he'd done every night for three years, he understood that he wouldn't do it anymore. "Love you," he whispered.

Before he slept, just for a moment, he smelled lilacs and spring.

And he felt hope.

Chapter Nine

Kelly Brennan was pale and listless. Her makeup was as perfect as ever, but it was more like a mask than an enhancement. Lucy felt sorry for her in spite of herself. She poured a cup of orange spice tea and set it in front of Kelly at the kitchen's island. "Would you like some breakfast?" she asked brightly. "I was going to make oatmeal."

The lawyer's glance was baleful. "I'd rather eat glue. I came over to talk to my brother and my aunt, and I'd like some privacy while I do that."

"Fine." Lucy went into the laundry room, closing the door with a snap that very nearly qualified as a slam—Lucy the Pleaser *never* slammed doors. She emptied the washing machine and carried the basket outside. Every bed in the house was changed on Monday morning. Gert was a modern thinker most of the time, but her evolution had stopped with certain housekeeping habits—even when Monday was a holiday. One of Lucy's favorite jobs was hanging the crisp white bedding outside. It was a dose of sanity on even the worst of days.

When the two sets of sheets from that load were flapping on the line, she went to the garden behind the garage, getting a hoe out of the shed. Jack did a good job keeping the weeds at bay, but there were always a few to take one's frustrations out on. She'd chopped up earth around the tomato plants and onions, pulled a handful of radishes, and was hoeing the beans when she heard a drawling voice behind her. "You were wearing those shorts when I met you. I liked them that day too."

She had to stop herself from saying something rude. It wasn't Boone's fault his sister was a pain in the backside. "Thank you," she said primly, not turning around.

"I'm going to drive out to the cemetery. You want to go? It's a pretty morning."

She'd had to call and order flowers for her parents' graves in Virginia after the fire fiasco on Saturday and she felt a sharp twinge of regret that she wouldn't be able to visit.

"Dad and I went every year. He made me," she murmured. She straightened and faced Boone, leaning on the hoe. "He'd sit on a bench and talk to Mom and I'd run around looking at all the names on the markers. There was an Isobel Dolan who was buried three rows away, and I used to put flowers on her grave. I just knew she was a long-lost grandmother." She smiled sheepishly and handed him the hoe to put away. "My grandparents are all buried in Ireland and I never knew any of them, but that didn't stop me from daydreaming." She nodded. "I'd like to go."

The Jeep was full of flowers. Some were silk arrangements, some real, their aroma sweet in the warm air. "You just want me along to help distribute all this," she accused, climbing into the passenger seat and accepting a bouquet of yellow roses from him.

Boone started the Jeep. "You got that right. Aunt Gert and Kelly will go to the cemetery today—it's one way we're all very traditional, I guess—but I always get to be the flower boy."

"These are gorgeous," she said, sniffing the flowers in her lap.

"They were her favorite."

Oh. "Her" must have been his wife. Lucy was surprised by the surge of jealousy she felt.

Now, *that* was a new and attractive development, being jealous of a dead woman. It wasn't as though she and Boone were going to have a real relationship, for heaven's sake. He'd be going back to Chicago at summer's end and Lucy would be staying here, too busy trying to build a life for herself to worry about including a terrible driver still in love with his wife within its boundaries.

No matter how good a kisser he was. No matter how good and warm and safe she felt in his arms. No matter how easy he was to talk to.

Nope, no matter at all.

So why did her eyes feel teary and her throat scratchy? It must be the flowers. She'd never had allergies before, but it wasn't too late to start. She sniffed.

"Oops, allergies?" He reached for the roses, causing the car to veer alarmingly. "Sorry. Let me put them in the back somewhere."

"No, that's okay." She held onto them—and to the upper edge of the door so that she'd have just the slightest chance of leaping to safety before he drove into a tree. Of course, chances were better she wouldn't be able to get her seatbelt unfastened and she'd be stuck in the Jeep with a bouquet of roses and a maple tree branch in her lap. "They might get damaged back there. I'm not allergic." She sniffed again. "Just a tickle."

At the small, shady cemetery, Lucy distributed arrangements where he directed, taking time to get them straight. "I always just toss them on there," he said.

"I'll bet you do," she said wryly, placing a spray of carnations on top of Michael Taylor's monument and a smaller one on the little marker next to it. "Susan Ellen Taylor. Gert lost a child?" she asked, taken aback. "She's never mentioned it."

"It's been a long time," he said. "She and Uncle Mike never expected to have children at all, then she found herself pregnant. I don't know how old she was, but I think her age may have been problematic. The baby lived a few months, but she was never healthy. I'm not sure what all was wrong. I can just barely remember my mom holding Aunt Gert while she cried. Later, Mom and Dad stood, real quiet, with their arms around each other, watching Kelly and me. It was the first time I had a clue how much kids mean to their parents."

Lucy nodded. "Dad said he and Mom were confused by it. They'd always been everything to each other, then all of a sudden there was this little intruder who became everything to both of them." Tears smarted in her eyes, and she blinked them back. "We were lucky, weren't we, having the parents we did?"

"I think we were, even though it didn't last nearly long enough for either of us." He knelt at his parents' graves. "Once we got past the worst of it, we were glad they'd died together. They were like your folks. They meant that much to each other. Took years to get to that point, though. I think Kelly and I both stayed mad about it till we were grown up." He shook his head. "For that matter, Kelly might *still* be mad about it. I don't know how to tell the difference with her."

A wind chime hung from a shepherd's hook on the next grave they came to. "Maggie Brennan, beloved wife and daughter," Lucy read to herself. "I'll wait in the car," she offered quickly, turning to leave, even though she wanted to straighten the flowers he'd stuffed into the vase on the base of the granite marker.

"No, that's okay." He stood silent, smiling a little, and she knew he'd gone somewhere alone. It didn't matter if she was there or not.

She straightened the yellow roses, rearranging the Queen Anne's Lace that was with them so it wasn't all in a clump. For the first time, she noticed the white sweetheart roses on the other end of the marker. She didn't remember having seen them in the car. She fluffed them anyway, stealing a few pieces of ferny greenery from the other container to make the little spray fuller.

Boone cleared his throat. "That was the second time I had a clue about what kids mean to their parents," he said quietly. "She was pregnant when she died. We'd just found out and—Jesus, we were happy. I was surprised two people could *be* that happy. As far as Maggie and I were concerned, it was the second perfect conception. Not immaculate, just perfect. I hadn't really had time to get used to having a baby, but that additional loss made it all so much worse."

Lucy's tears welled again. The cemetery was peaceful and pretty with its mature trees and neat hedges. The area was bright with Memorial Day flowers and the sun shone steadily, but she was still overwhelmed by the loss represented by the crosses and granite stones.

"How do you get over it?" she asked. "It was hard losing my mom so young, and I'm still like a boat without a rudder without my dad. Losing Maggie and the baby—I don't know how you survived."

His smile was crooked. "Sometimes, I'm not sure I did. But if you go through the motions long enough, pretty soon you start living again. When I was a kid, though, I don't know how long it was before I stopped expecting to see my folks in the bleachers at ball games."

Lucy nodded. She understood that. "I still think

I see Dad sometimes. Still listen for him when I wake up in the night. It's odd, too, because I don't really wish him back. The Johnny Dolan I knew would have hated the life Alzheimer's forced on him." She saw the path of pain on Boone's face. "But you went through worse."

"Remember that movie, *Pleasantville*, where they lived in a black and white world and only saw little patches of color at first?" He ran a hand lightly over the top of Maggie's headstone. "That was the way I felt after losing her."

"Is it better now?" she asked.

As they walked toward the Jeep, he reached for her hand. "A lot better."

She smiled. She liked to hear his voice. It sounded the way sunlight felt. "You're all about color," he said. "Your hair's the shade of Aunt Gert's butterscotch pie. You're always sunburned somewhere. You wear bright clothes. You even laugh in color, somehow. It's like reading the Sunday paper funnies after three years of the weekday black and whites." He dived in for a quick, hard kiss that took all the strength from her knees before opening the car door for her. "I draw cartoons for a living. I *love* color."

Gert came into the kitchen and frowned at the cake Lucy had covered with a particularly lavish amount of cream cheese icing. "Is that a butter pecan cake? Do we have a party tomorrow?"

"No party. I just haven't made one of these in

a long time. I thought it would be a good dessert." With her tongue caught between her teeth in concentration, Lucy piped loop-de-loops of caramel sauce over the cream cheese icing.

"Would be, except we already have angel food on the menu. Are we becoming a two-cake tearoom?"

"Nah. I just like this kind." It was her favorite, in fact. Her father had made it for her birthday every year until he died, even after he didn't know who she was anymore. Last year, her first birthday after Johnny's death, she'd ignored the day—there seemed little to celebrate. However, today, this particular Friday when she turned thirty-four, seemed like a fine day to have a good time.

"Anybody up for Trivial Pursuit?" she asked. "The game's still in the parlor from where some of the high school teachers had a tournament today. I don't know how they did, but they were laughing really hard and drank all of the beer we bought from that new microbrewery."

"Count me in. For the beer, too." Moving slowly with his walker, Sims came into the kitchen. He made his way to the island and sat down, gesturing toward the cake. "What's the occasion?"

"No occasion." Lucy put a bottle of beer in front of him. "Want a glass?"

"I don't need a glass. I'm not a sissy. Speaking of which, where's that boy at?" Sims grumbled. "Ethan and Jack ran the station yesterday and today both. Ethan's too old for that and Jack's too young."

"Boone went to Chicago for a few days. He flew

up on Wednesday," Gert reminded him, whacking his shoulder as she walked past, "and Ethan Walker's no older than you. Plus he doesn't have any broken bones and his head's not nearly as hard."

"Nancy says he's enjoying working in the station," Lucy said, sitting at the island with the older couple, "and I think Jack needs the money. He never says so, but he works really hard and is willing to do anything." She sipped her coffee. "Sissy? Did you really call Boone a sissy, Sims?"

"Yup. Always did. Him and Crockett both." Laughter gleamed from his blue eyes. "Called 'em that because they weren't."

"Let's go get the board set up." Gert held Sims's walker. "Just come in when you're ready, Lucy. Give me your beer, you old grouch. We've already mopped the floors once today."

"Calm yourself, woman, and make sure that bottle's still full when we get to the parlor."

They left the room, still grumbling at each other. Lucy smiled after them. She started to cover the dessert, then changed her mind. Today was her birthday, after all—they could eat while Gert trounced Lucy and Sims at Trivial Pursuit. Because there was no doubt that's how that particular scenario would go. Lucy rinsed her cup and got a miniature bottle of chardonnay out of the wine cooler. Might as well live dangerously.

She wondered if she'd ever grow weary of this house or of the mundaneness of living on Twilight Park Avenue. Would playing board games in the parlor and croquet in the back yard become boring with the passing of time? Would Gert and Sims become simply two old people she'd met instead of residents in the family portion of her heart?

Would she ever again start a day without wanting Boone Brennan to be part of it? She'd missed him since he'd given her a quick one-armed hug on his way out the door Wednesday.

To be real up front and honest about it she missed him pretty much all the time he wasn't with her. This was not something she was going to admit in a public forum of any kind, including the passenger seat of his Jeep. Or even the driver's seat, if Boone was smart enough to let her sit in it.

With a chuckle at her own foolishness, she left the kitchen, carrying the cake and her bottle of wine, going through the center hall of the house to the front parlor. The pocket doors were closed and she frowned in concentration. How on earth was she going to open them without dropping everything in the process? She'd have to do more than mop the floor again—she'd have to do the hands and knees scrubbing thing, and that wasn't going to happen. Not on her birthday.

"Gert?" she called. "Open the door, will you? Do I want to know what you and Sims are doing in there?"

The pocket doors slid open as though by magic, accompanied by a shout of, "Surprise!"

She almost dropped the cake, but Boone caught

it, handing it off to Landy Walker before bending Lucy back over his arm and kissing her senseless.

"How did anyone know?" she asked, hugging him hard and turning to face the people stuffed into the parlor like so many laughing sardines.

"That's pretty easy," Gert said. "It's on the partnership papers, then Boone the Intrepid snooped in your wallet just to make sure. The boy has no class at all."

"Boone the Intrepid?" Micah Walker snorted. "Sounds like another comic strip to me. Maybe we should start our own syndicate. I couldn't care less if you have any class or not, Boone. Actually, I'm used to you *not* having any."

Gert raised her voice. "Now that everyone's here, let's take the party outside so that we can actually have room to move."

The back yard was full of patio tables and chairs. "We cleared the neighborhood of lawn furniture and liquor," Boone confessed, "so if anyone calls the police—"

Tom Simcox spoke from behind Micah. "It won't matter, because I'm already here."

Lucy was busy hugging people. "I still don't see how you got it all past me."

"I had to keep grouching at you earlier to keep you away from the kitchen windows," Sims complained. "It was a stretch for me, I'll tell you," he added, provoking laughter from the whole crowd.

She'd never had a birthday party. Johnny always baked her cake, and the restaurant staff sang to her and gave her presents, but then they all went back to work and it became just another day.

"Do you want to play croquet?" eight-year-old Lindsey St. John asked. "Or can you still play? My dad says you're really, really old now. Almost as old as Mr. Sims."

"But still not as old as your dad," Lucy said into the laughter that followed. She hooked an arm around Lindsey's neck. "Let's play."

She lost, as she always did, but won at horseshoes. She danced, stood in a circle with other women and drank wine and talked about men, then danced some more. When she jitterbugged with Tom Simcox, they cleared the "dance floor," at least until Crockett swung past them with Gert on his arm.

She blew out what seemed like hundreds of candles, cut her cake, and opened more gifts than she'd had if you added all thirty-three of her other birthdays together. She sang karaoke and was booed off the makeshift stage. She laughed all night—the kind of laughter that made her hold her stomach and wipe her eyes, the kind she made into a memory to save for later.

People began to drift away at ten-thirty or so, and by midnight, the back yard was empty. Gert and Sims had hugged Lucy and gone to bed. Boone went in a few minutes later to see if Sims needed anything, leaving Lucy alone in the yard.

She sat at a lacy wrought-iron table that usually lived on the front porch, sipping coffee and playing with the bangles on her arm. They'd been a gift from Eli and Jessie St. John, which Lindsey assured Lucy she'd be glad to wear if Lucy didn't like them. She had on a musical-sounding charm bracelet too, which had been sent by Andy, the chef at Dolan's, and two of the waitresses who'd gone to work at the same place he had after the fire. A necklace which should have been gaudy but wasn't fit the curves of her neck, its pendant resting just below her collarbone.

"You never wear jewelry except for your earrings," Landy said when Lucy opened it, "and everyone needs a little artificial light sometimes."

Lucy fingered the peridots in her ears. They'd been her mother's, and she never took them out—it was a way of not letting go of Siobhan Dolan.

Boone came into the yard, reaching back inside the sunroom to turn off the outside lights so the only ones remaining were solar ones in the flower beds and a citronella candle that burned on the table where Lucy sat. "Happy birthday, Lucy."

"Thank you." She smiled. "I'm glad to see you, by the way. It was quiet around here while you were gone."

He pulled her up and into a loose embrace. "I missed you," he said.

She curved her arms around his neck, relishing his touch. She wanted him to kiss her in the worst way. "I've been happy at times in my life," she said. "Especially before my mother died and then for a long time before Dad got sick, but never more so than tonight."

"That's good." His lips hovered over hers. "So, what do you want to do now?"

"I'm tired," she murmured, rising—just a little—on her tiptoes so he could reach her mouth more easily. This wasn't a night for playing hard to get. "It's been a long day."

"Has it now?" He held her closer with one arm and lifted his other hand to shape her face, his thumb rubbing lightly over her bottom lip. "I love your mouth." His face was so close to hers she felt his breath on her cheek.

"Same goes," she said, and closed the distance.

Growing up in a restaurant kitchen, Lucy was well acquainted with "sizzle." However, kissing Boone Brennan in the back yard gave the word a whole new connotation. His hands slipped down her sides as they kissed, doing a little foray over her breasts that had her nipples pebbling up against the fabric of her bra. He held her hips, fitting her to him so she knew she wasn't the only who was being aroused.

His voice was uneven when he spoke against her mouth. "What would you say," he said, "if I invited you upstairs?"

It was as though her entire body was reaching for his. "I watch lots of old movies." Her voice hitched as his hands moved over her. "I'd probably say, 'Your room or mine?'"

"Yours," he answered immediately, and stepped away to snuff the candle on the table. "It's closer."

They were quiet going up, using the front staircase because it didn't have as many creaky spots as the worn treads on the steps from the kitchen. Lucy's room was in the back, with its own miniature sitting room, balcony and bathroom. The suite was a mirror image of Kelly's on the other side of the stairs.

Lucy was glad she'd remembered to make her bed that morning, although that didn't do much to calm her nerves. "It's been almost an embarrassingly long time. I don't know..." Her voice faded away as whatever it was she didn't know lost importance in the overall picture of things.

She was about to get naked with a man. *Oh, God.*

But first she was going to go on kissing him for a while. One of her favorite things about Boone Brennan was the way he kissed.

And touched.

And stroked.

And made her feel like she was in one of those movies where the camera lens cruised around the perimeter of the room while sounds of panting and sighs of satisfaction came from its center.

"I love that you wear dresses," he said as he lifted hers over her head and draped it carefully over a chair.

It was to her credit that she didn't dive under the covers. Even in the late night, her room wasn't that dark. She could see the glint of his eyes, his smile when he gazed at her, the brightness of the bracelets on her arm. She started to remove them, but he stopped her, sliding the metal up and down and kissing the inside of her wrist, lifting the chain from her neck and kissing the hollow at the base of her throat.

"Dresses are cooler," she said in a humiliatingly wobbly voice, though she didn't know if she'd ever feel cool again. His touch—and he seemed intent on touching everywhere—left heat in its wake. Undulating, liquid heat. When she unbuttoned his shirt—at least, she guessed she unbuttoned it, because it was open and sliding off his shoulders—the heat became more intense, the tingle between her legs a steady throb. He freed her breasts from the silky confines of her bra, and she marveled at the heaviness of them as he kissed and shaped them in his hands and teased the tight buds of her nipples with his teeth.

She wasn't sure how they came to be lying down, but she was glad they were, because it was definite that her legs wouldn't hold her up any longer.

He was already naked, and when he slipped her panties down her legs, following their progress with his lips and tongue and nipping teeth on the insides of the thighs, she was, too.

It had been so long.

She stroked the long muscles of him, thinking of the beauty there he was darkly tanned, but it was a careless tan, his left arm a deeper color than his right, his legs having lines that coordinated with the lengths of different shorts and swimming trunks. His skin was soft beneath the roughness of the hair on his chest and legs, and she delighted in the feel of it. Her fingers trailed—ever so lightly—down his belly and into the vee of his legs, finding what they searched for and circling and stroking.

His breath drew in, quick and sharp. "Careful," he murmured, though he didn't pull away even a little bit. "We'd like this to last at least a few minutes."

He kissed her, his hands slipping down her sides, shaping her hips, laying her on her back and teasing her knees apart so he could reach the throbbing core of her. His fingers found all the creases—behind her knees, between buttocks and thighs, inside the nest of curls—and stroked them lightly, causing her skin to shudder in response. When one finger slipped inside and his thumb began a rhythmic little rub near the entrance, she gasped and arched against him.

"Boone?"

"I'm right here." He moved on top of her. "Show time?"

She laughed, a gasping little sound, feeling the delicious pressure of his chest against her sensitized breasts, and welcomed him inside. Nothing had ever felt so good.

But a few minutes later, when he said, "Oh, hell, come with me, Lucy," and she heard a silvery, shivery moan that had to have been her, something felt even better.

Happy birthday. Oh, yes, happy birthday, indeed.

Chapter Ten

"I didn't give you a present last night and you didn't even notice. I'm wounded." Boone sipped morning coffee and peered over the cup's rim at Lucy. There were certainly worse ways to start the day than sitting across from her.

"There were a lot of presents there," she reminded him, but her cheeks were pink. "I've never had so many. Even Kelly gave me a picture frame."

He liked that he could make her blush. That was probably another segue back into pubescence, but he could live with it.

"What's for lunch today?" he asked.

"Chicken divan, which Gert's cooking. I'm doing the salads, some of the contents of which I'm going to go pull out of the garden. Pumpernickel or wheat bread. Angel food cake and fresh strawberries or ice cream for dessert. We picked the strawberries, but bought the ice cream."

He nodded at the tall angel food cakes under glass domes on the counter. "So when are you going to start baking your own bread?" he asked facetiously, knowing she'd spent most of yesterday afternoon on the desserts, not counting the time consumed by baking the birthday cake that had been eaten by last night's hungry hordes.

If she heard the teasing in his voice, it didn't show in her response. "In the fall. We'll sell loaves and half-loaves, too, along with dinner rolls. Oh, and honey and jams and jellies from Miller's Orchard. We'd sell wine by the bottle too, but Gert's picky about getting arrested."

"Really? I thought she only minded it when she had to go down to the jail and get someone out." He got up, going to put their breakfast dishes in the dishwasher.

Maggie had been a terrible cook. She'd been a great first grade teacher, a superb athlete and a talented musician—he'd finally donated her parlor grand piano to the elementary school where she'd taught because he couldn't bear the sight of it—but anything domestic had eluded her. "I'm the only person in the world," she used to say, "who can *dust* wrong."

They'd eaten out most of the time and hired someone to clean the apartment twice a week. It had never mattered if there was dust under the furniture or if the bed wasn't made or if the dining room table was completely covered with papers—as it often was. They had been so involved with each other that the rest of the world went largely unnoticed. They'd nearly missed Kelly's law school graduation because the invitation had been buried in a stack of books on the bedside table.

Life with Maggie had been fun and exciting and

intellectually stimulating. Their mutual devotion was so all-consuming that it had occasionally been exhausting. There were long days when he worked behind closed doors. Other times, Maggie retreated to her parents' home in Florida to spend time with them and her sister as just herself instead of part of a married couple. When they came back together after those separations, the reunions were joyous, with a sense of life going back on its track again.

That reflection drew Boone back into the present. Maybe it was happening again, that whole life on track thing. It was a good thought.

He refilled their coffee cups and returned to his seat across the island from Lucy. He thought about how she dusted, being so careful with Aunt Gert's collection of figurines. He remembered that she'd waxed the hardwood floors on her hands and knees and that her favorite thing on Monday morning was drying the bedding outside. When she woke in the middle of the night, she cooked.

She was so different from Maggie. So very different.

Damn.

For a moment, he felt an unreasoning and unusual anger with his dead wife. *Why can't you get out of my mind?*

"Would you tell me about her?" Lucy asked.

"What?" He met her eyes, startled.

"Maggie. Would you tell me about her?"

Talking about Maggie had always been painful, so he didn't do it. It had taken all the fortitude he had to have the discussion with Crockett, and so far, he wasn't doing that well with the letting go part of it, either.

Except for when he was with Lucy. When he'd held her in his arms the night before, he hadn't closed his eyes and wished she was someone else. He hadn't compared her compact body to Maggie's lissome one. She hadn't been a replacement he'd made love with out of physical need—she'd been Lucy.

"Tall," he said finally, "and she played piano and sports. She had a higher vertical jump than I did, and Crockett said she landed better too—as in it was almost always on both feet. She told bawdy, nasty jokes, and she told them better than most guys I know. We had a good life together. Now it's over." It surprised him when the words didn't have their usual sharp effect. Maybe Crockett was right. Maybe it *was* time…

He smiled at Lucy. "Do you want to go to the movie tonight? It's one of those chick flicks where the girl's strong and brave and gets naked and the guy's a total idiot. I always feel at home at those."

Lucy tore salad greens into easily manageable pieces and distributed them among mismatched glass bowls. She added radishes, carrots, and cucumbers, then ground fresh pepper into the bowls before adding a spoonful of chopped peppers and celery to the mix. She loved making salads. They were never the same two days in a row, which had earned them the name Lucy's Adventure on the blackboard menu.

The thermometer in the kitchen window declared solemnly that it was in the nineties, and even in the air-conditioned house, Lucy perspired while she worked. She filled a large insulated glass with ice and lemonade and took it outside.

"Drink this," she called to Jack, who was weeding flowerbeds. "Are you hungry?"

He shook his head. "Too hot to eat, but thanks for the drink."

"Well, don't work too hard. Gert will yell at you if you faint in her lilies."

"Yes, ma'am, your princess-ship." He smiled politely before returning to his task, and she wondered, not for the first time, what made a sixteen-year-old boy work so hard. She was almost certain he helped his family with the money he earned, since he didn't seem to spend any of it on himself, but when she asked about them, he said little. He did mention having younger brothers, so she always made sure to send cookies home with him for them.

The day seemed anticlimactic after the excitement of the night before. Even the lunch crowd in the tearoom seemed lethargic and overly quiet. When the last of them had gone, Lucy loaded the dishwasher and tossed the day's tablecloths into the laundry room. They could wait until tomorrow morning to be washed—she was tired. She gave the contents of her apron to Gert and dropped the customary handful of change into the pickle jar.

"I think I'm going to take a nap," she said. "I've never really gotten fully awake today."

Her landlady's eyes were merry and extraordinarily blue. "Something keep you awake last night, dear? I figured you'd slept through since there wasn't any baking done this morning."

Lucy felt color rise in her face. "I'm just tired." She fled up the back stairs, not wanting to see the knowledge in Gert's face.

She opened her bedroom door and shared a surprised stare with the tiny tuxedo kitten that sat on her bed. "Well," Lucy said. "Hello." She picked up the ball of black and white fuzz and held it in front of her. "Who are you?"

The kitten didn't blink, just lapped Lucy's thumb with a rough little tongue and continued its earnest blue-eyed gaze.

A wicker laundry basket was on the bed, too. It held a litter box and litter, food bowls, and kitten food, along with a miniature jeweled collar and a bag of toys. "She's six weeks old," the note in Boone's sprawling handwriting read, "and doesn't have a name yet. Hope you like her. Happy birthday!"

"Well, of course you have a name," Lucy whispered past the lump in her throat. Had Boone gone through her pickle jar? Even knowing he probably had, she couldn't summon up any indignation over it.

"Gert, did you see?" She thumped down the stairs, her heart feeling as though it were dancing in time. "Did you see what Boone left for me? Is it all right? I know she'll have to stay upstairs or in the sunroom most of the time, but isn't she beautiful?" She held the kitten up for Gert's inspection. "Kitty Kinsale, meet Gert Taylor. You have matching eyes."

"Kitty Kinsale?" Gert scratched the cat's chin, sending it into a squirming writhe of ecstasy. "That's a lot of name for such a little cat."

"We'll call her Kinsey," Lucy decided, "but my parents were from County Kinsale. Where's Boone? I have to thank him."

"He's working at the station." Gert glanced at the clock. "I thought you wanted a nap."

"I thought I did too," Lucy said dismissively, "but, Gert, I've wanted a cat since I was little. How did he *know?"*

"You've never had one?"

"Dad wouldn't let me when we lived over the restaurant, and when I got my own apartment, I couldn't have pets." She shrugged, cuddling Kinsey. "It wasn't a deal breaker or anything, but I always wished for one anyway." She went to the counter and dug through the pickle jar, coming up with a wrinkled and coin-marked piece of a green and white customer's check from Dolan's. "See?"

The strip of paper merely said, "Kitty Kinsale."

Gert laughed. "If anyone had found that, they wouldn't have known what it meant. It would be a good name for an exotic dancer."

Lucy grinned. "For when we open the bordello?"

"Right." Gert took the cat. "If you want to go over to the station, I'll take care of Kinsey. We'll chat about leaving hair on the furniture and climbing curtains and things like that."

Lucy hurried out, not even bothering to search for the bicycle helmet she tried to remember to wear, and rode her bicycle to the gas station. She regretted the decision halfway there when sweat was dripping off every part of her.

Boone, wearing perspiration better than anyone had a right to, was refilling the soda machine when she pedaled onto the lot. She dropped her bicycle and threw herself into his arms.

"Wow," he said, dipping his head and finding her mouth. "What's all this? Whatever it is, I'll do it again."

"The cat," she said between kisses. "I love the cat."

And you. I love you too.

His expression was bemused when he met her eyes, and she thought for a moment she'd said the words aloud. She drew away, embarrassed. "She's beautiful and her name's Kitty Kinsale only we'll call her Kinsey," she said, her words tumbling over each other, "but how did you know she was the perfect present?"

"Well, I didn't, but I did engage a personal shopper," he admitted, "Lindsey St. John told me if she was as old as you, a cat was what she would like."

Lucy laughed. "I'll have to thank her."

"Don't bother. Eli and Jessie told her the kitten

population was going to have to decrease at their house, so Lindsey was pretty much going door-to-door. Kinsey has siblings and cousins all over town."

A car was pulling up to the gas pumps. "I'll let you get back to work. Thanks for the cat."

"You're welcome. We still on for tonight?"

"The chick flick? You bet. If Gert and Sims will kitten-sit, that is. I don't want her to be lonely."

"We can't have that." He grinned at her, stepped close enough to kiss her hard on the mouth, then closed the soda machine before sprinting to the waiting car.

Lucy waved to the driver and got on her bicycle, thinking she might ride a little slower on the way home to try to beat the heat. Although she wasn't actually sure all the warmth she was feeling was weather-related.

Boone wondered if Lucy wore a dress to the movie because he'd told her he liked her in them. This particular one was green, which matched her eyes and contrived to make her hair brighter. "It's redder," he said, tugging at a curl that had come loose from its clip.

"That's because we had a spa night at Landy Walker's and everybody's hair ended up a little different color than when we came." Lucy gave him a mock-severe look. "That was over a week ago. It's good to see you're so observant."

"Oh." He remembered that. It had been on Thursday, poker night, and a few of the guys had been wondering what all they were supposed to notice when they got home. Micah had been smug, being pretty sure "the girls" would leave lots of food he'd be compelled to finish up.

Boone ran his fingers under the complicated strap system on the back of Lucy's dress, her skin warm and soft beneath his touch. "I like this, but how on earth do you get it off?"

"Oh, I don't." She fluttered her considerable eyelashes at him. "I wear it to protect my virtue."

"From what?"

She laughed and preceded him through the door of the theater.

The old Roxy, which had once been an ornate building complete with balcony, had been divided into two separate screening areas since he'd last been there. The balcony seemed to have disappeared altogether. When they'd found seats in the cramped room, he watched as Lucy took careful stock of their surroundings. She was, he realized when she relaxed beside him, checking for fire exits.

"I liked the building better the old way," he murmured. "You could sit in the balcony and make out. People in those days knew what movie houses were for."

"Not for watching movies?"

"Oh, well, sometimes, if you couldn't think of anything else to do."

Boone enjoyed the film, though the strong and

brave heroine never did get naked. “Not even once,” he complained to Lucy when the lights came up. “There wasn’t even a decent nipple shot. And there was plenty of chance for one, because all of her tops were too small.”

“You noticed that, huh?”

“Just in passing. It wasn’t important or anything.” He pushed open the heavy door of the theater. “What a relief. I think the humidity level dropped below a hundred while we were in there. What would you like to do now? We could find a drink somewhere or do a couple of laps on the River Walk.”

“Let’s do that. It’s nice being outside.”

They walked for over an hour. Boone pointed out old haunts and confessed to adolescent sins that had her covering her mouth to stop her laughter from bouncing across the surface of the Twilight River.

“We lived in Louisville before my parents died,” he said. “When we came here, to a town that’s smaller than our neighborhood was, I had no idea that if I sneaked into the theater for the Saturday matinee, the Methodists would be praying for my deliverance the next morning and passing it along to the Catholics at St. Charles. Uncle Mike went to one church and Aunt Gert the other, so the parishioners had us well covered. We’d probably been here six months before we knew it was universal—they prayed for all of us, not just the new kids from the city. Whoever first said ‘it takes a village to raise a child’ must have grown up in a place like Taft.”

She laughed. "Or inside a restaurant. It was the same way there." She peered up at the huge Victorian house that was the Methodist parsonage. "I think I've seen some of these houses on Christmas cards."

"They've probably been on them," he agreed, sobering, "but they don't necessarily have Christmas-card histories. Landy's first husband died in that particular one." He pointed at another of the large homes, barely visible through the trees. "The Ku Klux Klan used to meet there, and the one on the end was a house of ill repute owned by the same guy. Eli St. John grew up in the house where Micah and Landy live now, and it was a stop on the Underground Railroad during the Civil War."

Their meandering eventually took them to the front porch of Tea on Twilight, where they joined Gert and Sims. Boone went into the house to get iced tea and when he returned, Lucy was sitting in a wicker loveseat with Kinsey in her lap.

Boone sat beside her, reaching to tickle the kitten under its chin. "You do realize," he said, "that we left my car at the theater."

"Oh." She started. "We talked all the way home and I guess I forgot. Will it be all right there?"

"Yeah. I'll get it tomorrow on the way home from the station. I forgot it too." Because he'd been involved with her. With thinking of being alone with her. He wanted to make love with her again, to feel all that soft freckled skin under and around him, to get lost in the warmth of her green eyes and her generous mouth. To feel more than he'd felt in three long years.

"It's safer there anyway." Gert got to her feet. "All vehicles are safer when Boone's not driving them. I'm going to bed."

"Aw, Aunt Gert, you know you don't mean that." Boone rose to kiss her cheek and give Sims an arm up. "You need any help, you old goat?"

"Nah, just get the door so your aunt doesn't let it go and knock me over. You know how she is." Sims winked at Lucy and squeezed Boone's arm before he let go of it to grasp his walker. "'Night, young'uns."

Boone wondered what he'd be doing if he were in Chicago. He had acquaintances there, guys he played golf and basketball with and joined for beer and trivia at a local bar. He worked a lot, drawing and writing his comic strip and working at developing the new one.

"Elmer and Myrtle" appeared in enough newspapers to make him a minor celebrity in the city. He did workshops at seminars, appeared at fundraisers, and had been the keynote speaker at a few conferences. He took dates with him who wore slim pants and jackets that were too short and tight but whose conversation and flirtation he enjoyed. He never drew just in his spare time the way he did here—it had always been his primary avocation and he spent hours of every day doing it—but then he never pumped gas, bussed tables, or delivered pies to outlying areas, either.

"Do you get homesick for the city when you're here?" Lucy asked.

Boone blinked. How did she so often know what he was thinking?

"Sometimes," he said, "but when I go back, I'm homesick for here. More often, I miss some of what the city has to offer—you know, like you do—with public transportation being a biggie. Taft's idea of taxi service is to jump on and off the senior citizens' shuttle while it's still moving. I miss the White Sox, too, but not as much as I thought I would. The Reds are close enough if I need a major league fix."

Lucy nodded. "I keep thinking I'll get bored with knowing what to expect every day."

"Hasn't happened?"

She grinned. "I haven't had two days that were the same yet."

He chuckled and put his arm around her, drawing her to his side. "Are you sleepy?"

"No," she said, and promptly yawned. "Well, maybe." She tilted her head and smiled up at him. "It's been a nice evening. I hate to see it end."

"Me, too." He kissed her then, for a long time, even though they were right out in front of God and everybody and dollars would get you donuts the neighbors across the street were stargazing from their porch swing. "Do you maybe need help getting this dress off?"

She shook her head, her soft hair tickling his chin. "I need to think about what I'm doing." She raised her face so that their gazes met in the dim glow of the streetlights. “I don’t want to be like Crockett and your sister, barely speaking to each other because at some point in time, something happened between them that still stings. It’s hard on them and it’s hard on Gert. I intend to stay around, and I don’t want a broken relationship littering either of our paths.”

Anger stirred under Boone’s ribs. Holy horseshit, couldn’t they just have a good time? They were both adults, not the post-adolescents Kelly and Crockett had been when Kelly had decided she was in love with the guy who’d treated her like a sister most of her life.

“I’m not ready to make any promises,” he said, his fingers going still under the straps of her dress.

She stiffened—he could have sworn her skin cooled under his touch—but held his gaze. “I’m not asking for any, nor do I have any to offer in return, but sex isn’t casual for me. I’m not going to pretend it is.”

There was nothing casual about it for him, either. At least, not anymore. In truth, holding Lucy in his arms was about as un-casual as it got. It made him think of things like permanence and moving, lock, stock, barrel and baggage, to Taft. He’d even held Micah and Landy’s baby girl and exchanged solemn stares with her and thought maybe it was time to put that particular grief away and try again.

Live again.

Love again.

It scared the hell out of him.

"How about we just go slow?" He didn't want to argue—the relationship was too new to withstand the coldness of anger. He drew his hands away, then put them back on her shoulders, meeting her eyes again. "Slow, but not backwards. What do you think?"

"I'd like that." She smiled, though the expression was more wistful than happy. "And I won't expect any promises."

Three minutes ago, that's what he'd wanted, what he'd said.

A lot could change in three minutes.

Chapter Eleven

The smoke rose thick and acrid up the staircase as Lucy stumbled down it. She moved unerringly to where he stood at the huge commercial stove, pushing onions and peppers around in a sauté pan. He worked happily, singing something Irish in his rusty baritone. She grasped his arm, shaking it for emphasis.

"Dad? Come on. Let's get outside where it's safe. No, let's go out the back door. The fire's in the front."

In her dreams, she was always in time, and when she woke, she grieved again because she wasn't.

Johnny Dolan was dead.

She'd slept well lately. Even the night of the trash fire at Down at Jenny's, she'd gone to bed thinking of Boone's kisses instead of encroaching flames. Tonight, however, the dream had come again, and it had been real enough that she still smelled a faint whiff of smoke.

She knew she wouldn't go back to sleep—the sun was already up—so she dressed in shorts and a tank top before draping Kinsey over her arm and going down the back stairs. The house was cool, but the humidity of early August made it feel uncomfortably close, as though a headache were hovering around the ceiling searching for a place to settle in.

She filled her cup even before the coffeemaker stopped grumbling about being awakened and went toward the sunroom, draping a kitchen towel over her shoulder. "Let's go outside," she murmured to Kinsey. "And no chasing birds, okay? Those feeders don't hang in the trees to make things easy for you."

The cat was sidetracked by the food and water bowls in the sunroom, so Lucy pushed her feet into flip-flops and stepped into the back yard alone.

She wiped a patio tabletop and a matching chair dry and sat. She loved early mornings, although this one would have been better if it had started an hour or so later, without the dream as an unhappy impetus. As much as she enjoyed the hubbub of the tearoom, she cherished the quiet feeling of no one being awake but her and the birds. And one frisky tuxedo kitten.

The flower beds were still alive with color, but the grass was already the paler, dryer green of late summer. She'd given up on any semblance of neatness in the vegetable garden—it had been taken over by tomato plants and greedy melon and cucumber vines, all of which were producing far more fruit than they could use. It even *smelled* different than it had just a few short weeks ago.

Not just different.

It smelled like smoke.

As if on cue, the sounds of sirens sliced through the air. Lucy's grip on her cup was so tight her fingers ached with it. She looked around, unable to see the gray haze that she knew accompanied the smell.

Boone's voice preceded him into the yard.

"What's going on?" He carried coffee in one hand and Kinsey in the other.

"Fire." Her voice sounded as hollow as she felt. "Can't you smell it?"

"Where is it?" He handed her the cat and dried a chair with the damp dish towel lying on the table. He didn't sit, however, but prowled the perimeter of the yard.

"How should I know?" Lucy asked sharply, her gaze following his movements.

"Get over yourself," Boone suggested, scowling over his shoulder. "I wondered if I needed to try to spray down the house."

"Oh." She petted Kinsey much harder than the cat liked. She meowed a protest and jumped out of Lucy's lap, running to sit on the back stoop and groom herself.

The sirens came closer. Closer. And stopped. Lucy's stomach clenched. What if someone was hurt? Unable to sit still, she got up and walked around to the front of the house.

Two fire trucks, a sheriff's car and another emergency vehicle filled the street at the end of the block. Feeling like an ambulance-chaser, Lucy started toward the corner. People were already outside, some of them still in nightclothes, standing in the street and on the sidewalks. The sheriff waved them back.

By the time she reached the small throng, Boone was beside her, his hand clasping hers.

"What's burning?" he asked the group of neighbors.

"Stan Morgan's garage. It was full of crap. Kept trying to warn him," said Mr. Ballard, whose house was beside the Morgans'. "We'll be lucky if it doesn't take his house and ours with it, if the wind picks up."

As if on cue, the never-present August breeze paid a visit and the flames veered toward the Morgan house. A shout from the firefighters preceded a preventative stream of water. Lucy flinched when a window shattered.

"Where *is* Mr. Morgan?" she asked. Dread moved through her in shuddering waves. When Boone released her hand and put his arm around her, she leaned into him.

"He's over there." Mr. Ballard pointed. "He lives alone. His wife died a few years ago, and all the stuff in the garage was hers that he never could make himself get rid of."

Boone's arm tightened around her back, but the sensation disappeared so quickly she wondered if she'd imagined it.

"Come on." His voice was quiet. "Let's go home. There's nothing we can do here."

She went with him. "I feel as though I'm being followed," she said, glancing over her shoulder as they walked toward Tea on Twilight.

"Followed?"

"By tongues of flame or something. How long before everyone starts wondering about me like Kelly does? And who can blame them? As far as I know, fire isn't a commonplace occurrence in Taft. Or it wasn't before I came here."

"I don't think two unrelated fires create a pattern." Boone's voice was calm.

Gert was preparing breakfast when they got back to the house. "I heard sirens," she said, forking bacon onto a platter.

Boone explained while Lucy set places at the island.

"Stan Morgan was always a packrat. That didn't start when Winnie died. I thought it was healthy that you didn't keep Maggie's things," Gert said, "but I know it bothered you some giving them away."

"Keeping them was harder. Her sister still wears some of her clothes, and it startles me when I see them. After I gave her piano to the school, I used to go there and listen to people play it. Until it occurred to me exactly how sick Maggie would have thought that was." Boone laughed, and his aunt gave him a smile that was both surprised and pleased.

Sims came into the kitchen, his walker thumping in front of him. "Today's the day," he said, sitting down with a grunt of accomplishment.

"What day's that?" Although Lucy knew very well—he'd talked of little else lately. Landy and Nancy Walker were coming to serve lunch in the tearoom so Lucy could make the drive to Cincinnati. "Want coffee?"

When he nodded, Lucy poured his and carried the carafe around to refill everyone else's cups while she was at it. Once a waitress, always a waitress.

"My partner here and I are parting company." He rapped his knuckles against the cast on his leg.

"I'll be able to get out of your way and back into my own house." He frowned at Boone. "Reckon you'll be able to stop working at the station too, if this leg works. That boy Jack's pretty good help, though, for sure. Thought I might keep him on. He couldn't work all that many hours after school starts, but maybe we could stay open later, the way we did when you and Crockett were in school." His scowl beetled his heavy gray eyebrows. "Not that either of you did diddly, but just sayin'."

"Good idea, though I can still fill in if you need me to. I was planning on staying around till Labor Day anyway. That's another two weeks."

Lucy set down her fork and stared sightlessly at her plate. She'd known—of course she had—that Boone would leave. He had a home in Chicago, a life that had little to do with Taft, Indiana. His aunt and sister usually visited him, not the other way around.

"He and Crockett nearly always come during the Christmas holidays, though not necessarily on the day itself," Gert had told her the week before, "then for a few days at different times in the summer months. This year has been a social anomaly for both of them." Tears shimmered in her eyes for just a moment, and her gnarled fingers with their long, blood-red nails stopped snapping beans. "I miss the old days sometimes, when all the kids were here and the house was never quiet or neat."

Remembering the conversation, Lucy lifted her fork again and sighed. She was going to miss something too. Someone. This wasn't something she'd counted on when she moved to Taft. She was used to being on her own. She was good at it—she didn't need another family, much less a man. Specifically a man like Boone. Whatever that meant.

Across the table, Boone spoke. "I'll come back, though." He tried to capture her gaze, but she avoided his eyes.

"Micah and I are having a good time with the new strip," he said. "I'll come down to brainstorm with him."

What about me? Will you brainstorm with me too? Will we ever make love again or was that just a one-time thing? Was it casual for you after all?

"There's a soup supper in October," he said. "Want to go to it with me?"

She smiled at him, though her heart felt empty. "I'll be working at it. You want to help?"

"I can do that. I've cleaned a lot of tables at church suppers."

Gert snorted. "You were *supposed* to clean tables. You boys spent more time outside talking about football and embarrassing girls as they came in."

"We thought that was part of the job."

A shout of, "Good morning!" preceded Kelly into the kitchen. "It smells awful out there. Where's the fire this time?" Her gaze barely touched on Lucy as she poured a cup of coffee, cadged a piece of toast from her brother's plate and sat at the island.

"Morgans' garage." Boone raised an eyebrow. "New attire for court?"

She flicked a glance at her shorts and T-shirt. "Actually, it's attire for going to Cincinnati. I thought I'd take Gert and Sims over to get his cast off. Maybe I can get them to buy me lunch." She fluttered her lashes at Sims. "Whaddaya think?"

"*I* think you should have called." Gert's voice was sharp. "Lucy's taking us. Boone's riding shotgun."

"Oh." Kelly's face fell, hurt crossing her features. "I guess I should have," she admitted. She sipped her coffee and drummed her knuckles against the top of the counter, then took her phone out of the pocket of her shorts and started jabbing at the screen.

Lucy wasn't sure what Kelly was doing—her own cell phone was both old and featureless—but the other woman's fingers were flying over the miniature keyboard, her nails with their violet polish and embedded rhinestones sparkling.

"Why don't you and Boone go?" Lucy's suggestion stopped the fingers midflight. "I can do lunch today, save my day-off ticket for something more fun than spending it with a grumpy old man." She grinned at Sims and he glowered back. "Don't frown at me. I was talking about Boone."

Kelly brightened. "Oh, okay." She put her phone back into her pocket. "Thank you," she added briefly.

Lucy didn't know why she was surprised at

Kelly's instant acceptance of the offer, but she was. Not only surprised, but disgruntled. That was what came of being a pleaser. You ended up in situations where you had no one to blame but yourself.

"Lucy, if you have time," Sims requested, "would you go over and make sure the air's turned on in my house? Don't worry about food or anything like that. I just don't want to be walking into a blast furnace when I go home."

"Sure." She grinned. "Wouldn't want you to break into a sweat while you're dancing around the house."

One thing about having her plans changed was that it left her plenty of time. She'd done much of the day's work beforehand in preparation for being away from the tearoom. She would also—though he'd told her not to worry about it—fill his refrigerator. That wouldn't be hard because all it usually had in it was a half-gallon of milk and a twelve-pack of beer.

The day's lunch crowd was sparse, making the three hours she served drag. One man said his sandwich was "lousy" and pronounced to the room at large that she should be drummed out of business. A toddler gave a tablecloth a jerk that landed half the table's dishes in a shattered mess on the floor. A woman sat alone in the front parlor and talked on her cell phone throughout her lunch, broadcasting the details of her personal life. When handing change for a hundred-dollar bill to the person who hated his sandwich, Lucy inadvertently gave him twenty dollars too much, and he kept it.

"No, you didn't give me too much. You're trying to cheat me," he said when she attempted to correct her error. It was cheaper to let him have the twenty dollars—he obviously needed it more than she did if he was willing to lie for it. Taking the money out of her pickle jar to cover the shortage in the day's receipts, she decided some dreams came more expensive than others.

It had not been the best of days. She was almost afraid to go to Sims's bungalow at the end of the River Walk, for fear it would burst into flames at her approach.

However, everything appeared to be in order. She stocked the refrigerator with the staples and the leftovers she'd brought and turned on the central air conditioning. She changed the sheets on the king-size bed in Sims's room and hung fresh towels in the bathroom.

It was a nice house, she thought, locking its front door behind her and going to the van with her armload of laundry. She wondered, not for the first time, why Sims and Gert maintained separate residences. Perhaps Gert stayed in the Twilight Park Avenue house because it was Lucy's home, too, not to mention the place of business that supplied the younger woman's entire income. Gert being Gert, she wouldn't want to leave her boarder either homeless or jobless.

It was a singularly depressing thought.

* * *

Boone helped a scarcely limping Sims into his house. “Jack’ll close the station,” he promised. “Tomorrow’s soon enough for you to get back on the clock.”

“I own the clock,” Sims grumbled. “I should be there.”

“Tomorrow’s soon enough,” Boone repeated, trying to sound calm and unhurried. He loved his family and Sims, but the trip to Cincinnati and back had exhausted his social capacity. He needed some time by himself. Or with Lucy. Either way would work.

“The kid’s working a lot of hours and he’s on the football team, too,” Sims argued. “I wanted to let him have tonight off.”

“Then I’ll go close. Kelly can drop me off at home and I’ll ride my bike over.” Not the evening he’d planned—he was behind in his work—but he could catch up. He was just doing too much of that lately. It was easier in Chicago, where he was able to sort his time into neat little segments. Life in Taft didn’t lend itself easily to compartmentalization.

“All right. Go on then. I’ll be fine.”

Jack was cleaning the gas station restrooms when Boone got there. “Geez, kid, you wanting to clean your way to a raise?” Boone waved a hand when the bell from the pumps rang. “I’ll get it.”

He filled the SUV in the lot, ran the customer’s credit card, and cleaned his windshield. He was going to skip that, but there was no doubt someone would have called Sims by morning and ratted him out.

Jack was putting the mop bucket away in the storage room when he came back inside. “I don’t need help. Mr. Sims trusts me.”

Boone grinned, trying and failing to surprise an answering smile out of the boy. “I trust you too. But if you’re able to get the johns cleaned, I won’t have to, which is good for me.”

“I thought I was working till closing. I can. My mom doesn’t care. And I can use the money.”

“You’ll still get paid, but football season’s coming on fast. Aren’t you doing two-a-days? Those used to wear me down to not much more than a grease spot.”

“Coach gets it that some of us need to work. He busts our asses when we’re there, but there’s no penalty for having a job. It pisses off some of the guys who don’t have anything to do but play football, but them’s the breaks.” Jack shrugged, then hurried out when a car pulled up.

When he came back in, he put cash into the electronic register that Sims had fought acquiring for years. “Did Mr. Sims get to come home?”

“Yeah, and it was his idea to give you the night off. He doesn’t want you working too many hours.”

“But I need—”

“He’s the boss, Jack, and he’s no dummy. He respects you and he appreciates your work. There’s not a whole lot more you can ask from an employer.” *Oh, Lord, could I possibly sound any more like a high school principal taking his job way too serious?* Boone did a little internal eye-rolling. "Except more money, that is. Remember that raise I mentioned? By all means, ask Sims for one from time to time. It gives him a good chance to blow off some steam. He might give you one eventually, but not until he calls you Shit-for-brains and tells you you're the worst pump jockey he's ever had."

There was just a glimmer of a smile in the boy's eyes. "I've already heard that a couple of times. Scared the hell out of me the first time. I thought he was firing me because I had to be taught how to do an oil change. I'd never even lifted the hood of a car before. My dad always—" He stopped, his face going sullen again in the blink of an eye. "He used to bring his car in here for maintenance stuff, and I never learned how to do any of it."

"My dad died when I was twelve," Boone said, "but Uncle Mike—that was Gert's husband—taught Crockett and me how to check and change oil. Not that we wanted to learn, but he didn't offer us a choice. After he died, Sims took over." He laughed conspiratorially. "He wasn't a real nice-guy teacher, either, but I'm not telling you anything you don't know there, am I?" He checked the time. "Now, you need to get out of here, or Sims'll have my ass. Your pay won't be docked, but it's early enough to spend some time with whoever you hang with."

Boone sent Jack on his reluctant way and drew comics between customers. By the time he locked the station, he had "Eight Hours Work" ready for

Micah. He'd even started on the other strip, always the more labor—and imagination—intensive of the two. "Elmer and Myrtle" had supported him in fine style for ten years, but he was nearly ready to let them ride their vintage Harley Davidson off to the retirement home. Not that he was tired of them—that would be like saying he was weary of Sims and Gert—but he was having trouble with storylines.

Although Micah had been writing much of the new strip, he was reluctant to volunteer input into the content of "Elmer and Myrtle."

"You don't want to change its voice," he'd said when they talked about it one evening over Sam Adams and a plate of cookies someone had dropped off at the newspaper office. "We've done 'Eight Hours Work' together from the start. No one knows where you leave off and I start, but it would be different with this one."

Boone was still thinking about "Elmer and Myrtle" when he got home. He sat at a table in the back parlor and drew while Lucy arranged silk flowers in bud vases. "What do *you* think?" He watched her for a moment where she sat a few tables away near the bay window. "No fresh flowers?"

"We don't have any now that smell good. And if I use artificial ones, I don't have to wait till just before serving time to put them on the tables. Mornings are busy enough without that." She tied ribbons around the necks of the vases, her brow knit in concentration. "What do I think about what?"

"Do you think 'Elmer and Myrtle' have had their day?"

She lifted her head, her expression startled. "Good heavens, no. Why?"

He thought a minute, drawing with bold, minimalist strokes. "Well, we've done Sims's broken leg. A few years ago, I did the thing when Gert had to have a hip replacement. That was one of the most popular storylines ever, but I'm afraid it's going to become a hospital strip, one illness after another, because the protagonists are aging."

"Well, of course they are," Lucy said, a note of Myrtle-like long suffering in her voice, as though she were talking to someone who was challenging her last nerve, "but that's not *who* they are. You have to put in things like the pills they take in the morning *and* the broken leg. You need to show how hard it is for Gert to walk downstairs in the morning when she's stiff, but what's important is that they keep on going. They don't go to bed and let age happen to them."

Her hands went still, and even though she was gazing in his direction, he was pretty sure she didn't see him. "I used to try to remember that Dad was more than the disease." She started working with the flowers again, but slowly, thoughtfully. "Every now and then I was able to convince myself he was a nice man who liked to cook and just happened to live in my father's body."

Boone nodded. "Sometimes I get them mixed up in my mind." He drew the curved slash that was

Myrtle's hair. "I'll call Gert by Myrtle's name and she just shakes her head."

Lucy laughed. "She should talk. She goes through the whole list of your names whenever she talks to you, Crockett, or Kelly. I loved it when she started including me in that roll call—made me feel like part of the family. Not that I'm trying to take anyone's place," she added hastily.

"Speaking of Gert, where is she?"

"Over at Sims's. She's spending the night there to make sure he doesn't fling himself down the stairs or something. He's so happy to be mobile again, I think she's afraid he'll try that stair-step dance Shirley Temple and Bill Robinson did in the old movies."

Boone laughed. "There's a visual that will show up in the funny papers."

"Will I get a commission?" Lucy grinned and got up when the phone in the foyer rang.

He made a note on the back of his sketchbook and started another frame. He loved the drawing part of what he did—there just weren't enough hours in the day to do it the way he wanted to. The time had come to make changes in a life that had already been altered too radically too often.

The question was, which changes should he make? Which ones did he *want* to make?

Lucy came back into the room, wearing a bemused expression. "That was the realtor from Richmond. She has a buyer for the property where Dolan's was. He just now faxed her an offer."

"Is that good news or bad?" When she would have walked past him, he caught her hand so that she sat at the table where he was working instead of returning to her flowers.

"Oh, it's good, I guess. I can finish off Dad's medical bills and have a little nest egg set aside for when the van goes belly-up and Sims pronounces her dead."

"Do you need to go to Virginia?"

"Maybe to sign the papers, although I probably wouldn't have to. Everything's electronic now." She smiled, but her eyes were shadowed. "It's the end of my life there. I spent thirty-three years in Richmond, but the truth is I never need to go back, and it feels weird. Kind of lonesome."

He put down his drawing materials and got to his feet, pulling her up. "Let's take a walk."

They sauntered through the neighborhood, stopping to talk to Stan Morgan, who was in his garden. "It was my own fault," he said, gesturing toward the charred remains of his garage. "I had flammable stuff in there, and there were aerosol cans in my wife's things. It wasn't a good combination." He shook his head. "All the old wiring in the houses around here—it's a wonder there aren't more fires."

Boone felt Lucy stiffen beside him. He reached for her hand. "It's lucky you were awake," he told Stan.

"I wasn't. I'd have slept through the whole thing if it had been left to me. I'd probably be an old and soggy French fry. I guess someone was driving by and saw the smoke. Called 911. It was a good thing for me, I'll tell you." He leaned on the handle of his hoe. "Blessings come in strange packages sometimes."

"They sure do," Boone agreed cheerfully, winking at Lucy. "Let us know when you're ready to clean up, Stan. We'll be down to help."

"Will do. I appreciate it. And that lunch you brought down too, young lady. That was awful good." The old man extended his hand to shake both of theirs. "My wife always said I wasted more time holding onto things than I did enjoying them. I think maybe she was right."

As they walked back toward Tea on Twilight, Lucy frowned up at Boone. "Am I mistaken or did you just take the back door to referring to me as strange?"

"Why, no, ma'am." They stepped into the back yard and he pulled her into his arms, drawing her full length against him so that the heat and scent and motion of her became an instant part of him. "I was referring to you as a blessing."

Lucy didn't recall having been called a blessing before, but she liked how it sounded. It went right along with how it felt being in Boone's arms. She remembered what Stan Morgan's wife said to him about hanging onto things. Is that what Lucy did? Did she cherish the dreams in her jar so much that she didn't recognize others when they came along?

One of the notes in her pickle jar said, "Marriage. Children. Red SUV with a luggage rack."

Was she holding out for that even though Boone had already had the marriage with someone he adored, had already grieved a child, would probably drive an SUV as terribly as he drove everything else on four wheels?

While the knowledge that she was in love with him rocked and danced around her heart, she was just as certain he didn't return that love. However, he liked her, he wanted her, and he thought she was a blessing. She could, for the time being at least, live with that.

She lifted her face to his.

Kinsey was asleep in the sunroom when they went inside. She raised her head, accepted chin-scratches as her due and tucked her nose back into her tail.

They walked up the back stairs together without talking, but it was what Lucy had seen referred to in books as a "speaking silence." She understood that when they reached her room, he would go inside with her.

He did, and in the confines of her little sitting room, he took her into his arms and kissed her breathless. "Do you know how long I've been wanting to do that?" he asked, running his hands down her back until they came to rest on the curve of her hips.

"No. Tell me."

"Since the last time."

"Then maybe you should do it again."

"Now, there's an idea."

"I need a shower," she said a few minutes later, moving restively as his hands did an investigative foray inside her clothes. "I'm sticky with August."

He unfastened her shirt, concentrating on the small white buttons. His smile reached into her, sending delight cavorting right along her nerve endings. "That's a lot worse than sticky with July."

"It is," she said, "because I never really get dry before I'm sweating again."

"Well, then." He slipped her shorts down. "I'm probably sticky too. How are you about sharing showers?"

"Does sharing mean I get my back washed?"

"Uh-huh."

"Then I'm good with it." At least she thought she was. She'd never shared a shower outside of P. E. class before, and she thought it would be different standing under the spray with Boone than it had been with a cluster of other eighth-grade girls.

The water was warm and soft as it sluiced over them. Boone turned her so that her back was to him and lathered her washcloth with scented bath gel. He stroked the soft terrycloth over every inch of her back before re-soaping and kneeling to wash her buttocks and legs, his hands slipping casually between her thighs so that she gasped and leaned against the shower wall. "That soap stuff smells good," he said, seeming not to notice that she was turning into a quivering mass. "Turn around and rinse off."

She turned, feeling as though she were in a lovely kind of dream.

"Wow," he said, setting the cloth aside and reaching up with soapy hands. "Sticky breasts, too. You're just a mess." He soaped and circled, teased and taunted, before straightening enough to take first one stiffened nipple in his mouth and then the other. "Oh, gosh, yes," he said, "just an August sticky mess." He knelt again, licking her soft belly, dipping his tongue into her navel, and then lower still, tracing a light kiss the length of her appendix scar before using his thumbs to part her labia and dip his tongue yet again. Deeper.

Lucy thought she just might die right where she stood. Tried to stand. Her legs were going to give out any second. She'd never climaxed this way, not orally and not standing up. Was it even possible?

It was. Oh, dear, sweet Lord, it was.

She also found out multiple orgasms didn't only happen in books and in hushed conversations during which she'd always been silent. She thought she might still be silent, but no longer because she didn't have anything to add. No, she would be still because if there was even the slightest possibility that sharing the joy of this night would mean lessening its magic, that wasn't a chance she was willing to take.

Exhausted and a little sore, she fell asleep spooned into his long body, his arm lying heavy across her waist. When she woke, in that soft, inky darkness just before dawn, he was still beside her.

Chapter Twelve

August, unexpectedly and blessedly, cooled as it meandered along. By the middle of the second week, when entire departments of schoolteachers were meeting for long working lunches in the tea-room, the temperature and humidity had become downright easy to live with.

Lucy sipped coffee left over from lunch and re-read the letter in her hand. "Maybe I should go to Virginia," she said. "The buyers want to reopen the restaurant as 'Dolan's' and I haven't even met them. Andy—he started out bussing tables and ended up as the chef—called me this morning and said they asked him to come back to work there."

"Why don't you go? To Virginia, I mean, not to work at the new restaurant." Gert sat at the island with her calculator and the account books for Tea on Twilight. "You haven't taken two days off in a row since you got here in February. We have a strong backup crew when we need them. I'll be fine." Her eyes widened and she tore the paper strip off the calculator, passing it over to Lucy. "My goodness, we should give ourselves a bonus. This is the best week we've had all summer."

Lucy was tempted to take her partner up on the vacation-time offer. The last six months had been eventful and busy, so there had been little time for homesickness, but she'd like to see Richmond again, to visit her parents' graves and leave flowers for Isobel Dolan. She could meet Andy's new wife and visit with the other wait-staff who had been at the restaurant long enough to be family.

"Take Boone with you." Gert's eyes twinkled at her over the top of her reading glasses. "He's worked hard this summer. You could both do with a vacation. Spend a little time with Crockett. Maybe even drive over to the ocean for a couple of days."

"But you and Sims—"

"Will be just fine without anyone babysitting, though as soon as Kelly knows you're gone, she'll probably move in for the duration."

Lucy took a deep breath. "Gert, Boone and I—"

"Are adults." Gert closed the account book and pinned Lucy with a direct blue gaze. "What you do in your free time is your business."

"I'm afraid we'll hurt each other," Lucy admitted, "and put you in the position of siding with one or the other."

"You probably *will* hurt each other. That's what happens in relationships. But I'm going to love you both, just like I love Kelly when she's being awful and Crockett when he's being melancholy, and I'm not taking sides. Period."

"Then I think I'll ask him. He won't go all macho on me and want to do the driving, will he?"

"Fly," Gert advised. "He never bothers the pilot. At least, I don't think he does. You might want to talk to him about that before you make reservations and then take a separate plane if necessary."

"Oh." Lucy's stomach began to quiver. She'd never been on a plane. Not that she was afraid to fly. At least, not really. She and her father had just never taken vacations beyond the very occasional weekend at Virginia Beach—a habit she'd continued as an adult. When she was engaged, she and Scott planned to honeymoon in Gatlinburg, an easy-enough drive from Richmond. The trip to Atlantic City in her early twenties had been on the train.

Well, there was no time like the present to change that. "We could, couldn't we? If Boone wants to go, that is?"

"Go where?" He spoke from the doorway, and she glanced up, startled. When had he come in? The last time she'd seen him, he'd been in the back yard with Kinsey and his laptop.

"Richmond," Gert said, "and maybe the beach if Lucy can detach herself from the tearoom long enough. You should check on Crockett while you're there. I worry about that boy."

Boone rolled his eyes. "That boy's pushing thirty-seven, Aunt Gert."

"So are you." His aunt whacked him with the account book. "Though you're a few months behind him. You're also close enough to keep an eye on right now. He's not."

Lucy held up the papers she'd received from the realtor. "I wonder if Kelly would go over these. I'm afraid she'll get mad if I ask her to and even madder if I ask someone else."

"That's probably how it would go," Boone agreed unhelpfully. "So when are we going to Richmond?"

"This weekend?" Lucy asked. "Come back Tuesday? We don't have to go to the beach."

"I'll get the plane tickets," he offered, "but I want to go to the beach. It's been too long since I've seen an ocean."

"Take the whole week," Gert suggested. "We're going to be busy for a while when you come back. Everyone whose kids go back to school is going to be having lunch here over the next few weeks."

"Everyone?" Lucy raised an eyebrow. "Do I sense some wishful thinking going on?"

"No, you sense a newspaper ad. Twenty percent off the last week of August and the first week of September. The beauty shops, the nail salon, and that store that sells makeup and bath and body products are all doing the same thing. We're going to split the cost of a full-page ad in the *Trib.* Micah offered it at a back-to-school special price." Gert's eyes shone and she was once again the woman Lucy had met when she'd first come to town, before Sims's injury. Energy bundled in Birkenstocks. "I know I should have run this past you, but I feel as though you do the lion's share in this partnership anyway."

Lucy snorted. "I do the grunt work, which is exactly what I'm suited for. It takes a much sharper mind than this one to do the business parts."

"So, are we going?" Boone's gaze caught Lucy's, and she stopped moving, unable to break the connection.

This was what it was like, she realized, when you really fell in love with someone. It took over a part of your heart you didn't even know you had.

And now that she knew she had it, she wasn't sure what to do with it. "Yes," she said, "I'd like to go."

"Good." His smile wrapped itself around her. He gestured at the papers she still held. "It's poker night and we're meeting for beer and brats first. Do you want me to drop those off at Kelly's office on the way? She'll still be there."

She tucked them into a manila folder and passed it to him. "Thanks."

He kissed her, a leisurely meeting of lips and just the very edges of tongue that did strange things to her pulse rate, right there in front of Aunt Gert and the nosy kitten sitting in the flower pot on the kitchen window. "Later."

She nodded.

When he'd gone, she went to let Kinsey into the sun porch, picking the cat up to exchange solemn stares before delivering a head-scratch. "What do you think about the situation?" she asked.

Kinsey bumped her fuzzy black head against Lucy's chin.

"You're absolutely right." She stroked the cat and put her down. "Definitely some new clothes."

Boone smiled at the receptionist at the law firm. "Is Ms. Brennan busy or is she sleeping again?"

"I heard that!" came from the wide hallway between the two rows of offices. Kelly appeared, her arms full of file folders. "I'll see him, Bridget," she told the woman at the front desk, "but don't worry about coffee. He'll probably spill it on the carpet. Come on back, Boone." When he joined her, she handed him the folders. "Here. Make yourself useful."

Her office was large and bright, and he glanced around appreciatively, his gaze coming to rest on the framed cartoon panel across from her desk. "Ah." He walked over to it, reading the introduction of Daphne into the "Elmer and Myrtle" strip as though he hadn't written the words. He turned to his sister. "Did you know right away Daphne was you?"

She rolled her eyes at him. "Duh. A lawyer wearing a beauty pageant sash and a prom gown into the courtroom? Giving the judge a ration of shit right off the bat? What was my first clue?" She took the folders and set them on her desk.

"As I remember it, you did have a fondness for formalwear." He grinned at her, wishing it could always be like this when they talked. He didn't really know why or when they'd started creating sparks of contention with nearly every conversation, but he'd like to end it. To go back to being the protective older brother she liked.

"I still do," she admitted, "but I never entered any beauty pageants and I never wore taffeta to court. It wrinkles too easily and has to be dry-cleaned every time you wear it."

He nodded toward the panel. "Did it bother you?"

"At first it did, but then it became an asset being thought of more as a wardrobe and a hairstyle than as a litigator. Going up against an opposing attorney who doesn't take me seriously can be a good thing."

"I'm proud of you." Then he wished he'd kept his mouth shut when tears flooded her eyes.

"Thank you," she said quietly, and went behind the desk, staring fixedly at its messy slate top. When she looked up, her eyes were clear again. "You've never told me that before. I wanted that so much, you know. When I graduated from Notre Dame, then law school. When I passed the bar. And, Lord, when I made partner damn near right out of the gate…it was… I just wanted so much for you to be proud of me. I wanted to be as important to you as—oh, not Maggie, but Crockett, anyway."

"Kelly." Boone stood still, stunned by her words. "Of course I'm proud of you. I've always been—"

Her laugh sounded more splintery than mirthful. "Well, if you have, I haven't known it. I knew Uncle Mike and Aunt Gert were, but you were always more in tune with Crockett—then with Maggie—than with me, I always felt like Kelly the after-thought who couldn't be anything but pretty and dumb. That's why Daphne was hard to take at first.

I knew you took care of me, sort of, but you hadn't had any choice after we lost Mom and Dad."

"You're my little sister," he protested. "Taking care of you and pissing you off are parts of the brother job description I took very seriously and still do. And you've *never* been an afterthought."

She nodded at the cartoon panel on the wall. "Perception, you know—maybe mine was off. I don't know. But when I was in love with Crockett, I felt like his relationship with you was more important to you both than his with me was. When he fell in love with Maggie, then when *you* fell in love with her too, it was the loneliest I'd felt since the accident."

Oh, good God, why didn't I know? How could I not know? "Kelly," he said again, moving forward, toward her. "I didn't realize how you felt. I'm so sorry if—"

He stopped halfway to the desk when she shook her head quickly, sharply. "No. I'm mature enough to know it was me, and God knows, I loved Maggie too. No matter how I tried to put how I felt into words, it sounded as though I blamed her, and I didn't. Ever. When she died... God, I'd have gone in her place if it had kept you from being hurt that much. I would have, Boone, I swear. But then I couldn't help you. Even though you and he barely spoke, it was Crockett who was able to bring you comfort. That one day you came back from sitting by the river and he was there with you? It was as though you'd been delivered."

She tried to laugh, but it caught in her throat. "And I was glad. I was. But I was jealous too. I wanted to be the one who was there for you, not Crockett. I feel as though you never want to spend time with me."

"That's not true." He hesitated. "Well, maybe sometimes it is. Because you act as though you're the only one with work to do or a schedule to keep. I *want* to be there for you, but you never *have* the time. Isn't that true, too?"

She lifted her chin. "I don't want to be just a responsibility, Boone. To anybody."

"You're not *just* a responsibility, but you're my little sister," he repeated. "I'm always going to feel like watching after you is my job. But if you're bitchy every time I see you, if you're pissy with Aunt Gert because she doesn't let you boss her around, if you're constantly rude to a woman I care a lot about, then you're right—I don't want to spend a lot of time with you." He caught and held her gaze. "That doesn't change anything. I'm still proud of you for what you've accomplished."

"Well." She cleared her throat and reached to straighten the stack of files threatening to slide off the desktop. "What brings you down here? You haven't visited my office since… Well, ever, I guess. Even when you and Maggie made out your will, we did it at Aunt Gert's, not the office."

He handed her the folder containing Lucy's papers from Virginia. "Lucy asked if you'd take a look at these when you have a spare minute. They're about the sale of her property in Virginia. You can bill her if you want to."

"Oh." She scanned the letter on top. "She'll probably be glad to get this behind her."

"I don't know about that. I don't think she does, either. She feels about it a lot the way we feel about Louisville. It's not home anymore, but yet it is."

Kelly waved him toward a client chair. "Did you ever read the news stories about the fire in their restaurant?" She sounded professional—cool without being cold.

He stiffened. *Let it go, Kelly. Let it go.* "No."

"I did. Long before she told anyone what had happened, when Aunt Gert was still telling me to mind my own business. I know you don't want to hear this, but it was ugly, Boone."

"She told Gert. That was all that really mattered."

Lucy's file slipped from Kelly's hand. She pushed it aside. "She did? When?"

"Before they decided to open the tearoom. She didn't want there to be any unpleasant surprises."

"Why didn't Aunt Gert tell us? She knew we were concerned." Kelly pasted on a smile when the receptionist arrived with coffee. "Thanks, Bridget. Did you bring my brother a bib?"

"I figured you'd loan him one of yours," the woman said cheerfully, setting the tray on the credenza under the window. "I'm off now if you don't need me for anything else. Don't forget to go home at some point." She smiled at Boone. "I enjoy your cartoons. Especially Daphne. She reminds me of someone—I just can't think who." Her gaze slid sideways toward Kelly.

"Thank you." He accepted the cup Bridget offered and waited until she'd left the room, grinning back over her shoulder at her boss. "Aunt Gert doesn't want us breathing down her neck, second-guessing her decisions. You know that."

"I know." Kelly sipped from her cup, scanning Lucy's papers with sharp eyes. "These seem to be in order, though I'll read them more thoroughly. Did she have any specific questions?"

"I don't know. Do you want her to call you?"

"No. I'm going over to have dinner with her and Aunt Gert. I'll ask her then." She shuffled the letters into a neat pile, taking longer than necessary to straighten five or six sheets of paper, then pushed them back inside the folder. "Don't you ever worry about these fires, Boone? Don't you wonder? There was another trash fire yesterday in the Dumpster behind the library. Abby, the librarian, just happened to see the smoke when she came back from an appointment. I know Lucy'd been there because I saw her when I dropped off a sack of books for the book auction."

He didn't answer until she lifted her gaze to meet his. "What I wonder," he said quietly, "is what made you decide you weren't going to like her. She hasn't done anything to anyone, yet you made up your mind the first day she came to Taft—before you knew anything about the fire or her father—that she was bad news. You had no idea Gert was going to ask her to be a business partner or I was going to...like her, yet you took it upon yourself to judge her and find her lacking."

Kelly's face lost color under its perfectly applied layer of the Lancôme he was pretty sure she owned stock in. "Her license plate—" she picked up the pen he and Maggie had given her when she graduated from law school and bounced the end of it on the blotter, "—showed she was from Richmond. Before she ever mentioned Crockett's name—she called him Noah or Father Crockett, I don't remember which—I knew they were connected. There she was with that hideous old car and no money to speak of, dressed like a 1960s flower child. For all we knew, she was someone Crockett found on the street, but Aunt Gert greeted her like a long lost and dearly loved relative."

"Kind of like she and Uncle Mike greeted us."

Irritation flashed across Kelly's features and the pen thumped again. Harder. "You're comparing apples to oranges. We were children. We *were* relatives. By marriage, I know, but they never made any differentiation between us and Crockett."

"Relatives who moved in and turned their lives upside down."

"We made them happy." She stopped. The expression in her eyes was heartbreaking in its anguish. "Didn't we? They gave us everything. Didn't we at least give them that?" *Thump, thump, thump.*

"Of course, we did." Boone kept his voice patient, reaching across the desk to take the pen out of her hand and lay it down. "Lucy does too. Aunt Gert is crazy about the tearoom, and Lucy works herself to a nub to make sure it goes okay. I don't really think she does that just for herself, do you?"

"That's my whole point. She's a stranger to all of us. How should I know why she does it?"

"You know everything else," he pointed out, "and you still haven't given a reasonable explanation for not liking her. It's like you're jealous of her."

Kelly got up, going to the credenza for the coffee carafe. She came back and refilled their cups. Her hand shook a little—the rhinestones on her nails twinkling with the tremor. "Maybe I am." She sat down again, cradling her cup as though she were cold. "Unless I miss my guess, you're falling in love with her. Aunt Gert thinks she's in line for sainthood. Crockett—" She stopped abruptly.

Crockett. Ah. There's the rub.

"They're friends, Kell." Although once upon a recent time he'd wondered. "And he's a priest." It was a cruel reminder, but he knew as well as anybody what it did to a person to want what couldn't be had. Maggie's face and the sound of her voice flitted across his consciousness with the thought.

It made him smile.

"I know." Kelly picked up the pen.

"Lucy and I are going to Virginia this weekend. We'll be seeing him." Crockett had been excited when they'd called to see if he'd be available for the weekend. He offered up a friend's beach house for their use.

"Give him my best."

Kelly's voice was so prim it made Boone want to laugh, but he didn't. Sadness lurked in the depths of her brown eyes and removed the humor from the situation. "Okay." He sighed and got up. "I'm going to be late for beer and brats." He leaned across the desk to kiss his sister's cheek, taking the thumping pen out of her hand again. "See you later."

"This seems all right." Kelly came into the kitchen and handed a file folder to Lucy. "If you have objections to them naming the restaurant Dolan's, we can see what we can do, but it doesn't appear they're trying to take something that's rightfully yours."

"No." Lucy slid the folder under the pickle jar. "It's kind of nice, really, that Dolan's will still be in that spot. Mostly I wanted to be sure that I'm not selling the name. Although I don't plan to open a restaurant aside from the tearoom, if I ever did, I'd want to be able to call it Dolan's."

"You can do that."

"Thanks for checking." Lucy gestured awkwardly. "Will you send me a bill or would you rather I wrote you a check now?"

Kelly hesitated, her gaze slipping away from Lucy's. "Neither." Her smile was small, but it was there. "Let's call it a favor."

Lucy thought she'd almost rather be beholden to the devil himself. She swallowed. "I don't—"

"I owe you." Kelly's voice was brisk. "That day when Crockett came, you rescued me and I never even said thank you, though I probably did say some other things."

"Oh." Lucy shrugged. "That was a girl thing. I imagine you'd do the same thing for me." She wasn't sure she really believed that, but it was something she'd like to be wrong about.

"I don't know." Kelly smiled again, albeit ruefully. "Do you still carry around a broken heart and a grudge you should've gotten over fifteen years ago?"

Lucy shook her head. "No, but it's probably only because I saw the movie *Pollyanna* about a hundred times so I was able to convince myself I was glad Scott Knight jilted me. You know, *before* I found out he was an asshole as opposed to after the wedding."

"Girls." Gert's head appeared around the door into the sunroom. "You need to come on or I'm going to eat without you."

"You and Boone are going to Virginia this week?" Kelly led the way to join Gert at the table.

"For a few days. Even playing tourist at Virginia Beach."

"That will be fun."

"I hope so. I've never been on a real vacation. When Dad and I went somewhere, it was to check out other restaurants. Get new ideas. Recreation was secondary." She smiled, remembering. "When I drove to Taft, it was the farthest I'd ever been from home, and it was an adventure even before the van decided to require hospitalization. I ate fast food, spent a night in a motel all by myself without waking up every ten minutes to check for fire and find my father…" She stopped, the words fading away as pain took an uninvited twirl though her.

"Kelly and I took a trip like that after Mike died." Gert passed the mashed potatoes. "The boys were in college, and we drove all the way to Pennsylvania to watch them play basketball. Remember, Kell?"

Kelly's eyes softened. "I do. It was fun. We stopped and did things just because we could and no one got mad when we had to go to the bathroom. It was the first time I ever drove on an interstate highway."

"And even then she drove better than Boone," Gert said dryly. "It explains a lot. Law school and those kinds of things. She always knew where she was going."

"Yeah." Kelly spoke quietly, as though she were talking to herself. "And God forbid I ever admitted to taking the wrong direction, since I knew where I was going and all."

"Sometimes, though—" Lucy formed her potatoes into a rose with her spoon, "—you can only get to the right turn by going the wrong direction to begin with. Don't you think?"

Kelly's expression was skeptical. "Is that your story? Yours and Pollyanna's?"

"Sure is." Lucy grinned at her. "And we're sticking to it."

Chapter Thirteen

The new property owners were nice people who owned other restaurants in other cities. They wanted to hang a large picture of Johnny and Lucy in the foyer of the new Dolan's. Lucy gave them a copy of her favorite photograph of her father.

"He was the heart of it, not me," she said. "And there are still people who think I had something to do with the fire in the building. He'd appreciate your respect for what he did." She hugged Andy, the chef, and drew away. "You're part of that heart too." Her throat felt raw. "Thank you for being the brother I never had."

He nodded, squeezing her hands. "I'd rather work with you than anyone I know."

When she left the site with Boone, she knew she probably wouldn't go back. Her stomach shifted as it had when the plane had taken off from Louisville. But flying had been a pleasant new experience—saying the final goodbye to Dolan's and Andy left her more than a little melancholy.

"Let's go to the cemetery," she suggested, "then pick up Crockett and drive on out to the beach. I don't think there's anything left here for me."

"Works for me." Boone grinned. "If you'd feel

safer, we can fly to Virginia Beach. They have shuttles, and I don't badger the drivers to go faster, no matter what Aunt Gert may have said about that. At least, I don't anymore."

She laughed. "I'll risk the drive. I'm brave."

The cemetery was quiet, but bigger than she remembered. For a couple of minutes, she stood frozen in place outside the rental car, confused and feeling a vague sense of loss because she wasn't exactly sure where Siobhan and Johnny were buried. "Over here," she said finally. "I think."

"I was mad at my parents for a long time for leaving us." Boone handed her one of the bouquets of flowers they'd brought. "Well, Kelly and I both were, I guess. Did you feel that way with your mother?"

"Not that I can recall. Dad kept her so alive for me. I don't even know how much of what I know about her is memory and how much of it is what he told me." She arranged the flowers and ran a hand over the rough top of the stone at the head of her parents' graves. "I'm fine," she told them quietly, then went to leave a spray of mums for Isobel Dolan.

Lucy walked away from the memorial park with a sense of finality, much like the one she'd felt when they'd left Dolan's. She'd probably come back someday, but she no longer needed to.

Before they went to pick up Crockett, Boone talked her into showing him the high school where she'd graduated nineteenth in her class, the swimming pool where she'd learned to swim—though never very well—and the house with a tower room and two stained glass windows that she used to dream of living in.

"Living in an apartment above the restaurant was okay," she said, leaning out the car window and smiling at the big gray house and the white fence that surrounded it. "We had plenty of room for privacy and there was even a patio so we could sit outside, but it wasn't like having a real porch. We didn't even have a kitchen table or island, because we never ate or entertained up there. It wasn't that I was ashamed of our apartment. I just wanted to be like everyone else." She drew her head back inside the car and grinned ruefully at Boone.

He smiled back. "What everyone between the ages of ten and eighteen or so wants, I think."

She closed her eyes, wandering into the past. "My girlfriends loved Dad. He was the ultimate charmer. And they liked the restaurant because it was elegant in a family kind of way—we used to do our homework around the fireplace and the waitstaff would serve us milk and cookies. But I loved my friends' houses, their family rooms with clutter and dog hair and nosy little brothers. Andy was like a brother to me, but he had his own home, his own family." She sniffed, embarrassed by the tears that pushed at the backs of her eyes. "They all had mothers."

He nodded, the pain slipping across his features quickly enough she almost thought she imagined it.

But she knew better. She'd never had a single feeling of loss that he hadn't experienced himself. In her whole life, she'd never felt as close to anyone as she was to the man beside her in the car.

"I still miss her," she said. "Dad, too, but in a different way because he didn't die young the way she did." She laughed, though it caught in her throat. She was a little embarrassed by her own sentimentality. "It's as though she's the music in my heart. She called me Lucy Goosy once in a while, not often, and I can still hear her saying it. And sometimes I smell something that helps fill the hole that was made by her absence. Lavender-scented soap or those pomanders made from oranges and cloves."

Before she knew it was coming, without so much as a tingle on her eyelids, the storm of weeping took over her senses. Boone's arms came around her and she sobbed into his shoulder, her fingers clutching the soft cotton of his shirt.

"Shh," he whispered, his fingers tunneling gently through her hair. "It'll be okay. Really it will."

Just as she had never cried this hard or this long over the loss of her parents, she'd also never felt this depth of comfort. No one's voice besides Boone's had ever soothed her very soul. No other arms had made her feel safe, as though everything would indeed be all right.

The unmistakable sounds of a basketball game in progress reached them as they approached the doors to the school gymnasium across the street from the church where Crockett served. They stepped inside to see a three-on-two shirts-and-skins competition. The trash talk was loud and colorful. Lucy, a self-proclaimed prude when it came to language, felt a blush climb up her cheeks.

"Yo!" Boone yelled, and caught the no-look pass from Crockett. Boone dribbled onto the court, tossed the basketball into the waiting hands of a kid poised just outside the three-point line, and leaned past the opposition to shake hands with the sweating priest. "Why are you so wet? Are you ready to go to the beach?"

"Will be as soon as we take care of these limp—these young men here. It shouldn't take us long. You up for it?"

"Oh, hell, yeah."

"He's pretty old, Father," commented a young black man whose vertical jump ended somewhere around Boone's chin. "Ain'tcha worried he might croak on you?"

"Don't say 'ain't,' Anton." Crockett slapped the ball right out of the boy's hands. "Got it, Boone?"

"Yup." Boone dribbled outside the key to give his own best effort from the three-point line.

Swoosh! Nothing but net.

Hot damn, he didn't know he had it in him.

Crockett beamed at him. "Not bad for an old guy."

"We let him," jeered a kid whose shorts were hanging down around his ankles, "on account of he's your company, Father."

"Let me?" Boone cut in, then stole the ball. "Old guy?" He wondered how these guys could run without losing their pants altogether. Of course, if they did lose them, it would give a much-needed advantage to the geezer group.

They all kept their pants on, though just barely, and, unlike him, they weren't winded after two trips up and down the length of the basketball court.

"Are we ahead?" He hoped he didn't hyperventilate in front of Lucy and everybody. That would be so damn embarrassing, but his lungs were rattling with every breath.

"Almost." Crockett, whose vertical jump was marginally higher and a whole lot more graceful than Boone's, rebounded neatly and passed to him. "Bring us home so we can get out of here without being completely humiliated."

"I can't usually do this more than once." Boone dribbled toward the corner of the key. "Don't run over me," he warned the kid who was guarding him. "I'm old and I'm the Big Daddy there's best friend and that's my girlfriend over in the bleachers. I don't want to look bad in front of her."

"Not to mention you could show up in the comics." Crockett hipped in front of the kid so Boone had a clear shot. "And he's not a good enough artist to make you come out pretty, Moses."

Boone made the shot. Nothing but net *again*. Better quit while he was ahead.

"We're done." Crockett echoed his thoughts. "See you guys next week. Don't forget to go to mass. I'll be gone, but Sister Joseph will be watching."

"She's a whole lot scarier than you, Father," one of the boys mumbled, hiking his pants up.

Crockett pulled Lucy into a hug and spoke over her shoulder. "And don't forget it. Also remember that the old guys just beat you. It was a good lesson in humility."

"More like that one's a ringer." The one called Moses jerked a thumb in Boone's direction.

"Let me grab a shower." Crockett locked the gymnasium doors when they left "Then I'll be ready to go."

A few hours later, Lucy pulled the rental car into the carport of a large stucco house on a relatively uncrowded stretch of beach. "This," she said, getting out and gazing around, "is a whole lot different from a two-star motel. Are you sure we can be here, Crockett? I don't have enough money to bail you guys out if we're breaking and entering. Even if I *wanted* to bail you out, I mean."

"I'm sure." The priest, wearing decidedly secular and very old Notre Dame shorts and a ragged T-shirt, bounced his fingers on the keypad of the door lock. "It belongs to my dad."

"Whoa." Boone spoke from where he was getting things out of the trunk of the car. "When did he move down here?"

"He didn't, but he bought this house. A one-up on my mother, I suppose. You know, a way to show that he's so devoted to spending time with their son that he's willing to buy a vacation home for that purpose."

"Hmm." There was no reason to state the obvious, that such devotion was a long and too-late time coming. Boone stepped inside behind Lucy. "Nice place."

"It is. There are four bedrooms upstairs and they all have their own baths. I always sleep in the green one. Take what you want from the others, though I don't recommend the master suite. Someone went a little overboard with brocade and velvet—nightmare stuff."

It was a little uncomfortable being with a priest and a girl you had a fairly complicated relationship with. Were he and Lucy to the sharing-a-room point yet? Even if they were, would she want to do that when Crockett was there? More importantly, would she want to do…other things when Crockett was there?

"You can take my stuff upstairs and give me whichever room has the toilet seat down in the bathroom." Lucy answered the uppermost question in his mind. "I'm checking out the food situation and making a list, because I want to cook in this glorious kitchen."

"Is she always this bossy?" Crockett asked, heading toward the stairway that was in the dining room.

Boone nodded. "Usually."

"Good. I like that in a woman."

"I didn't think you were allowed to like anything in a woman."

"I'm a priest. I'm not dead."

There was something in the testy response that made Boone say, "You okay?"

Crockett turned enough to meet his gaze, and Boone was surprised at the turmoil in his friend's expression. He felt Crockett's pain as certainly as he had when they were joined-at-the-hip adolescents. "Can I help?"

"Counsel the counselor?" Crockett asked dryly. "Nah, I'm fine, Boone, but thanks." He gestured. "Give Lucy the blue room. It's girly."

"Speaking of girls, Kelly said hello." Boone set Lucy's suitcase on the end of the white wicker bed. Crockett was right—it was girly and she would like it.

"Did she? Tell her hey back." Crockett's answer was polite, his face impassive.

Boone rolled his eyes. Whatever had happened between his sister and his best friend was years old—it needed to go away. Kelly had still been in high school when she'd had her painful and unrequited crush on Crockett, who had been horrified by the turn of events.

"It would be like doing the nasty with my sister," he'd told Boone at one point. "That would be something you'd have to beat the hell out of me for and we both know I can kick your ass from here to kingdom come."

They'd laughed, but it hadn't been quite comfortable. Kelly's infatuation had thrown a cog into the smooth wheel of the relationship the three of them shared, one that Boone and Crockett got past fairly quickly, but Kelly did not. Boone thought of saying something now, of suggesting Crockett make his peace with Kelly, but then Crockett opened the door of the room beside Lucy's. "If you take the yellow room, you and Lucy can sneak back and forth and I'll never hear a thing."

The moment passed.

Lucy loved the kitchen at Tea on Twilight, but she had to admit it was technologically inferior to this one by a couple of decades and thousands of dollars.

"There's not a squeaky cupboard door in the place," she marveled when the men came into the room, "and if there's a junk drawer, I haven't found it."

"What kind of kitchen doesn't have a junk drawer?" Boone looked up at the complicated ceiling structure with its hanging pot racks and skylights.

"One like this." Crockett went to the coffeepot and filled three cups with the fresh-ground brew Lucy had just made. "I tried to establish a junky little area in the pantry one time when I was here, but when I came back, it was gone."

"You made that up," Lucy accused, opening one of the doors to the refrigerator. "Fresh shrimp and strip steak? Someone knew we were coming, right?"

"I called ahead," said Crockett, "and I did make it up, but I want you to be comfortable here. However, fresh meat and produce aside, Boone and I thought we'd take you out to dinner tonight—" he arrowed a sharp "go-along-with-me" glance at Boone, "—in the hope that you will cook for us tomorrow."

"Oh, is that what you thought?" She eyed them across the counter, her gaze moving from laughing Irish blue eyes to fathomless dark brown ones.

She really wanted to lose herself in the brown ones. The hairs on her arms stood up just thinking about it.

"How about we go out tomorrow?" she said. "I'll cook tonight. Breakfast tomorrow is up to you, Crockett, and Boone can do lunch. Sound fair?"

By the time they sat at the table on the deck with grilled steak, shrimp scampi, and a bottle of wine Lucy was certain hadn't come from the cheaper end of the aisle at the supermarket, she was feeling at least a modicum of the comfort Crockett had mentioned.

"Have you decided what you're going to do about the strips?" Crockett asked Boone, scooping rice onto his plate and passing the bowl.

Lucy looked up in surprise. The comic strips? Boone had mentioned ending "Elmer and Myrtle" once, but had never brought it up again. He wouldn't, would he? It would be like sending Sims and Gert to the old folks' home.

"Not really. Micah's doing more of the writing than he wants to. He still has a family and a paper to run, not to mention poker on Thursday nights—

the dude has his priorities. I need to hire an assistant to work with me in Chicago, but I'm reluctant..."

"Maybe it's time to move on," Crockett suggested.

Boone's eyes gazed toward the Atlantic's crashing waves. He seemed a million miles away. "Maybe it is." He sighed. "Of course, after eating this dinner, I won't be able to move at all."

He was, though. When Crockett offered to load the dishwasher, Boone grabbed Lucy's hand. "Come on. Let's hit the beach before he changes his mind."

"I've got calls to make anyway." Crockett held up his cell phone. "Take your time."

"Your bookie again?" Boone shook his head. "You oughta be ashamed."

"And you oughta be locked up. Lucy, take him away."

"Come on, doofus." Lucy laughed as she pulled Boone out of the house and down to the water. "Oh, isn't it beautiful?" Her voice bounced up and down with the roar of the waves, making her laugh again.

"It is."

They walked along, stepping into the water now and then, pointing at far-off sailboats and the swirling colors of the evening sky.

"What did Crockett mean when he said it was time for you to move on?" she asked, giving up the whole notion of minding her own business. "Are you still thinking of retiring 'Elmer and Myrtle'?"

"No. It would be easier if I was. Crockett was just telling me to fish or cut bait with the new strip.

It's a good one and my syndicate has indicated they would buy it. Lots of the papers that publish 'Elmer and Myrtle' would probably take on 'Eight Hours Work,' too, but it's more than I want to do. That being said, the idea of just turning it over to someone for them to choose who writes and draws it is a lot like giving away a pet after you've already housebroken it and let it sleep on your bed."

"Then don't give it up. Just hire the assistant you were talking about, and if you ever want it back, it will be there. Shedding on the sheets and chewing your shoes." *You've already had to give up too much.* She stepped into the water, holding up her long skirt. "Think about what you want to be doing with your life in ten years." She didn't meet his eyes, afraid of what he would say. Or wouldn't.

His arms came around her, pulling her full-length against him. His cheek sandpapered against hers, and she smiled at the sensation.

But he didn't answer.

Boone crawled between the sheets in the yellow room, thinking of the suggestion Lucy had made a couple of hours before. *Think about what you want to be doing with your life in ten years.* He'd be nearly forty-seven. Would he still be living on memories and regrets over things lost? Dancing on the edges of relationships because he knew beyond all doubt if he moved to the center, there was no going back?

"Probably," he muttered aloud, pulling the sheet

over his bare shoulder and closing his eyes to listen to the sound of the ocean. It was like Lake Michigan on steroids. He fell asleep almost instantly, soothed by the raucous lullaby, wondering somewhere in the back of his mind what Lucy wore to bed.

He didn't know what woke him before dawn. He put on the shorts and T-shirt he'd worn the night before and stepped out onto the deck. Even now, the beach wasn't deserted. A few joggers ran close to water's edge, walkers with dogs sauntered at a safe distance. A runner with a familiar gait was directly behind the house. Boone walked toward the water and fell into step beside him.

"Far be it from me to criticize anyone for running from their problems," Boone said dryly, "but doing it in the middle of the night is just crazy."

Crockett's sidelong glance was half irritation, half amusement. "You should know. I seem to remember a few three a.m. runs with you."

"You listened. It was a big help."

"I wasn't listening. I was winded and couldn't talk."

"Bullshit."

They ran for a long time, breaking the silence only with heavy breathing and the occasional grunt when the sand was too wet and sucked at their feet. "I'm at the same place you are." Crockett's voice sounded hollow in the night. "In a way, at least. At a crossroads, not having the slightest idea which way to go."

"You thinking of leaving the priesthood?" It had

been difficult to become accustomed to Crockett as a clergyman—now it was hard to imagine him *not* being one.

"I don't know. Sometimes I feel like it's leaving me." Crockett shook his head, drops of perspiration flying from his dark hair. "I'll be fine. What should happen will happen. What about you, though? When are you going back to Chicago?"

"Two weeks, if the guy living in my apartment finds a place to live. I haven't pushed him."

"Living in the big city losing its charm?"

"No." *Living alone is.* He left the thought unspoken, but an eye roll from Crockett made him realize he might as well have said it aloud.

"You don't want to leave Lucy." Crockett said it for him.

"No."

"But?"

"We're both just getting free. I'm giving up a past life I didn't want to end and she's just signed the papers releasing the only remaining connection to where and how she spent the first thirty-three years of her life. I'm not sure either of us is ready to tie ourselves to another person."

"And?"

"And what? Holy shit, Crockett, isn't that enough?"

"Maybe, but there's more."

"Sun's coming up." Boone gestured toward to the light working its way over the water.

Crockett nodded. "So it is. Does it every day, so

I'm told. You going to talk to me or am I going to have to go put my collar on and call you 'my son'?"

"Lucy asked me, sort of, where I wanted my life to be in ten years." It was hard to breathe, harder to talk. "It bothers the hell out of me that I don't know any better now than I did when the high school counselor asked the same fricking question when I was sixteen."

If anyone had asked, Boone would have said they were too winded for talking, but he'd have known that wasn't the reason for the silence that fell between them. No, the reason was that they didn't have any answers.

Chapter Fourteen

"The sorority wants the pies delivered to the event center out by the lake at noon because the party's at two o'clock. I can't begin to make sense of that, but it's what they wanted and paid extra for." Gert peered at the schedule on the kitchen chalkboard. "Neither of us can possibly leave here at eleven forty-five on a Friday. Where is Boone, anyway? It's just like a man to not be around when you need him. Maybe Jack can take them. He only has half-days at school this semester. Classes start at a quarter till one and he's mowing here this morning."

Lucy set pumpkin custard pies on the island to cool and replaced them in the oven with Dutch apple and blueberry. "Boone left yesterday to speak at a conference in Louisville, remember? He was whining about eating mystery meat and lime gelatin with fruit in it." *And talking about what he'd like to do with me and a whole vat of lime gelatin.* She smiled with the memory of that particular conversation.

She and Boone had grown closer in the week since they returned from Richmond, spending most of their evening hours and many of their late-night ones together.

"I can take them." Kelly—who'd joined them for breakfast and helped with tablecloths and flowers for the tearoom while she was there—turned from where she was curling her eyelashes with the toaster serving as a mirror. "I'm having a working lunch meeting in another room at the center. Only thing is, I need to borrow one of your cars. I left mine with Sims this morning to change the oil and filters and all that under-the-hood stuff."

"You can take mine to the office," Gert offered. "We'll load the pies into the van and you can drive that when you go to the meeting."

Lucy grinned. "Just don't tell anyone where you got the car or they'll all want one. I'm pretty sure that blue-and-rust combination is going to start a whole new trend."

"You should buy a new van, or at least a newer one," Kelly advised, getting Gert's keys from one of the hooks on the inside of a cupboard door. "It could be a company car for the tearoom."

Lucy shook her head. "The tearoom can't even afford a company bicycle yet, although Gert's last newspaper ad was inspired. Even with the percentage off, we've had record revenue."

Kelly went outside, only to come in again thirty seconds later and exchange sets of keys. "You're parked behind Gert, Lucy. I'll just take your car to work and the pies can go in hers."

"Musical vehicles this morning." Gert smiled at her niece. "Reminds me of when you kids were in high school and needed to go in three different directions—we'd play car tag all day long."

"Anything to keep Boone from driving," Kelly said, and went out the door again, laughter following her.

Lucy went to the refrigerator and stood staring at its contents, trying to remember what she needed. "Gert, do you—"

A panicked shout from outside interrupted her. She pushed the refrigerator shut and ran out through the sunroom, Gert close on her heels.

Kelly was in the yard, her cell phone at her ear. Jack, white-faced, had abandoned the lawnmower and was dragging the garden hose from beside the garage, aiming its spray toward the van that was rapidly losing much of the blue paint left on it to the flames that were bursting from under its hood.

Lucy stood still, watching in silent horror as yet another fire laid insidious siege to her life. "Don't get too close," she shouted to Jack. She ran across the drive to pull Kelly away from the burning vehicle. "Stay back. Did you call 911?"

It was a revisit of the fire in Mr. Morgan's garage. The same fire trucks and ambulance filled the street in front of the house. The same volunteer firefighters unfurled the big hose. Tom Simcox stepped out of his cruiser and held up a beefy arm and traffic stopped as if by magic.

Sims, his face as white as Jack's had been, arrived in Kelly's Volvo, running over a flowerbed and striding across the yard with scarcely a limp to take Gert in his arms.

In the end, the only lasting damage was to Lucy's van, which was totaled, and the flowerbed.

When the last of the emergency vehicles and the backed-up traffic had gone, Tom came to where Lucy stood. "The fire marshal will release it after he investigates. You'll want to call your insurance agent too."

Tom was burly enough to be scary if you had a guilty conscience, but non-judgmental and soft-spoken right along with it. If Lucy had been drawing a prototype of everything she'd want in a law enforcement officer, he would have fit nicely onto the page. His wife was Lucy's doctor and one of the tearoom's best customers. One notable Tuesday—traditionally a slow day for Tea on Twilight—all the tables had been full at once and the sheriff had donned an apron and helped Lucy serve. A picture of him graced the bulletin board in the kitchen. When he'd jitterbugged with Lucy on her birthday, everyone had stood around and clapped.

But now, with his attendance at the third fire where Lucy was also present, his smile was conspicuously absent and suspicion had erased the kindness in his eyes.

"We have to stop meeting like this." His voice was calm.

"That would be perfectly all right with me." She tried to smile, but her cheeks trembled with the effort so she gave it up.

"Kelly was getting ready to drive the car, right?"

"Yes." Kelly stood between Gert and Sims. The accusation on the attorney's face made Lucy want to cringe, but she didn't. "I don't know if she'd started the car yet."

"Okay." He gave her shoulder an awkward pat and went over to the others. "Kell, you okay?"

Lucy didn't hear her response, though she knew what it was. She'd already checked, had already shouted, "Are you all right? Are you all right?" in Kelly's shocked face, grabbing her hands and shaking them for emphasis.

"Yes," Kelly had said, and it was as though ice ran through the words. "Did you think I wouldn't be? Or hope it, maybe?"

Lucy didn't answer the accusation, just dropped her hands and ran to Jack. She'd rubbed at the soot on his face. "You're not burned?"

"I'm fine." He'd pulled away from her, not meeting her eyes, going to coil the garden hose before someone tripped over it.

She felt accused again. Although the temperature was above seventy, she was freezing. And she was alone. As alone as she'd been since the day Johnny died. She hadn't realized she was running away when she came to Taft, but maybe she was. Not from Richmond, not even from loss, but from fire.

She hadn't run far enough.

She went into the house to take the pies from the oven and make sure it was turned off. That would be the icing on the whole nasty cake, if fire followed her right into Tea on Twilight.

Moving on automatic pilot, she boxed pies and wrote up an invoice for Gert to mail to the sorority treasurer. She took the stockpots off the deep shelf in the pantry and put them on the stove. Friday had become soup day in the tearoom. Today's choices were chili and vegetable. They'd also have a smaller pot of the vegan potato soup Jessie St. John had taught her to make. She needed to assemble meat and cheese and relish trays for the wedding shower that afternoon. Lucy would just concentrate on food, preparing it, cooking it, arranging it neatly on antique platters.

For now. It was the only thing she knew to do, the only way to stop herself from running screaming toward—toward what? She had no idea.

Gert came in and went to work beside her, browning the ground round and just a "smidge" of sausage for the chili while Lucy sautéed the peppers, garlic and onions.

After a few minutes, Gert broke the silence. "I don't know what you're thinking, Lucy, but I'm pretty sure it's wrong."

"I'm thinking maybe I should leave." The words felt like fishhooks coming through her throat.

Gert shook her head, clearing her throat. "That's just foolish."

But Gert hadn't seen Tom Simcox's face, hadn't seen the progress Lucy and Kelly had made toward sharing the planet in peace drain away in a fiery moment. Hadn't seen the way Jack avoided Lucy's eyes as though he hated her. Gert wasn't considering that just maybe her business partner was a pyromaniac in some deep, dark identity no one knew existed. Gert wasn't wondering what was going to burn next and if Lucy was going to be the one to start the fire.

No, Gert wasn't wondering any of that.

But Lucy was.

Boone loved cartoonists' conferences. He liked interacting with others who shared his interests and his talents. He even liked being a featured speaker. It used to scare the bejesus out of him—it was nothing in those early days to drain four glasses of water during a twenty-minute speech. He always prayed there was a restroom somewhere close to the lectern because he would be in dire need of it as soon as he said, "Hey, thanks for listening," and unhooked his microphone. Nowadays, though, he was comfortable with what he had to share and with the audience. The Q and A portion of his presentation always lasted longer than the talk itself, and that was fine with him.

His favorite part was the schmoozing time spent in the hotel bar. He'd spent the evening there last night, catching up with colleagues he saw only a few times a year, and he'd planned to go back after dinner, but the truth was that he was ready to go home. He wished he'd brought Lucy to the conference with him, but she'd pushed him out the door.

"I've got a living to make," she said. "My vacation's over."

"Aw, come on." He swept her into a hug and kissed her for a long time before letting her go and meeting her gaze. "I'll miss you, Lucy John."

He'd been flirting, teasing, because he was actually looking forward to a few days of single guy time. He and Lucy were nearly always together these days and even though he liked it, he liked being single too. Sort of. Although he thought he was ready to love somebody again—better be, since he already did—he didn't think he wanted the same kind of closeness he'd had with Maggie. They had, he could admit in retrospect, damn near smothered each other from time to time.

So he was surprised to find himself leaving the conference hotel almost immediately after his presentation. He'd be back on Twilight Park Avenue in time for supper. He might even call and see if Lucy and Gert wanted him to pick up pizza on his way.

Then again, he might not. He whipped into the right lane of the interstate and set the cruise control for five miles an hour over the speed limit. He rarely did that, because no one knew any better than he did what a lousy driver he was, but a sense of urgency was humming along under his skin that he couldn't explain. He just knew he wanted to be home. He thought maybe Lucy needed him.

Arson.

Lucy folded freshly laundered tablecloths slowly,

matching corners so the creases would be in the center of the tables when she set them. She loved the autumn colors of the table covers. Gert had been aghast when Lucy suggested seasonal cloths instead of white, but she'd come around the day Lucy walked in with thirty yards of fabric she'd found at a garage sale. The two women had unearthed Gert's sewing machine and borrowed Kelly's and spent every evening for a week cutting and hemming tablecloths and coordinating toppers for the tearoom's fifteen tables.

They'd bought the tables off an internet auction site and driven to Lexington, Kentucky in a rental truck to pick them up. The creamy old dishes and thick, faceted drinking glasses had been in the kitchen of the Knights of Pythias lodge hall, along with most of the mismatched wooden chairs. The Knights no longer met and Sims had bought the building to do something with—he hadn't decided exactly what.

Lucy stopped folding, remembering washing the dishes by hand that first time and praying silent thanks that the temperamental van had died in front of Gert's house. She'd only intended to spend the afternoon with Noah Crockett's aunt, just long enough to receive advice about apartments and jobs in the Taft area. But it took a few days for Sims to get the van back into running condition, and by that time it was too late.

She was home.

Even though she hadn't meant to be. She hadn't

intended to go into business with someone she liked and admired. She'd never expected to meet Gert's other nephew, the one who made Father Crockett's eyes light with laughter whenever he mentioned him. Once she'd met Boone, she'd absolutely never meant to fall in love with him.

When she'd asked him, back in Virginia, what he wanted to be doing in ten years, she'd known beyond all doubt what *her* answer was. She wanted to be running a restaurant of one kind or another. Children running through its kitchen. A house to go to when the workday was done. A red SUV with crayons and coloring books in the back seat and a CD player for playing Christmas songs from the first week in October until New Year's. That was the biggest dream in her jar.

Except for the one she'd never written down. She wanted Boone. Oh, yes, she did.

But that was before another fire had burned a scalding inroad into her life and her dreams. Before the fire marshal and the insurance adjustor wore a solemn and angry face and said the word *arson.*

"Do you have any enemies, Miss Dolan?"

Not that she knew of. But did she? The fires were coming closer. Would the next one be in the house? Would it hurt one of these people she'd come to love?

She stared down at where she held the corners of a pumpkin-colored tablecloth. Her hands weren't pretty, with their short fingers, nails bitten to the quick and pale burn scars mingling with the freckles on the backs. Johnny and Andy used to shake their heads at her because no matter how careful she tried to be, she always managed to burn herself.

Even in cooking, her favorite thing in the world to do, fire was her enemy.

"Luce?" Boone's voice preceded him into the room. He carried his laptop and Kinsey trotted in beside him. The kitten's second-favorite person was home, and she pranced with the delight of it. Boone smiled into her eyes, the expression warming her through and through. It was the first time since this morning she hadn't had to stop herself from shivering.

"What's the black spot on the driveway? Jack burning leaves already?" He laid down his computer case and plucked the tablecloth from Lucy's hands so he could take her into his arms. "I missed you."

"I'm fine." She raised her face for his kiss, putting her arms around his neck for just a minute. Just a minute and then she would let go. Really she would. "I missed you too. The black spot's where the van used to be."

He raised a questioning brow. "Sounds ominous. Did it finally kick up its tires?"

She drew away, reaching for the tablecloth he'd taken from her hands. "In a manner of speaking." She folded it, having trouble getting the corners to match because her hands were shaking. She picked up another one, this one the color of paprika.

"Lucy?" He stood still. Kinsey wound around his ankles, then Lucy's.

The cat's long fur felt good on her cold skin. She folded, though her hands still shook. "There was an engine fire. It doesn't take much to total out a twelve-year-old car, so I guess it did kick up its tires."

Her voice sounded hollow in her ears, like it belonged to someone else. She wished it did, because she didn't want to tell him about the fire. She didn't want to talk about it at all.

But, as anyone else would, he said, "What happened?" He took the cloth out of her hands, finished folding it, and laid it neatly on the stack on top of the dryer. "Come on." His arm went around her waist, and he pulled her into the kitchen. "Sit down and tell me."

He got an opened bottle of rosé out of the wine cooler and sloshed healthy amounts into a pair of water goblets. He sat on the barstool around the corner from hers and set the drinks in front of them. "Lucy?"

She told him. It took the whole glass of wine, but she got it said. She kept her gaze on his and held her eyes open wide. They felt hot and dry and soulless, as though they were separate from the rest of her. But if she looked away, he would think she was lying. Wouldn't he?

At the end, he put down his nearly full glass and reached for her hands. "No one—you, Kelly, Gert, Jack—none of you were hurt?"

"No. Not physically. But you need to call Kelly. Make sure."

"Where's Aunt Gert?"

"With Sims. They were going to drive till they were hungry, stop and eat, then drive till they were tired and stop and stay. I think they just wanted to be alone together." *And not with me.* She was glad she'd stopped herself from saying it, but she couldn't seem to stop thinking it. "I'm—" She hesitated, pulling her hands from his, though her fingers felt icy as soon as he wasn't touching them anymore. "I'm not very good company tonight, Boone. Why don't you go over and see Kelly instead of just calling her, make sure she's all right? I'll be okay here."

Indecision flared in his eyes, and Lucy could read his thoughts. Should he go to the sister he'd been looking after her whole life, who he loved unconditionally, or should he stay here, where God only knew what Lucy would do next?

"I'm tired and you are, too," he said quietly. "Let's both stay here. Why don't you order pizza while I call Kelly?"

Because arguing would have required more energy than she had, Lucy nodded acquiescence. She got up, snagging the phone from its cradle and going into the sunroom with Kinsey at her heels.

After ordering the pizza, she stayed in the sunroom, sitting at the table and thumbing through the cookbook she'd left there earlier. Through the French doors, she saw Boone get up from the island with his cell phone at his ear. He walked the perimeter of the kitchen, stopping to sip his wine occasionally as he listened.

She closed her eyes and catalogued in her memory his chocolate eyes and chiseled features, the sun-streaked brown hair that was never quite neat. She thought of how his laughter sang along her nerve endings and remembered thinking his voice was the stuff her dreams were made of. It still was, whether it was soft and sexy in the darkness of the night or loud and intense when he was making a point.

Years back, when she'd been engaged to Scott Knight, this was how she'd wanted to feel. She'd wanted to love his touch, his laughter, had wanted to feel a little explosion of joy whenever he entered the room. But she hadn't. Not even once.

As she watched, Boone disconnected his phone and plugged it into one of the trio of battery chargers that lay on the counter beside her pickle jar. He stood still for a minute, and Lucy wondered what he was thinking. What had Kelly said?

The front doorbell rang, and Boone went to answer it. Lucy went into the kitchen. She got out plates and forks for the pizza, setting them on the island, and poured glasses of iced tea. Going through all the motions of ordinariness.

But the truth was that for Lucy, normalcy was as unrealistic as the dreams in the big glass jar. Like the spot in the driveway, there was nothing left but ashes.

* * *

The pizza was good, although Boone hadn't been hungry after his conversation with Kelly. Lucy's face told him she wasn't, either, but they polished off the twelve-inch combination pizza and the small order of breadsticks.

She asked about the conference and he answered her. He asked about the shower that afternoon and she answered him. They discussed the weather. The emptiness of the conversation was pervasive.

Finally, she threw out the gauntlet. "What day are you leaving for Chicago?"

"A week from tomorrow. I have meetings on Monday and I want to spend Sunday settling back into the apartment." He needed to make it home again. It hadn't been, not a single day since Maggie died. No amount of sound, not even music or laughter, had been able to fill the echoing silence.

"Why don't you come up with me for a few days?" He asked the question even though he knew she wouldn't come. The fire in the driveway had destroyed more than Lucy's van. It had burned away whatever self-confidence seven months at Tea on Twilight had given her. He waited, dreading what she would say next.

"I don't think so." She picked up a piece of crust from her plate and began breaking it into little pieces. "It's time for me to move on, Boone, before someone gets hurt." She smiled, although her eyes were dark with pain. "Too bad I don't know how to ride a horse—I could just go off into the sunset with Roy Rogers singing 'Happy Trails' after me like he did in all those old TV shows."

"Like people won't be hurt if you move on?" He got up, feeling hemmed in by the house and the happenings of the day. "Let's go for a walk."

They put on hooded sweatshirts in deference to the coolness of the evening and left the house. Boone lifted his gaze to the trees that canopied the street. Their leaves were beginning to change color, with yellows and oranges peeping through the green. "I'll miss Taft. I always do when I leave it. And I miss Chicago when I come here."

He steered her around a tree root that had split the sidewalk. The next question was obvious, but he didn't want to ask it. If he didn't—if he kept walking without addressing the issue, maybe she'd stay put here on Twilight Park Avenue. Maybe she'd… Oh, for God's sake, like that was going to work. "If you leave," he said, his voice firm, "where will you go?"

"I don't know. I haven't gotten my mind completely around having to go." The unhappiness in her voice was so deep it was painful to listen to.

"Then don't. No one thinks you started the fires. You weren't even there when they started."

"No one? Kelly does. I think Jack does. Tom Simcox is beginning to wonder. *I'm* beginning to wonder. I'm afraid to light candles in the house, even more than I usually am. On nights I don't have dreams, I still get up to make sure the oven's turned off. Gert's already said she wants to have fires in the parlor fireplaces this winter while the tearoom's open—it'll drive me crazy."

"So you're just giving up."

He felt her rage, knew she wanted to scream at him that of course she wasn't giving up, she just wanted everyone to be safe. But he also knew the woman who referred to herself as Lucy the Pleaser. He felt her words before they left her mouth and lodged themselves between them.

"Yes," she said. "Yes, I am."

"Stay through the end of the year. We have enough party bookings that we might have to consider remodeling the garage," Gert said firmly, zipping the bank bag that held Tuesday's receipts. "If, after that, you're still determined to go, we'll close the tearoom and cut our losses."

"You don't need to close it," Lucy protested. "It's viable. It's gone like gangbusters ever since we opened. The backup crew is as good as we are. I'll bet Nancy Walker would buy me out in a heartbeat. Jack will help more, both outside and in the house. You know he's always wanting to earn more money."

Gert put the bag into her purse for the trip to the bank the next morning and got up to refill their coffee cups. "I know I could count on Jack, and Nancy probably would buy you out if we suggested it. She'd be an excellent partner, but the truth is that Nancy and I have both retired once. She was a teacher for thirty-five years and I was a financial planner for thirty. Neither of us wants to be a career woman anymore. I like cooking sometimes and having you do most of the work. Nancy wouldn't do that and Jack won't wear aprons, especially the cute ones like yours."

Lucy burst into laughter, thinking even as she did that it had been too many days since she'd laughed without tears pushing the sound out. "You and Nancy both can work me under the table and you know it. And Jack would do anything you asked of him."

"Lucy, dear." Gert's voice was gentle. "Please."

Without answering, Lucy left the room. She went into the den, with its three intimate tables for two that were often pushed together to make a long table for eight, then through the two parlors and the dining room—four tables for four per room. There was room for more, at least in the parlors, but they hadn't wanted the rooms to be crowded.

"I want to be able to wait tables without saying 'excuse me' every time I walk through," Lucy'd said, and Gert had agreed.

The rooms were decorated for autumn, with pumpkins and cornucopias on the mantels and garlands of artificial leaves around every window and doorway. A basket of shiny apples sat on small side tables in each room.

Lucy loved every square inch of Tea on Twilight.

She went back to the kitchen, and stood inside its doorway, watching as Gert emptied the dishwasher, stacking the plates on the open shelves.

They still washed the glassware and flatware by hand, drying them on soft old towels so that they maintained their shine.

Gert was probably seventy or so—no one really knew—but was as lean and energetic as a woman half her age. She had a bigger personality than anyone Lucy knew. And love. Regardless of all she'd lost, her capacity for loving had only grown with those losses.

Lucy loved her too, had wondered in moments of whimsy if not only Crockett but the spirit of Siobhan Dolan had sent her to the house on Twilight Park Avenue. *I can't be there for you, Lucy Goosy,* she could almost hear her mother say, *but Gert can. You be the daughter she lost, and she'll be your mother.*

"I think—" Lucy had to clear her throat, "—Christmas trees in the front parlor and the dining room, and a small one in the den. In the second parlor, we could—I don't know. What do you think?"

"We could make it a gift room." Gert's voice sounded a little ragged too. "The crafters and stitchers in town have mentioned it before. They could bring in their Christmas things and we could sell them on consignment. They'd get their eighty or ninety percent, whatever the going rate is, and we could donate our percentage. We could offer gift-wrapping for a further donation."

"Oh, I like that."

"So you'll stay?"

"Till the first of the year." Lucy let the decision slip into a place of semi-comfort in her heart. "After that, we'll see."

Chapter Fifteen

"Just keep the Jeep. I can fly back to Chicago or you can drive me back." Boone scowled at Lucy, the expression so alien on his face that she couldn't help laughing at him. "The van had hardly any insured value and you can't be going into fall and winter without a vehicle. I, on the other hand, live in the city where I can walk, take a taxi, ride the train, or get delivery. I could even buy another car. Elmer and Myrtle have taken good financial care of me over the years."

It would be their last hike around the River Walk before Boone's return to Chicago the next day. They ambled along in the golden sunlight of early fall.

She wanted the afternoon to never end.

"I'll get a car, a used one, probably next week," she promised, "and I can afford payments. There just hasn't been time this week to go shopping for one. That newspaper ad of Gert's has kept us hopping."

"Have Sims check it out before you buy anything," he advised. "He's the best mechanic around."

"I will."

He stopped walking, pulling her into the warm arc of his arm. "You know I care for you, don't you?"

"I do." She met his gaze, memorizing the planes of his face so she'd be able to close her eyes and see him even after he'd gone. "I care for you too." *I love you, is what it is, and I always will, but I'm not what you need. You don't need a pleaser who gets followed around by fires and keeps her dreams and her savings in a pickle jar.*

"Are you sure you won't come with me for a few days? We can walk up and down Michigan Avenue and pretend Lake Michigan is really an ocean."

"No." *It will be even harder then. To say good-bye. To start over.*

"I'll be back down in a month. It's not as though you're getting rid of me."

"I know. The weekend of the soup supper at church. And you're going to help, right?"

"Well, I thought I'd stay outside and tell people where to park. You know, wear one of those nifty orange vests with the duct tape stripes."

"And talk about football and flirt with girls."

Boone nodded somberly. "Yeah, it's a big responsibility. I think Crockett's coming up. He can help with the parking too."

Lucy laughed, the sound ringing in the clear air. Oh, she would miss him when he was being funny. And when he wasn't.

His laughter joined hers and he swung her into his arms, dancing her down the cobblestone path and around the park benches and lamp posts that were interspersed along it. When they stopped, they were both breathless and at the end of the Walk, where the cobblestones segued into a concrete sidewalk that led to the street.

"Promise me."

She met his gaze, startled by the starkness of his words after the laughing dance. "What?"

"That if you ever need me, you will call."

I need you all the time. "Boone, I have to stand on my own."

"Promise me."

"I can't—"

"Listen to me, Lucy. I know you don't even trust yourself right now. You think you might have some kind of weird alter ego who runs around starting fires. My sister the idiot—she's a lawyer, remember, and if her own brother can't make snide lawyer remarks, no one can—is half-inclined to agree with you. And you're both so full of it, I swear. I know—did you hear when I said listen to me?—I *know* who you are, that you won't even light a match unless there's a bucket of water at your elbow, that you'd jump into the fire yourself before you let someone else get burned."

"If you know that," she said, unable to get her voice above a whisper, "why are you leaving me?" She hated sounding like a woeful, unloved child, but devastation drained her, leaving pride somewhere deep where she couldn't find it.

"I'm not." He framed her face with his hands and bent his head to kiss her. He lingered, his tongue teasing, until she opened her mouth under his. "I'm not leaving you, Lucy." He smiled before kissing her again, but the sadness she remembered from early summer filled his eyes. "I'm finding me."

She found the car she wanted the Monday after Boone went back to Chicago. The "new" SUV was three years old with less than 30,000 miles and a functional CD player and air conditioner. It was canary yellow, which Sims said meant they should've paid her to take it off the lot. And Lucy loved it. It was quiet and comfortable and in only four years, providing she made timely and not-too-big payments, it would be completely hers.

Micah Walker ordered a magnetic sign that advertised Tea on Twilight and she slapped it on the driver's door and left it there.

The days, once she got past the horrific one when Boone left, moved along easily. Business at the tearoom boomed. Tom Simcox said the investigators had found nothing new concerning the burning of her car. "It could be random vandalism," he'd said one day when he and Maria came for lunch. "There's no denying it happens. Just watch your back and make sure 911 is on speed-dial."

"Do you believe I didn't do it myself?" She hadn't meant to ask the question, no matter how badly she wanted to know its answer. Her breath stopped in the middle of an exhale and she bit down on her bottom lip.

"I do."

"Thanks, Tom." She'd smiled past him at his wife. "He's not bad sometimes, is he?"

Maria'd laughed. "No, and he's cute in an apron, too."

Leaves began falling in early October, and as always in the Midwest, its residents remarked that fall was early this year. Or late. Or dry. Or exceedingly wet. The tearoom dispensed as much mulled cider at lunchtime as it did coffee and tea. Homemade soup was so popular they served at least one kind every day. During a business meeting held while Gert counted money and Lucy made piecrust, the idea of opening seven days a week was discussed and dismissed to the great relief of both of them.

The Friday before the church supper, Lucy was loading the day's tablecloths and napkins into the washer when Gert carried the phone into the laundry room. "It's for you," she said, and sneezed.

"Bless you." Lucy took the phone. "Hello?"

"Thank you, and bless you too." It was Kelly. "Jack's got a football game tonight."

"I know. We sent cookies over for the team. Do you have any idea how many cookies thirty teenage boys can eat?"

"No, and I don't think I want to know. You should feed the cheerleaders instead of the players—it would be much cheaper. The thing is, Jack doesn't have anybody to be there for him. His dad's in jail and his mother just started working nights at the casino in Rising Sun. Even his little brothers are in foster care. I don't feel like going by myself. Would you go with me?"

Lucy took the receiver away from her ear and

stared at it for a moment, wondering if Kelly remembered who she'd called. "Well, sure," she said. "I can do that."

"I didn't ask Aunt Gert." Kelly answered her unspoken question. "She doesn't sound too good."

"She's catching a cold. She'll be happy to stay here with Kinsey, I imagine."

"I'll pick you up at six-thirty."

Still feeling nonplused, Lucy thanked her and hung up, putting the phone in her pocket and turning concerned eyes on Gert. "Why don't you get ready for bed?" she suggested, closing the washer and starting its cycle.

"It's three-thirty in the afternoon."

"And you're about to collapse. Take some cold medicine, or a shot of something. I'll bring you some soup and tea and you and Kinsey can take the rest of the day off." She grinned. "Sims might come over and sit with you if you ask nicely."

Gert snorted. "You and Kelly going out?"

Lucy explained, lifting the next day's tablecloths and napkins off the shelf above the dryer. She had time to set the tables if she hurried. That would keep Gert from doing it while she was gone.

That whole idea didn't work, of course. Gert followed her, sitting down to fold the napkins in artistic shapes Lucy had never mastered. "That's nice you girls are going. Give him a thumbs-up from me."

"I've been here since February, see Jack almost every day, and love him to death, but I still don't know much about him," Lucy said. "I have the impression he's had a rough time. Is that right?"

"Yes, he has. Still is, I think." Sadness settled on Gert's already pale features.

After settling Gert in, Lucy dressed in jeans and a red and black Taft High School sweatshirt she'd bought from one of the St. John children who'd been selling them as a fundraiser. She flat-ironed her hair so that it lay neatly on her shoulders. Kelly was prompt, as Lucy had expected, and she ran down the front porch steps to slide into the passenger seat of the Volvo.

"I haven't been to a football game since I was in high school," she said, "and not very many of them then. Friday nights were busy in the restaurant."

"Just yell when everyone else does and make sure you don't say anything less than complimentary about a particular player. If his mother hears you, she'll never forgive you *and* she'll tell all her friends."

Lucy smiled across the car at Boone's sister. Kelly was extraordinarily beautiful. Slim but still curvy, with skin Lucy would have been willing to bet had never seen the business end of a tube of Clearasil. If there were flaws, they were invisible ones. Even her clothes were the prettiest Lucy had ever seen. "Were you a cheerleader?"

"From sixth grade all the way through college. I even tried out for the Colts and the Pacers cheerleading squads, but when I didn't make it, I went to law school instead." There wasn't much humor in her smile. "I'm still not sure that was a good choice, but changing my mind at this point would be a pretty expensive option."

"So how did you know about Jack's family? He's never mentioned any of them except his little brothers. He used to take them cookies and talk about them sometimes, but he doesn't anymore. He hardly talks at all."

Kelly didn't answer right away. She drove to the high school campus on the edge of town, waving at the deputy who was directing people into empty parking spots.

"His father embezzled money from the place where he worked," she said finally. "I'm the assistant prosecutor and I drew the short straw. He was a popular man, a husband and father, a model citizen who'd never been in trouble, even a deacon at his church. But he was in over his head and he stole money and I helped send him to jail." Without waiting for Lucy to answer, she got out of the car, slamming the door.

Lucy got out on the other side and spoke across the top of the Volvo. "Well, obviously it bothers you, but weren't you just doing your job?"

"It does and I was. The judge was unbelievably severe, slapping my hands because I didn't ask for enough of a penalty. The guy was a first-time offender, for God's sake, no more a threat to society than I am, but His Honor was in a punitive mood that day, and Jack's dad's paying the highest price that could legally be charged." Kelly led the way toward the entrance gate to the football field. "Unfortunately, Jack and his family are paying the price too, and that payment's just going to keep rippling out. You have little boys who only know the father they worshiped is gone, a wife who's so overwhelmed she doesn't know which end is up, and—" her voice caught, and she struggled for a moment before going on, "—you have Jack, trying to be a man before his time."

"It's a shame." Lucy remembered when her father had hired Andy. Johnny had caught him sneaking out of the restaurant without paying and hauled him to the police station himself, scaring the stuffing out of him all the way. After a great deal of huffing and puffing and yelling while they were at the precinct, he'd dragged the boy back to the restaurant and shown him how to bus tables and run the dishwasher—shouting the whole time. Andy'd never left. "Did you get Jack the job with Gert?"

"Yes." Kelly hesitated. "But that's—"

"It won't go any further," Lucy promised. "I just wondered." And was glad to know.

They paid their way in, bought coffee at the concession stand and took seats in the home-side bleachers, waving at the fullback wearing number thirty on his black jersey. He nodded slightly in their direction, and the women grinned at each other. "I don't think he wants anyone to see he knows us," Lucy said. "You suppose it's because we're too old?"

"Can't be."

Lucy nodded. "You're right. You still sort of resemble a cheerleader. Daphne with an edge."

Kelly's whoop of laughter reminded Lucy painfully of Boone. As if in response to the thought, the cell phone in the hand-warmer pocket of her sweatshirt rang.

"Gert said you two were at the game," he said without preamble when she flipped the phone open. "Don't embarrass the kid. When it's over and everyone talks to the players in the parking lot, don't hug him. Just say 'good job' and go on so he can pretend it's no big deal you guys came to watch him."

"His mother's not here. She works nights. And his dad's in jail."

"Yeah, I knew that part." He was silent for a few seconds. "Okay, go ahead and hug him. Try to rub the sweat line from his helmet out of his hair so he'll be embarrassed—he'll like that. Tell Kelly 'hey.' I miss you."

"Same goes." She closed the phone and put it back into her pocket. "He says—"

"I know." His sister waved a hand. "He says 'hey.' I miss him something fierce. I didn't expect that after all the time he's lived away, but I do."

"Me too," Lucy said, and stood for the national anthem.

Taft's Warriors won the game. Lucy surprised herself by yelling until her throat hurt and even occasionally being able to find the football in the swarm of players on the field. Following Boone's suggestion, both women hugged Jack in the parking lot before heading back to the house.

It was easy to forget that the tall and well-muscled boy was just that—a boy. But there was a still-young fragility to Jack that Lucy felt when she'd hugged him, a narrowness through his ribcage that made her hold him an extra few beats in time. She'd wanted to cry, but knew he'd neither understand nor thank her for it.

"I want to check on Gert before I go home." Kelly got out of the car and followed Lucy inside.

"I'm going to get her some hot cider. Want some?"

"Yeah. Thanks."

A few minutes later, Lucy carried a tray with three mugs of cider into the room where the other women were talking. She sat in a wing chair with her feet on the bed while Kelly leaned up against the headboard beside her aunt.

"We used to do this sometimes when we were kids." Kelly reached for her cider. "Only I sat in the chair and the boys sprawled across the foot of the bed. They'd get to wrestling and Uncle Mike would toss them onto the floor. Then they'd pull him down there with them and they'd all wrestle."

Gert chuckled, though she coughed on the end of it. "Those were the days, weren't they?" She stroked Kinsey, who lay across her lap, and the little cat's constant purr became a rumble. "When my baby died, I thought my life was over. Then we lost your parents, Kelly, and you and Boone came here to live and Crockett came, too, a few months later. That was when I found out your family lives in your heart, and it doesn't matter a damn who gave birth to them." She hugged Kelly to her and reached to pinch Lucy's sock-garbed toe. "Nope, not a damn."

There you go, Lucy Goosy. What'd I tell you?

Boone hung up the phone from calling Lucy for the results of the football game and went back to the drawing board. There was Daphne, sitting in the bleachers in her formal gown with a beauty-queen sash across one bare shoulder, her hair swept into an elaborate updo. Her makeup and jewelry were exaggerated the way they always were, but she was still beautiful. Next to her sat—

Who?

Drawing her was no problem. She had big green eyes and curly red-gold hair and wore a sundress with an apron even in the bleachers. She was Daphne's friend—probably a bit of a stretch—but what was her *name?*

He called Lucy back when he had the panel done. "You asleep?"

"No, I'm baking pecan pies for the soup supper," she said cheerfully. "But it *is* two o'clock in the morning. Stranger things have happened than people being asleep at that hour." Her voice changed perceptibly. "Are you calling to tell me you're not coming down tomorrow?"

"No, why would you think that?" Although he

wasn't hurt by the disappointment he heard. Nope, not one bit hurt.

"Because it's two a.m. and you have a six-hour drive in front of you."

"Nah. I'm flying down. Crockett will get in at almost the same time and we'll be at the house about noon. Sims is picking us up. What I called to ask is, what did you want your name to be when you were a kid?"

"Anything but what it was."

"Aw, come on, give me something to work with."

"No, seriously. I love Lucille Ball, but when I was a little kid named Lucy with curly almost-red hair, I didn't. The only thing worse would have been Ethel."

"So what name would you have chosen?"

"Let me think a minute. I'm going to put the phone down while I put the pies in the oven. Don't hang up."

He pictured her moving the pies to the oven racks, her bottom lip captured between her teeth in a usually vain effort to keep from spilling something. God, he missed her. Noon seemed a long time away.

She returned in a couple of minutes. "Okay, you still there? I remember now. There was a waitress at the restaurant who taught me to make salads when I was little. She had bright red hair that came from the same bottle Lucille Ball used and big boobs that may or may not have been real, and she wore big earrings. Sparkly dangly ones, with bracelets to match that slid up and down her arms. Her name was Gladys Marie, so for a year or so there, that's who I wanted to be. How's that?"

"Perfect. What was her last name?"

"Vojtasek."

"What?"

Lucy's laughter was like music. *Oh, Lord, Brennan, you've got it bad.* "Vojtasek," she repeated. "There's a 'j' in there—that's how I learned about silent letters. I was the only kid in the first grade who knew what they were before we learned to spell 'comb.' The teacher was really impressed with me until she found out I could spell 'Vojtasek' but not 'comb.'"

"So how *do* you spell it?"

"C-o-m-b."

"No, I mean Vo—" Her snort stopped him, and he grinned into the phone. "Never mind. What's your favorite color?"

"Green."

"Yeah, that's—"

"Sometimes. Sometimes it's blue. And I love fall colors."

He sighed. "What was your mother's maiden name?"

"Doyle. She used to say she married Dad because she already had monogrammed linens and that way she didn't have to change them. Of course, she didn't. Have monogrammed linens, I mean, though I've got a few pretty things that were hers. I think my grandmother made them. Not borrowed-grandmother Isobel, but real-grandmother Abaigeal. My mother's mother. She died before I was born."

For a minute there, he considered "*Abaigeal*," but he knew he couldn't spell that, nor could he insert the Gaelic accent that had slipped effortlessly into Lucy's voice. "Okay. I'm good." He scribbled "Gladys Doyle" on the paper in front of him. "So. What are you wearing?"

In the moment of silence that followed, he closed his eyes and imagined her trying to decide what to say. He chuckled silently, waiting.

"Why do you want to know?" she asked cautiously.

"Phone sex. I've never done it, but I haven't seen you in two weeks and I'm willing to learn."

"We'll have a study session on it." He could have sworn her voice was blushing. But she laughed again, too, and he closed his eyes to store the sound behind his heart. "I'm hanging up now, Boone. See you tomorrow."

"'Night, Lucy John."

He disconnected and pored over the panel he'd drawn. It was good to be back in his studio. Convenient. But he didn't like the rest of the apartment anymore. It had been home with Maggie, a place they'd both loved. Now it was just a place.

Suddenly tired and aware he hadn't packed for the weekend at home—at Taft—he turned off the lights in the studio and went through the apartment, stopping to stare at the empty space in the dining room where Maggie's piano had sat. He remembered when he'd given it away. He'd felt relief, as though he were shifting a weight off his shoulders.

He'd sorted things then, that same day, choosing remembrances for himself—her favorite coffee cup, the CD of children's music she'd recorded, a few photograph albums, notes they'd left each other. A few weeks later, her sister and brother-in-law had come from Florida to visit and Boone had asked Emily to take what she wanted of Maggie's clothes and other personal items so he could give the rest to Salvation Army. Another weight'd gone away.

But the empty places remained. He'd never put a desk where the piano had sat, had never stored winter clothes in Maggie's closet or filled the shelves where her books had been.

He packed quickly and went to bed, lying in the room he'd shared with her and staring at the ceiling. He gave himself the luxury of thinking about his wife. Remembering the fun and funniness of their life together. But the memories were fading around the edges. He no longer recalled the exact sound of her voice or feel of her hair between his fingers. When he listened for her laugh, it was Lucy's he heard.

It was strange how it worked. The idea of Lucy replacing Maggie was untenable to even think about. People couldn't replace other people, couldn't fill those spaces left by loss. But when they created places of their own, it was like the candle thing Gert had told him and Kelly about when they'd felt disloyal by being happy with her and Mike after losing their parents. She'd lit a whole box of candles, explaining that each of the tapers stood for a person, and the more you loved—or lit—the brighter the love and the light.

He turned on his side and stared toward the windows. The Chicago skyline was out there, beautiful and alive, and he still loved the excitement and convenience of the city. But he didn't want to live here anymore. It was no longer home.

Chapter Sixteen

"I haven't missed a soup supper in over twenty years. They *count* on me. I can't believe you expect me to miss this one because I have a sniffle." Gert punctuated her tirade with a series of sneezes.

"You'll be there in spirit." Lucy handed her the dose cup of cold medicine. "I read the alcohol content in this. You'd be way over the legal limit anyway and Eli would be using you for an example from the pulpit. How embarrassing would that be?"

Gert swallowed the orange liquid with a grimace. "Did you get all the pies taken over to the church without those boys getting into them?"

"I took them this morning before they got here. Eli helped carry them into the church, so I'm sure they've been gotten into by now."

"Probably." Gert sighed, but she smiled at the same time. The pastor was one of "her boys." She handed the dose cup back to Lucy. "There's that birthday party here at seven-thirty. I can be up in time to help with that."

"No, you can't. Kelly and I will both leave the church at seven so we'll be here for the party. Everything's already set up or on low in slow cookers in the kitchen. All we have to do is get the food into the dining room then stand aside in case anyone needs anything." Lucy handed the cup back. "Drink it all, like a good girl, and you can have a cookie."

"Make them leave by ten. They probably have a curfew anyway." Gert drained the cup. "I'll want a snickerdoodle. Actually, I'll want two. I earned them swallowing that stuff."

"The birthday girl is sixty and this is a get-together with her friends from high school, so they can probably stay out late."

"They can, and they'll think they want to, but the truth is they won't be able to stay awake. Take it from someone who knows." Gert gazed out the window of her room at where Crockett, Boone and Jack were raking leaves into huge piles and scooping them into orange plastic bags with jack-o-lantern faces on them. They were throwing nearly as many leaves at each other as they were getting into the bags. As Lucy and Gert watched, Crockett and Boone picked Jack up and tossed him into a freshly raked pile.

"I hate to admit it," Gert said, "but I wish they'd move back home. I miss seeing them."

Me too. One of them anyway. But Lucy didn't say it aloud. It might not be much of a secret, this love that seemed to be taking her over, body and soul, but she thought she'd try and keep it to herself anyway.

The four "young people," as Gert referred to them, walked to the church together. Crockett and Kelly were sarcastic and silent in turn, and Boone and Lucy finally rolled their eyes at each other and separated them. "I'm telling Aunt Gert," Boone complained, pushing Crockett and glowering over his shoulder at Kelly, "and she'll ground your asses, is what she'll do."

Eli St. John issued neon orange vests to the men when they got there. "We're playing poker after the supper. We put it off till the weekend so you two would be here. Maria's on call, so we're playing at Tom's house. She said we could as long as we cleaned up after ourselves and didn't let Tom gamble with the kids' college funds."

Boone frowned at him. "Does the congregation know you're a card shark?"

Micah joined them, reaching for his vest. "We know he *thinks* he is, but since he usually loses, we overlook it. Of course, there's the drinking, too."

Crockett and Boone spoke in unison. "Drinking?"

"Yeah, and he's not choosy. If someone else pays for it, he'll drink it."

Eli cleared his throat and took a moment to glower at everyone. "You are to tell people where to park. This does not mean we want them parking over at the Catholic or Baptist churches—they have their own dinners on different nights. This also doesn't mean you're to run into the middle of the street and tell people they *have* to come here. We want our customers to be willing and generous. You cannot accept tips. This means you're not to go around hiking up your pants leg, Boone. That doesn't work anyway."

"Told you it wouldn't." Crockett nodded sagely at Boone. "Especially with those legs."

Lucy snickered, then smiled brightly. "I've tried to tell you that about your legs, but you never listen to me."

Eli grinned. "If anyone asks you to park their car, because the parking lot gets a little wonky as it fills up, that's fine," he continued, "but don't let Boone do it. The church doesn't have enough insurance."

"I'll see you whenever you get back to the house," Lucy told Boone. "Kelly and I are going to work the party at seven, so don't come in drunk and disorderly while there are people there, okay? At least unless you're prepared to sing and dance."

Boone sniffed righteously. "I won't, but I'm not being responsible for Crockett. He's older than me so he should know how to behave, but you've seen for yourself how he is. We had to separate him and Kelly while we walked over here, for heaven's sake."

"Come on." Kelly pulled on Lucy's arm. "I don't want to have to dip vegetable soup. I get it all over me."

Lucy did too. The difference was, she didn't care, so she wasn't surprised to find herself at the stove, wearing an apron streaked with chili, vegetable, and oyster soup.

"You're awfully good at his." Jessie St. John, Eli's very pretty wife, took a bowl from her and handed her a glass of cider. "Are you having a good time?"

"I am." Lucy sipped. "This is from Miller's Orchard, isn't it? It is so good."

"The next church supper is in March, when we have the Welcome Spring ham dinner. Will you chair it?"

"Sure." Lucy nodded, smiling.

But I'm leaving after the first of the year...

Well. She set down her glass and ladled a bowl of soup for Landy Walker, then shared noisy giggles with Jenny from the café over the unfunny subject of serving food to the same people no matter where they went. Lucy wasn't going to think about leaving. Not now. She was having too much fun.

"Being sixty doesn't mean calming down a lot, does it?" Kelly swept up confetti and cake crumbs while Lucy stripped the tables. "That's encouraging."

"It is, isn't it?" Lucy loaded the washing machine and came back with a bottle of white zinfandel. "I have no idea what one of them was doing in the laundry room—they must have gotten lost searching for the john—but this was sitting on the washer. It's been opened and it's still cold. What do you say?"

"Do you know how to play poker?"

"Badly."

Kelly grinned, leading the way into the kitchen and putting away the broom and dustpan. "All the better."

"The cards are in the junk drawer." Gert, in a robe, white socks and Birkenstock sandals, came into the room with Kinsey draped over her arm. "I'm feeling much better. I can enjoy some wine and something to eat. Lucy, can you loan us some change?"

Lucy dug handfuls of quarters out of the pickle jar, accepting bills in exchange. "We brought you home some stuff from the soup supper," she said, "but we were hungry for something besides *hors d'oeuvres* and birthday cake crumbs after the partiers went home, so we ate most of it."

"It's all right." Gert came out of the pantry with a jar of the salsa Lucy had made and a bag of tortilla chips. "I'm feeling snacky anyway. How was the supper?"

They gave her a blow-by-blow report on the soup supper, lying shamelessly about Crockett and Boone's performances while they told attendees where to park. "I doubt they're really playing poker." Kelly dealt five card draw as she spoke. "They're probably in jail. Tom can only cover for so much before he has to quit being the buddy and be the law."

Lucy groaned. "Oh, yuck. You deal like a lawyer."

"I *am* a lawyer."

"Not in your heart. In your heart, you're…well… not. I'll take three cards."

After winning the first hand, Kelly asked, "So what *am* I in my heart?"

"I don't know." Lucy flinched at the hand she'd been dealt. She'd thought she and Kelly were getting along better, but there was no way a friend would do this to her. "Maybe a used car salesman? I'll take three. Again."

"None for me." Gert smiled smugly. "I don't need them."

It was almost midnight when Lucy threw up her hands. "I'm done. I've lost my entire twenty dollars."

"And I don't have to be a lawyer anymore because I won it." Kelly put the deck back into its box. "I need to get home anyway."

"No, you don't. You need to stay here. That glass of whatever it was you and Lucy concocted from fruit juice and beer *after* you drank a bottle and a half of wine sent you right over the edge." Gert waved toward the back stairs. "Your room's always ready."

Kelly nodded, her eyes dark with fatigue. "I'm not going to argue. I'm too tired. Although it does bear mentioning that Lucy and I didn't drink that wine by ourselves, Aunt Gert. You swilled at least a water glass full of it."

"It was purely medicinal."

Lucy and Kelly both snorted. "For sure," Lucy said. "That'll hold up in court, all right."

They loaded their glasses and plates into the dishwasher and went to bed, Kinsey trotting along beside Lucy.

"Got any PJs I can wear?" Kelly asked from behind them. "I think the only ones in my room are from junior high and have rock stars on them.

Remember Mr. Big? I was in love with their lead singer."

"Sure." Although Lucy didn't remember the band Kelly mentioned. The radio in Dolan's kitchen had always been tuned to a news channel and the music in the dining room was Irish—she hadn't been to a concert until her one-time fiancé had taken her to see Bruce Springsteen. She'd been so enthralled by the Boss she hadn't wanted to leave.

Barely awake but with a Springsteen song playing in her head, Lucy gave Kelly a pair of pink plaid pajama pants and a matching tank top. "Sleep tight."

"Thanks. You, too." Kelly hesitated. "I was wrong about you, Lucy."

Lucy shrugged. "You were protecting your family from an unknown quantity who came out of nowhere. It's hard for me to fault that."

Kelly shook her head, a skeptical smile on her face. "Good God, woman, don't you ever hold a grudge?"

"Nope. Life's too short and I'm way too sleepy. Not to mention all the times I watched that movie."

"Point taken, Pollyanna. Good night."

Lucy put on pajamas, tossing her clothes in the general vicinity of the hamper before crawling into bed. Kinsey crept up to lie in the curve behind her knees, and Lucy reached to scratch her head. "It was a nice day, Kinsey," she murmured, and was asleep in minutes, the words and music of "Born to Run" a lullaby for her mind.

* * *

While it was true that her purr was lusty enough to nearly shake a bed, Kitty Kinsale scarcely ever meowed, and when she did it was very soft and polite. Gert said the little cat was asking, "If it wouldn't be too much trouble, would you feed me now?" Boone called her rude names, but he spent as much time petting her and catering to her gently placed requests as everyone else did.

This being the case, Lucy was surprised to be awakened by an insistent cat patting her face and meowing. The clock on the table by the bed said it was 1:07 a.m., and she groaned. Even though she didn't usually sleep through the night, her uninterrupted slumber almost always lasted at least a couple of hours. "What's wrong, Kinsey?" She scratched the cat's head and tried to make her lie down, but Kinsey responded by biting her chin.

"Ouch!" Lucy pushed her away and sat up. "What's gotten into you?"

Kinsey ran to the bedroom door and scratched at it, another first, and Lucy climbed out of bed. Her eyes felt as though they were full of crumbled saltines. She pushed her feet into flip-flops and stepped into the silent hallway. Even though there was a nightlight on the wall, the steep back stairs seemed unusually dark as she followed Kinsey toward the kitchen.

Halfway down, she smelled it.

No, no, no.

She twisted around on the staircase and rushed back up, crossing the wide hall to Kelly's room and bursting in. She ran to the bed, yelping in pain when she tripped over the shoes in her path. "Kelly!" she yelled. "Kelly, get out now!"

Kelly moaned, yanking loose from Lucy's grasp. "I just went to bed, for Chrissake. Where's the frickin' fire?"

"I don't know, but it's there somewhere. I can smell it. Come *on!"*

Still groggy, Kelly followed her from the room.

"Go down. Get Gert out. I'm going to get Boone and Crockett." When Kelly hesitated, Lucy yelled again, "Go now!"

Kelly headed down and Lucy went up, shouting all the way. She expected the men to meet her halfway, but they didn't, and she ran across the sitting area of the third floor to Boone's door, pushing it open.

The room was empty, the bed still made. Lucy slammed the door and opened Crockett's. Empty too. They weren't even home yet, and she'd wasted precious time searching for them. The thought made her angry, even though the part of her mind that wasn't scared to death understood that they were adults who didn't have to report their comings and goings to her.

She dashed into her room for her cell phone, punching in the emergency number as she ran down the stairs.

"They're on their way. You're the second caller," the dispatcher said tersely. "Get out of the house now."

There was smoke in the kitchen and the sunroom, though Lucy didn't see flames anywhere as she burst out of the house. Kelly was in the driveway, and Lucy cast a wild gaze around. "Where's Gert?"

"I couldn't find her," Kelly said. "She must have gone over to Sims's. Her car's gone."

"No, she didn't. She's still not feeling that well, plus she'd have said something if she left. You know she would have."

"Her car's gone, Lucy." Sharpness and weariness laced through Kelly's voice. "It's gone. She's got to be all right. I checked her bedroom and bathroom and she wasn't there. She's probably—"

"No." Panic washed over Lucy in a wave accompanied by nausea that would have brought her to her knees if there'd been time. *Oh, God, please, please, pleasepleaseplease.* "Crockett and Boone have her car. She has to be inside. Wait here."

And she ran back into the house.

"I can't believe we played cards this late." Boone yawned. "If Gert catches us coming in, we'll be grounded."

"Nah. You're not driving, so she won't care. She trusts me." Crockett turned off the River Walk to head through the three blocks of Taft's downtown. "Do you hear sirens?"

"No." Boone rolled down his window. "Yes." He listened. "Lucy's got me as paranoid about fire as she is. Sirens even make me jumpy in Chicago."

Crockett didn't answer, but he pushed his foot

down on the accelerator to go through a yellow light and didn't slow down even when he made a hard left onto Twilight Park Avenue.

Boone didn't see flames, but smoke was rolling from behind Tea on Twilight. When Crockett turned into the driveway, the headlights lit immediately on Kelly. She wore pink pajamas and had the garden hose in her hand. She was spraying the house.

Before the car came to a complete stop, Boone was out of it, sprinting across the drive to his sister. "Where's Lucy?" he demanded. "And Gert?" When she didn't answer immediately, he shouted, "Kelly! Where are they?"

Her eyes were wide with horror when she turned to him, part of the water shooting uselessly at the grass, the rest tumbling to her bare feet. "I couldn't find Aunt Gert, so Lucy went back in and she hasn't come out. When I tried to go in again, I couldn't get past the smoke. She hasn't come out, Boone. She hasn't come out."

"Oh, God." He grabbed the hose from her, soaking his shirt with the water. At some level, he felt his sister clutch his sleeve, but he pulled away and went into the house, holding his wet shirttail over his mouth. "Lucy!" he yelled. "Gert!"

Panic roared through his voice, the sound rushing in his ears. His heart felt as though it were trying to burst through his chest. *Stay calm. Stay calm. Oh, dear Jesus—* "Lucy, where are you? Gert!"

He moved forward slowly. Even as adrenaline surged, so did terror. He prayed in a silent, trembling voice. *I'll go, God. I'll go. I'm scared and I'm not worth a damn, but if they can be safe, I'll go. You have Maggie. You have Mom and Dad and Lucy's folks. Please don't...* "Lucy!" he shouted again. Or tried to. Smoke was splintering his voice.

He moved again, bumping the corner of…something with his hip. Where was he? What had he run into? He tried to judge how far he'd come into the kitchen and which direction he was going. "Aunt Gert, where are you? Lucy?"

At least if he lost her…them…he wouldn't have to learn to live with that new emptiness, because he wasn't leaving the house without them.

Crockett, I hope you're praying—you're a priest so He has to listen to you, doesn't He? Take care of Kelly, okay?

Boone was losing focus. Not consciousness, because he was still thinking, still praying, still scared—oh, hell, was he scared—but he was lost in the maelstrom of smoke. Lost. He didn't know where he was. His throat hurt. His chest hurt. It was…oh, holy shit, it was hot. And he couldn't find them. Despair tore a jagged trail through him, the pain so acute he nearly doubled over with it. Instead, he went to his knees. "Lucy?" he rasped. And again. "Lucy?"

"We're here."

Lucy's voice was close, but when he tried to pinpoint its source, the smoke was impenetrable—he couldn't see anything at all. God, what did they do in the movies when there was a fire? Why hadn't he taken classes on what to do or at least paid attention when someone told him? *Noise. Yes, noise.* “Bang on the floor so I can find you.” He was afraid to breathe, even more afraid he’d pass out if he didn’t.

Something thumped the hardwood floor and he went toward the noise—at least he hoped he did—and nearly tripped over Gert. “She’s unconscious.” Lucy was there, her voice hoarse and barely audible. “I did something to my ankle. I can’t walk. Take her out and I’ll crawl behind you.”

Boone drew Gert into his arms, one arm behind her knees. What if she was more than unconscious? What if she… *Please, God.*

“Here.” As he had for two thirds of their lives, Crockett showed up at Boone’s side. His voice was low and calm. “The experts are right behind me. Let’s make a chain. Stay down—” he pushed Boone back to his knees when he tried to rise with their aunt in his arms, “—we’ll pass her man-to-man.”

It was probably less than a minute later that Boone carried Lucy outside, followed and supported by a firefighter, but it felt much longer. A lifetime longer. Emergency medical technicians were already lifting Gert onto a stretcher for transport. There was a mask over her face, and Boone exchanged a look of dread with his sister and Crockett.

“I’m fine.” Lucy drew his attention by arguing with an EMT in a raspy voice. “Put me in a chair and go to the hospital. Take care of Gert.”

“Pardon me, miss.” The technician shook her head. “You need to go too. Smoke inhalation’s nothing to mess with. Your family can follow the ambulance."

Boone met Lucy's eyes in the harsh light from the vehicle. It was like seeing a scream. "Go. Take care of Gert for us till we get there." That would make her go. He knew now—if he hadn't before—that there was nothing Lucy wouldn't do for Gert Taylor.

A black Blazer parked in front of the house and Tom Simcox and Micah Walker got out, running up the driveway to where Boone stood. He ignored them, watching helplessly as the EMTs aided Lucy into the ambulance.

Crockett came to his side, grasping his arm. "Can you stay?" he asked the newcomers. "We need to go to the hospital with Gert and Lucy, plus idiot-man here needs to be checked out, too."

Micah waved them away. "We'll call Eli. He'll meet you there."

Boone got into the back seat of Gert's car. *Eli? Why would they call Eli?*

But then he knew, and the knowing increased the horror he felt. Eli was Aunt Gert's minister. He would need to be there if she was dying.

Chapter Seventeen

Twilight Valley, the community hospital, was small. In serious emergency cases, patients were stabilized and transported to Lawrenceburg or Cincinnati—there were no specialists on staff at the Valley.

Gertrude Taylor didn't give a good damn. She wasn't wearing one of those gowns that gaped open all the way up the back, she wasn't going to be quiet and by God she wasn't going anywhere. Except home, that was, thank you very much.

Lucy, her ankle wrapped in a bandage and throbbing nicely, felt relief flowing through her in spite of the pain. Anyone able to complain as much and as loudly as her business partner surely couldn't be too sick.

"It's bronchitis, is all," Gert wheezed. And coughed. Her face, already an unbecoming shade of pale, grew even more ashen.

"What were you doing in the den, Aunt Gert?" Kelly asked. She stood beside her aunt, rubbing a trembling hand up and down her arm. Up and down. "We all went to bed at the same time, but then, I couldn't find you. Thank God Lucy did, but what were you doing there?"

Maria Simcox picked up Gert's other hand. "You

going to tell your family or am I going to accidentally let it slip in front of them here and have you go to all the trouble of suing me for not respecting patient confidentiality?" She laid the thin hand on the coverlet. "You can, you know. Kelly's my lawyer and she's real good so I'm pretty much fearless."

"I'll tell them when I want them to know." Gert glared at the circle of faces.

"That should be any minute now, right, Aunt Gert?" Boone asked easily, standing at the foot of the bed with Crockett.

They were shoulder-to-shoulder, both still filthy and wet, their arms crossed over their chests. Lucy wasn't sure she would have argued with either of them. "All right, all right." Gert's glare was gone, replaced by a sulky expression. "I love you children."

"We love you too." Crockett didn't relax his stance even a little bit. "And?"

"And I have a minor heart problem."

Maria snorted. "You *had* a minor heart problem. It's not so minor now. You're agreeing to see a cardiologist or I'm transferring you to Cincinnati. Then I'm going to fire you as a patient and leave you there. I'm not sure, but I think I can fix it so you have to pay me unemployment insurance."

Gert ignored her. "My medication was in the den. I'd gone there to get it because I had a little pain."

"Were you overcome by the smoke?" Kelly asked.

"No, there wasn't any smoke."

Maria rolled her eyes. "She had a heart attack," she explained. "If it hadn't been for the smoke, she'd probably still be lying there. Not that the smoke in and of itself was good for her—oh, God, no—but it may well have kept her alive."

A spate of curses from the hallway drew their attention. Maria stepped outside the cubicle, to return a moment later with Sims. He kissed Gert's forehead and sat beside her on the bed, taking her hand in his.

"You make that appointment," he told Maria, his gaze never leaving Gert's. "We'll see she keeps it. I don't know much about that S and M business, but I got no problem with tying her up to get her there."

"Now just a damn minute, Josiah Sims. I can make my own appointments when and if I choose to." Gert tried to pull her hand free, but he held it fast.

He shook his head. "If that were true, you'd have already done it. Is she spending the night here, Maria?"

"Yes." The doctor's voice was pleasant but firm. Lucy thought she'd be entirely capable of handling Gert if the patient got too recalcitrant. "Maybe two. I'll decide tomorrow. Unless you'd rather go into Cincinnati, Gert?" She raised an elegant eyebrow at her patient. "Didn't think so. Now, the rest of you need to leave so that we can get her into a bed. She's going to have a good, long sleep."

"Except me," Sims said. "I'm not going anywhere."

"Except you." Maria pressed his shoulder. "We'll get a cot in the room for you."

"I'd sleep better at home," Gert complained, "and I need to see the damage."

"You'll see it tomorrow or the next day—whenever you get to come home. We'll take care of things tonight." Boone bent to kiss her, followed by the others. Lucy went last, and when she would have walked away, Gert reached for her hand.

"Thank you."

Lucy shook her head. "It was Kinsey. She woke me up." She knew if she said anything more about the missing cat, she'd end up blubbering, so she forced a smile. "See you tomorrow, Gert. Rest now."

In the hallway, they spoke with Eli.

"I'll spend a little time with her before she goes to sleep and make sure Sims settles in too," he said. "Rest easy." He shook hands all around and offered up a beatific smile at Crockett and Boone. "After all, your money's safe with me."

The emergency vehicles had left and the buildings seemed to be intact when Boone, Crockett, Kelly and Lucy got home. Micah's Blazer was still on the street and he and Tom were raking ash away from the house. Jack was with them, and Lucy checked the time in consternation. What was he doing out at this hour? Even on Saturday night, she was sure his curfew was midnight. His mother worked nights at the casino, but Lucy would have bet the boy honored her wishes.

"Maria called, so we know about Gert. We already contacted the cleaning service," Micah said. "They'll be here Monday morning, but you'll be able to go in tomorrow. The only smoke and water damage is in the back of the house—the kitchen and laundry area and Gert's suite of rooms. The fire started in the leaves and it damaged the back wall, but nowhere else on the outside of the house—although it came close. Even the roof and the eaves are intact."

Boone and Crockett's faces were stricken. Lucy knew they were wondering if the fire had started because they'd piled the leaves too densely.

"The fire marshal's already been here?" Kelly asked.

"Yes. The insurance adjustor was too. He'll come back tomorrow for further assessment in daylight, but we're cleared to start clean-up. Landy called and reserved rooms for you at the bed and breakfast on the edge of town if you want them, but you'll be back in the house in just a few days. Martha Mayhew, the proprietor, said not to worry when you came or even if you did—it's late enough no one else is going to request the rooms." Micah yawned hugely and leaned his rake against the garage wall. "I'm going to go home now. My wife would notice if she got up for church and I wasn't there."

"Hold up and you can drop me off." Tom held up a hand. "The deputy took the cruiser."

"I still don't get how it started." Boone pulled Lucy to him with an arm around her waist. "There are stacks of leaves everywhere this time of year.

Why would the ones in Aunt Gert's back yard ignite?"

"Because someone lit them." Tom's voice sounded calm and furious at the same time.

Lucy thought she might have fainted if Boone hadn't been holding her. The pain in her ankle seemed far, far away, replaced by a sense of dread and guilt. She didn't know what the latest fire had to do with her, but she hadn't known with the others, either, and still they had occurred. She should have left after the car fire. If she wouldn't have stayed, this wouldn't have happened. Gert wouldn't be in the hospital. Kinsey wouldn't be gone. She sobbed before she could stop herself, and Boone held her closer, his lips brushing the top of her head.

Tom spoke again, still the voice of reason, still with that anger whistling through the reason. "Let's sleep on it. Everyone is safe for the moment. The deputy will patrol through the night. I'll be back here tomorrow at—what time was that adjustor coming tomorrow, Micah?"

"Ten."

"Just hold off on everything until then. Everybody get some rest." Tom wiped an arm over his sooty forehead. "Jack? What are you still doing here, son? Your mom know where you are?"

The boy kept on raking. "She's workin'. It's not a problem. She'd want me to help Mrs. Taylor."

"That's good, Jack." Crockett's voice was heavy. "Aunt Gert will appreciate it, but you need to go home. We'll get started on this again tomorrow, and we'll welcome your help then."

"But I can—"

"No." Boone was never stern—his idea of being authoritative was not sharing his tuna sandwich with Kinsey—but his tone brooked no argument. "This day needs to end, Jack. One of us will take you home. Tom, can we go into the house long enough to get a change of clothes?"

They could, going in the front door and feeling like thieves in the shadowy house. After an exhausted discussion about who would go where, they divided by gender. Lucy went home with Kelly. Boone and Crockett drove to the bed and breakfast, agreeing to drop Jack off on their way.

"This has grown up a lot since we were kids." Crockett looked around at the cookie-cutter ranch houses in Twilight View, the neighborhood where Jack lived. "The honchos who owned the brewery also owned the land this development was on. It used to be like three streets, all named something beer-related. Long Neck Lane and Tall Cool Avenue and—what was the other one, Boone?"

"Six Pack Street," Jack supplied from the back seat of Gert's SUV. "That's where I live. The new roads are tree streets, like Elm and Maple. I guess some people thought that made the neighborhood sound more respectable-like."

"Micah lived on Long Neck," Boone remembered. "Everybody called it the Bowery in those days, when it wasn't nearly as nice as it is now. The trees were all shorter than I am and about three inches around and there weren't any sidewalks or curbs. Do they still call it that, Jack?"

"Yeah, but my mom was all excited when we moved here—we'd always lived in an apartment before. I didn't know Mr. Walker was a Bowery rat, though. He seems all professional and educated. Slick."

Boone snorted. "He's educated, all right, and professional too, but not a bit slick. I think *not* being slick is what won him some major journalism prizes before he came back to Taft."

Crockett turned onto Six Pack. "Which house, Jack?"

"The one on the end with red shutters and the garage turned into a family room. Ma calls it a Cape Cod, but I think it's just a box."

A sign was in the front yard of the pretty little house. The property was being offered for sale by a Lawrenceburg mortgage company. Boone exchanged glances with Crockett but didn't comment. Even he, a fiscal idiot and fairly oblivious to what went on in the world around him, knew what the sign meant. It didn't happen a lot in Taft, but even the utopian little town didn't remain untouched—the house was in foreclosure.

It also seemed lonely. Not empty precisely, or even neglected. Just…lonely.

"Is anyone here, Jack?" The grimness in Crockett's tone drew a sharp glance from Boone.

The kid's sixteen. He's old enough to stay by himself. Let it go, Crockett. You don't have to be Father Noah right now.

"No. I told you, my mom works nights. She won't get home till about eight. And you know where my dad is. Everybody knows that."

Boone remembered how hard it had been just telling people his parents were dead. Because every time he said it, he had to know it again—there was no pretending they were just away for a while and would be back in time for the ball game or eighth-grade graduation or Kelly's eleventh birthday party at the ice skating rink. He couldn't imagine being a kid and having to tell people his dad was in jail. It had been awful enough that everyone felt sorry for him. Having them be suspicious of him—mentally visiting the sins of the father on the son—would have been even worse.

"Where are your little brothers?"

The boy hesitated. "Staying with somebody right now."

His voice sounded like a toothache feels. Crockett's question had hit a nerve.

They let Jack out of the car in his driveway. Boone was sure Crockett shared his reluctance to just drop him off, because they started to speak at the same time. Boone gestured for him to go ahead, and Crockett said, "You sure you'll be okay? You can go with us. We'll text your mom and let her know where you are. Well, I will. I don't think Boone knows how to text."

The attempt at humor fell flat. Jack's face and voice remained grim. "I'm fine. I stay alone all the time while she works. I'm a big boy."

"We're big boys too." Boone leaned over to meet Jack's eyes. "But the truth is Aunt Gert will kick some major ass if we don't watch after you. Lucy will help her because I think she's become the big sister you never had and probably never wanted. Crockett pretends he's not scared of them, but I know better. You're coming to help at the house tomorrow, right?" He glanced at the clock on the dash. "Well, later today?"

"Yeah. I'll be there."

"Keep track of your hours," Crockett advised. "You'll get paid."

"Jesus! Sorry, Father, but…Jesus! Mrs. Taylor's been great to me. Can't I just help her?"

"Sure you can. And she'll appreciate it." Crockett spoke quickly, in a soothing Father Noah voice. "See you tomorrow, Jack. Sleep well."

They waited until Jack was inside to back out of the driveway. Boone frowned at the house as they drove away. "He didn't turn any lights on."

"I don't know if they *have* any lights."

"Damn. Lucy's been worried about him all summer, and Kelly's driven herself nuts trying to take care of him without him knowing it." Boone had spent guy-time with Jack, treated him with careless affection, but he hadn't gone out of his way to learn about the inner workings of the kid's life. All kids' lives were a mess, weren't they? Not only that, they didn't generally thank grownups for trying to fix the messes, either.

Boone wished he had. Even if Jack had told him to butt out, he wished he'd tried.

"Kelly's hands are tied." Crockett's defense was sharp and instant.

"I know. She knows it too, but sometimes, more often lately, I think, the real Kelly Brennan—the one we used to know—shows up." Boone chuckled, thinking of his sister. "I like it when she does. I like *her*."

Crockett was silent for so long Boone thought he wasn't going to respond. It wasn't until he pulled Gert's car into the curved driveway of the bed and breakfast that he spoke. "Yeah," he said, his voice morose, "me too."

Chapter Eighteen

Kelly's condo was lovely, with large rooms and acres of hardwood floors. Lucy would have been afraid to sit on the furniture even if she'd been clean, which she most decidedly was not. "I'm afraid to take a shower here," she said, standing in the doorway of the guest bath Kelly showed her to. "What if all this soot clogs the drains?"

"We'll call a plumber and say we have no idea where all the crud came from, since I'm as filthy as you are."

Kelly smiled at her and Lucy marveled that even with the dreadfulness of the night, it was one of the most genuine expressions she'd ever seen on the beautiful face.

Twenty minutes later, they met back in the living room. Kelly handed Lucy a cup of tea. "With any luck, we'll get to sleep before daybreak and no one will call before at least ten."

As if in direct response, Lucy's cell phone rang.

"I just wanted to hear your voice, even though it does sound like you swallowed gravel," Boone said. "You feeling all right? How's your ankle by now?"

"I'm fine." She turned her leg to check its mobility and had to stifle a gasp of pain. "It's a little swollen and a lot bruised. I kept trying to wash the dark off because I thought it was soot. But it doesn't hurt much." A little white lie never hurt anything. "You and Crockett okay?"

"We're good. At least, he was when he went to his room."

"How about Jack? He's never very talky, but he was even less so tonight…last night…whatever this is."

"Kid's got a lot on his plate." He hesitated. "Lucy?"

She sipped the tea, feeling the warmth wash through her. It made her feel boneless and seemed to turn the stressed exhaustion into a tiredness that was calm, nearly pleasant. "Hmh?" she asked drowsily.

"I know you didn't have anything to do with the fire at Aunt Gert's. We all do. You're not having any weird thoughts in that direction, are you?"

"Born to Run" played in her mind again, Springsteen's voice softened and mellowed by the influence of the tea—what had Kelly given her anyway? Lucy had to force her voice to work. "I don't know." She sipped again, her exhausted body enjoying the languor that was stealing its way into her limbs. Even the throb in her ankle dulled. "I don't know," she repeated. "We need to get some sleep, Boone." Her voice had the same clear enunciation Gladys Vojtasek's used to get when she stayed after work and shared a bottle of wine with Johnny.

Great heavenly days, was she drunk?

"I know." God, she loved his voice. "Sleep tight, Lucy Goosy."

"You too," she whispered. *I love you.*

When she'd disconnected, she frowned over at Kelly. "What on earth is in this tea?"

"It's some stuff Bridget—my secretary who knows everything—gave me to help me sleep. It's all natural." Kelly grinned at her. "I asked Maria if it would hurt you on top of the pain meds she gave you. She said it wouldn't, but that you might feel just the slightest bit inebriated. Appears as though she was right."

"No, she was wrong. I think I'm three sheets to the wind. I could probably get arrested." Lucy finished the tea, which was most likely a mistake but it tasted really good. "Of course, maybe I *should* be arrested. I don't know how I could be responsible for the fires, Kelly, but I'm sorry. I'm so sorry." Tears—she didn't know where they'd come from—dripped from her cheeks, dampening the front of her tank top.

Kelly sat beside her on the leather sofa, her arm coming around Lucy's slumped back. "It's not you, Lucy. I don't know who it is or why it is, but it's not you."

As far as eloquence went, the succinct statement didn't have much to recommend it, but the guilt that sharpened the edges of Lucy's mind waned for the first time in what seemed like days. When she climbed into the queen-size bed in Kelly's elegant guest room, she fell asleep so instantly she didn't even say the prayers that had been a habit since she'd knelt beside Siobhan Dolan every night.

She was grateful when she woke that "the slightest bit inebriated" hadn't left her with even that much of a hangover. Kelly handed her a mug of steaming coffee. "What's in it?" she asked suspiciously.

"Just coffee," Kelly promised. "I called the hospital while you were in the shower. Aunt Gert had a pretty good night, but I don't think Sims did. Either way, Maria said she's keeping her another night. Boone and Crockett will meet us at the house."

The two men were already working when they arrived, tearing scorched siding off the back of the house and arguing loudly about the proper manner for doing so. Jack loaded the debris into a wheelbarrow and transferred it to the Dumpster already in place at the edge of the property.

"You can go inside," Boone called from a point halfway up an extension ladder. "Power's been turned back on—no wiring damage. Adjuster's already been here. Tom was with him. He'll be back soon."

"We'll work inside." Kelly exchanged nods with Lucy. "Jack, make sure those two don't fall off those ladders, okay? Aunt Gert will blame Lucy and me if they do."

"And rightfully so," Boone said.

"You'll have to do the telling so Aunt Gert doesn't realize Boone was just being his usual clumsy self," Crockett advised Jack. "I would tell her, but I took vows about lying."

"It seems to me, you change those vows you took to whatever is convenient at the moment," Boone complained. "When we were working at the station while Sims was laid up, you said you took a vow not to mop bathroom floors."

"Believe me, sometimes there's nothing convenient about vows." Crockett sounded grim.

Lucy thought she heard his sigh from twenty feet away. She smiled at the priest and stepped onto the back porch to follow Kelly inside.

"If the coffeemaker's intact and there's coffee inside a sealed container, we could probably drink some," Boone called.

"I was going to make it," Crockett added, "but I took a vow—ouch!" He ended on a yelp when Boone threw a handful of leaves at him. "Hey, those might have hurt," he protested when everyone laughed. "There was no telling what he'd loaded them with. And I really did take a vow not to make coffee, way back in seminary days. Mine was so bad, they made me promise."

The damage, in the light of day, wasn't as severe as they'd feared, although the mess was horrendous. Lucy started the dishwasher and the coffeemaker while Kelly swept broken glass from the pantry. She took trash bags in to clear the shelves.

Lucy stood in the middle of the kitchen, not sure what to do next. It was as though her mind was numb. She washed the cups in the sink—although she had to scrub the sink first—preparing a tray to take outside. A scratching sound made her turn toward the sunroom, expecting Kinsey to be sitting there, asking politely to be allowed inside.

Even before her mind registered the empty spot where the kitten always awaited entry, she remembered. And her legs nearly collapsed under her. She knew Kinsey might have survived the smoke, but it wasn't likely. The more probable scenario was that the cat went off by herself and died.

You've lost your parents, the place you grew up, everything that ever mattered to you. Shouldn't that have been a clue? But, no, you make people who don't belong to you into some kind of pseudo-family. And you fall in love with a silly little cat without any thought of how it would feel to lose her. You're an idiot, Lucy Dolan.

"I can't do this now," she said. "I'm sorry. I just can't." Moving almost blindly, she poured coffee into a thermal server.

"It's okay. We don't have to. The cleaning service will take care of it." Kelly's voice was soothing beside her. "Let me help take this out. And we'll stay out until you're ready."

I'll never be ready. But Lucy didn't say the words, just nodded and picked up the tray. "Will you get the door?"

Tom was there when they went outside, helping Jack with the mess Crockett and Boone made. His blunt features were grim. "Eli said everybody missed you at church this morning," he said. "He told them to stay away until at least Tuesday to give Gert time to settle in."

Lucy set the tray on the wrought iron table. Leaves stirred, and a flock of ducks flew overhead. They sounded querulous in their traveling conversation. Apprehension, unexpected and unwelcome, prickled on the back of her neck and she shivered in response. *What now?*

Crockett crossed the yard and poured himself a cup of coffee. "I don't understand," he said, shaking his head. "Gert's never hurt anyone in her life. Why would someone want to damage her home, maybe even cost her her life?"

"Maybe this time," Tom said quietly, "we'll get a viable answer to those questions." He pushed the wheelbarrow to the back of the house and turned to face them, his hands hanging loose at his sides. "What do you think, Jack? Got any answers?"

It took a moment for the meaning of the sheriff's question to sink in, and when it did, the strength left Lucy's legs. "I need to sit down."

It appeared they all did, and they moved to the chairs around the table. Except for Tom and Jack, who were engaged in a stare-down.

The boy looked away first and, for a moment, Lucy thought he was going to run. But he didn't. His shoulders, broad for a boy his age, seemed slim when they drooped inside his ragged denim jacket. She remembered that vulnerability she'd felt in him when she'd hugged him. *Oh, Jack.*

"How'd you know it was me?" He maintained

eye contact with the sheriff. It was probably easier than facing Gert's family—the people who had shown him only kindness. Even as anger flickered to life within her, Lucy ached for him.

"You're sixteen years old and you showed up here in the middle of the night and started working without being asked. There was a first report to the fire department—before Lucy called—made by someone with a young, panicky voice." Tom held something up. "We know where that call came from, and then we found this in the alley behind Gert's house earlier today." He tossed the wallet to the boy. "I reckon you wanted to get caught, didn't you, son?"

"That's just crazy. Why would I want to get caught?" But it was as though Jack was going through the motions of being a tough guy. He seemed tired more than scared, resigned rather than angry. And though he still looked sixteen in his frayed jacket and soot-streaked jeans, his eyes were much older. Older and sadder, surrounded by dark circles of what could have been either stress or fatigue. Or both.

"Jack." It was Crockett's voice, deep and gentle. "Maybe you should tell us what's going on."

The boy spoke directly to Kelly, his voice strained. "It was you. You ruined our family. My dad's in jail, my mom's working all the time, and my little brothers are living with people who don't really know them—who won't even let them have a nightlight. And they're still little. Too little to..." He swallowed hard, his eyes shiny with sudden moisture. "I wanted you to know how it felt."

Kelly, her face drained of color, shook her head in confusion. "But it wasn't me you hurt. It was Lucy. And Gert."

"But it was people you cared about, and that hurts worse than if it was you. I'd be okay, but my little brothers aren't. They're scared and lonesome and they think they must have done something bad to make things turn out the way they have."

Lucy met Boone's and Kelly's eyes in turn, understanding that they'd all felt that way about different circumstances in their lives. Understanding that whether he wanted to admit it or not, Jack thought he'd done something bad, too. Even before he did.

Kelly's face was ravaged. "I still don't get it," she said raggedly. "Jack, I was doing my job. You *know* that. I did the best I could, really I did."

"Maybe you did." Jack stopped to take a breath and regain control of his voice. "But my brothers are still in a foster home and my mom's still working double shifts. You're still living in that fancy place by the lake and we're losing ours. Do you know how long and how hard my folks worked for that little piece-of-shit house? How hard *I* worked to help Mom keep it so they could start over when he gets out of jail? Do you have any freakin' idea? And it's all been for nothing."

"I couldn't make your dad not guilty." Kelly spoke quietly, hopelessly. Tears streaked down her cheeks. "You shouldn't have had to grow up so fast.

I'd have given so much to keep it from happening, but I couldn't, Jack. I couldn't."

His shoulders sagged even further in the jacket. "I know. In my head I know it. I always knew it. But I still wanted you to feel as bad as I did. As bad as my mom does."

"Lucy and I weren't even friends," Kelly said. "I was mad at her."

"I know, but Boone liked her, and Boone's your brother. Mrs. Taylor liked her and you love Mrs. Taylor." Jack covered his face with his hands for a painful space in time. When he took his hands away, his eyes were tearwashed and dark. And still much older than sixteen. "It was the long way around, but I found stories about Lucy on the internet after she got here. I read about the fire in Richmond and I knew if I went through her, I could get to you. She didn't start the fire, but she was scared of it. She won't light candles or anything. Even birthday cakes make her antsy. She had me set buckets of water in the tearoom when there were birthday parties."

She had. She'd decorated the buckets and set weighted champagne bottles in them, but they'd been full of water. Jack had rolled his eyes, but he'd never argued with her about setting them out.

"It was easy to start the first trash fire behind Jenny's," Jack continued doggedly, once again raising his gaze to Tom's impassive face. "I didn't plan the one at the library, but Kelly and Lucy were both there that morning, so I lit it anyway." The tears leaked from the corners of his eyes, but he didn't wipe them away.

Lucy felt her heart break, the anger slipping away as quickly and quietly as it had come. Boone scooted closer and his arm came around her. She longed to bury her face in his shoulder and wish away the story they'd just heard.

"What about Stan Morgan's garage?" Tom asked.

"I didn't—"

"You don't have to answer that," Kelly interrupted, her voice so crisp everyone started at the sound of it. Her face was still pale and tear-streaked, her hand shaky when she raised it to forestall Jack's reply. "You're not under arrest, nor are you in the official presence of counsel."

"It doesn't matter. I'm done. I didn't start Mr. Morgan's fire. I never meant—" He stopped, tears robbing him of his voice. "No one was ever supposed to get hurt. I didn't want anything to be damaged. Even Lucy's van—I just meant to have a bunch of smoke come out from under the hood. I read how to do that but the instructions were wrong."

"Jack—the house." Tom pointed at the scorched siding and the ash and cinders they'd raked into piles away from the foundation. "Does that look to you like nothing was damaged?"

"I know." Jack flung his arm out as though to encompass the yard and the back of the house. "I didn't aim for it to burn, just the leaves. Most of them were in bags back there by the alley, so I thought it would be like the trash fire, only somehow it spread and the door to the sunroom was on fire before I knew what was happening. I called the fire department, but the smoke came up faster than I expected. When Kelly and Lucy came out and the fire trucks were coming, I thought it was going to be all right."

"All right?" Tom's voice was quiet, but anger was deep and deadly within it. "Son, Gert was in there. Lucy went in after her. They could have died."

"I didn't know Mrs. Taylor was here. Honest to God. Her car was gone and I figured she was with Mr. Sims. She stays over there sometimes." Anguish broke through and the tears came faster, making wet, heartbreaking trails on the boy's thin face. "She's going to be all right, isn't she? Isn't she? I wouldn't hurt her for anything. Oh, God. I wouldn't. I wouldn't."

Lucy exchanged glances with Kelly and saw the same emotion in the other woman's face that she felt. They'd hugged him just thirty-some hours before and wanted to protect him from all harm. There was no denying the fact that they still did.

Kelly pulled a tissue out of her pocket and gave it to him. She stroked a hand through his hair and he didn't pull away.

"She'll be all right." Boone held Lucy's hand. "Lucy's ankle will heal. She'll probably get over losing Kinsey, too, sometime. But how do *you* get over it, Jack? What do you do next? Torch Kelly's condo? Life's a bitch, son. It's a pain-in-the-ass-sure-as-the-world-gonna-kill-you bitch. But you can't survive on the backs of other people. You just can't do it."

"Like I said, I'm done. I promise. *I promise.* I'll make it one of those vows like Father Noah has—only for real." He sat down as though his legs wouldn't hold him anymore, wiping his face with the already soggy tissue. "My dad said he got into something and he didn't know how to get out. I didn't believe him. I was—God, I was so mad at what he did to our family. If he'd said something, you know, I would have helped. I could have quit school and worked. But now I know how it can happen, that you know what you're doing is wrong and someone could get hurt, and you never intend to do it again."

He got up, pacing a short, agitated path. "But then something else comes up, like when they took my little brothers and they didn't want to go. They were crying and promising they'd behave and begging me to come and get them. And I couldn't. I couldn't." His voice broke all the way then, and he buried his face in his hands, his shoulders shaking with agonized sobs.

Crockett went to him, but Jack avoided the priest's touch, shaking his head. He accepted the new tissue Lucy offered with a nod of thanks, then stepped away long enough to blow his nose. The gaze he turned toward Kelly was dark with torment and weariness. "Last night, when you and Lucy came to the game and then stood in the parking lot afterward, it was like having a family again. It was that way today too, when we were raking out here and throwing leaves and even when you guys threw me into them…but then I went home and there wasn't anybody. My mom was working and things are packed up because we have to move. My brothers' foster parents won't even let me see them. There's a part of me that understands it's not really your fault, Kelly, but most of me is still mad."

He then met their eyes in turn. "I'll pay for the damages. It might take a while, but I can do it. I swear I can." He turned to Tom, straightening. "I'm ready to go wherever I have to. Can you not call my mom till later this afternoon? She's sleeping now."

Boone's hand tightened on Lucy's fingers so much she tried to pull away. He loosened his grip, but didn't let her go.

"Wait." Four voices spoke at once.

"No charges have been filed, Tom," Lucy said, "and I don't think any of us want to file any. Can't you just let him go home?"

"It's not that easy. Arson's a felony."

"It was vandalism," Boone argued, "and he's going to pay the damages. Every damn dime of them, and if he has any thought we won't stand over him and make him do it, he's sadly mistaken."

"You can release him to us," Crockett suggested. "We'll take him home and talk to his mom."

Tom scowled. "You guys aren't even residents."

"Lucy and I are," Kelly said, "and if his mother was able to be here, you'd release him to her, wouldn't you? Or to Aunt Gert if she was home. You're scared of Aunt Gert. She made you and Micah and Eli come and clean the windows when you used paraffin on them that year." Kelly sounded smug, and Lucy shot her an admiring look.

"All right." Tom lifted his hands in surrender. His face was still grave, but his eyes were smiling. "We'll talk about this Monday morning in my office. Nine o'clock sharp. Your mother will need to be there, Jack. Can I count on you showing up or do I need to send a deputy to the high school in a cruiser?"

"Yes, sir. I mean no, sir. I'll be there." His eyes were red from weeping, their expression weary, but hope glimmered in their depths, too. He didn't smile—it wasn't time for that yet—but the hopelessness was gone from his voice. He sounded almost like the kid Lucy had poured ice over. The kid they all loved.

"There's another part to this, too." Boone was somber. "If it hadn't been for the smoke, we don't know if anyone would have found Gert in time—she had the heart attack before the fire. There's nothing that makes what the kid did all right, but that goes a long way."

When it was sorted out, Crockett and Boone took Jack home again, staying to inform and reassure his mother. When they asked if Jack could come back to Twilight Park Avenue with them to work a few more hours that day, beginning his time of restitution, she agreed.

Lucy called and suggested they stop at McDonald's to pick up a late lunch for everyone. They bought Jack two Quarter Pounders with cheese and a large order of fries.

"I can't eat," he protested. "I'll get sick."

But he was sixteen. He ate. Including the cherry turnovers Kelly and Lucy didn't have room for and the fish sandwich that had been placed in the sack by accident. And he didn't get sick.

Boone, Lucy, Crockett and Kelly visited Gert in the hospital, telling her and Sims the necessary details. While they were there, Jack came in. He was carrying a bouquet of mums. "Mr. Morgan sent them. There's something I have to tell you, ma'am."

"All right, Jack. Have a seat." Gert regarded her niece, nephews and Lucy over the top of her glasses. "They were just leaving. They're going to Down at Jenny's to get me a large glass of sweet tea, because this hospital can't seem to make it so a body can drink it."

When Lucy and Kelly returned to the room with tea for Gert and coffee for Sims, Jack was sitting on the edge of the bed playing cards with the older couple. His eyes were red again. So were theirs. And whatever their conversation may have been, they weren't sharing a word of it.

Lucy and Kelly went back to meet Boone and Crockett at Down at Jenny's. A sense of relief gave them an appetite. The men and Kelly told stories on themselves that had them all helpless with laughter.

Lucy recounted tales of growing up in the kitchen of a restaurant, adding Johnny Dolan's brogue to her voice.

Afterward, Kelly returned to her condo and Crockett went to talk to Father Fitzpatrick, the rector at St. Charles. Boone and Lucy walked back to the tearoom, quiet after the emotional night and day.

Inside, at the foot of the front staircase, Boone drew her into his arms, holding her close. "Hey," he said, after a kiss that stole both her breath and the strength from her knees, "I'd like to make love with you. What do you think?" He kissed her again, his hands warm where they touched, eliciting heat even where they did not.

She wanted it more than anything. Wanted the excitement and the joy of being with him. Wanted the exquisite release of… Well, of release. Wanted that few minutes that she was always sure he loved her as much as she loved him. Oh, yes, she wanted it.

And she didn't think she could bear it. Not now. Not when every single feeling she possessed was as raw as if she'd just run her box-grater over each of them. "No," she said. And for the second time that day, "I'm sorry. I just can't."

She ran upstairs, not wanting to see his face if he was angry, because she didn't think she could stand it if he was. A minute later, when she was dropping a soft cotton nightgown over her head, he tapped softly at her door. "Sleep tight," he said through the panel.

"You too," she called.

She took pain-relievers to ease the steady throb

of her ankle, then slipped between the sheets of her bed. She lay on her side and took a deep breath to relax. And another. And one more.

Only then did she allow herself to think about Kinsey and weep hot, forlorn tears into the pillow.

Chapter Nineteen

"It wasn't that bad, ma'am." On Wednesday afternoon, the owner of the cleaning service held open the new door to the sunroom for Gert to step inside. "I had a full crew in here and Sam from the paint store brought in another crew and we got it cleaned up, painted, and fresh-aired in no time flat. You'll want to change your curtains and throw rugs, but other than that and replacing your food, you're good to go." She beamed at Lucy. "You should be able to reopen by Friday, I reckon, and we'll be here for lunch."

"It'll be on the house," Lucy promised. She opened the doors into the kitchen, allowing Gert to precede her, turning to wave at the cleaning crew as they got into their van. "Sit down," she ordered. "You can make a list of what we'll need."

Gert took her usual seat at the island, reaching for a pen and her notebook. "Are you going to spend the next six months telling me to sit down?"

"Probably."

"You're staying, aren't you? There's no longer a reason to leave, not that there was ever a rational one, anyway."

Lucy peered around at the big kitchen, amazed.

If she hadn't known the room had been full of smoke, water, and broken glass only a few days ago, she'd never have believed it. But the notes that always covered the refrigerator were gone, the pantry was empty. Even her pickle jar had been removed from the counter. She hoped it was around somewhere, but it was hard to think about dreaming right now anyway.

"We need all the staples." Gert was scribbling busily. "You can go to the wholesaler for those." She looked up. "Lucy? You didn't answer me. You are staying, right?"

Lucy went to stand at the window, gazing out at the driveway. Jack was there, having come straight from school. He was wheeling the power washer out of the garage. He met her gaze through the wavy old glass and smiled tentatively.

In this family that had become hers, he was the wayward little brother as surely as Gert was the mom and Sims the dad. Crockett was the handsome older brother, Kelly the grouchy sister. Boone was…he was…

He was back in Chicago is what he was, drawing cartoons and finding himself a new life without the wife he'd loved. It remained to be seen if there would be room in that life for Lucy.

And what if there wasn't? What if they ended up as "just friends," that classification Crockett and Kelly were trying to attain? Could Lucy stand it? For a minute, the thought made breathing difficult, made her eyes sting.

But the alternative—moving on down the road until she found another place that might be like home, saying goodbye to Gert and Sims and the kid in the back yard and even to Kelly—that would be worse.

She smiled back at Jack and raised a hand in greeting. "Yeah," she said, going to sit at the island with Gert. "I'm staying."

Boone peered into the kitchen area of the old Knights of Pythias building, then checked the restrooms again. The plumbing was good, Sims'd said, but the fixtures needed replacing. Did they ever—all that was missing were chain-operated toilet tanks on the walls. The wiring, on the other hand, needed a complete redo. He was pretty sure knob and tube wasn't even legal, plus God knew that if anyone could electrocute himself with it, Boone was that person.

The meeting room was perfect for a studio, and there were smaller rooms along the west side of the building that would work for private offices. There was a storage area upstairs as well as a spacious three-bedroom apartment complete with two fairly modern bathrooms. The "bones" of the building were sturdy, with recently replaced windows and roof.

"What do you think?" Crockett asked, coming to stand beside him at one of the big palladium windows that displayed the Twilight River. "Think you could work here?"

"Yeah. I found out this summer that I can work most anywhere. If I'm here, I can keep the strips going and have artistic control of both of them. If I hire another artist plus an assistant, I can even keep reasonable hours, like a real person." He laughed. "'Eight Hours Work' can be a reality."

"That apartment's pretty nice. You going to live there?"

Boone hesitated. "No. I want a house. But I was thinking maybe Jack's family could live there. He and his mom could be caretakers for the building in lieu of rent, so she could cut back on her hours at the casino. I know it won't be the same for them as having their house, but they wouldn't have to worry about foreclosure, either. Kelly's almost positive once they're in a stable home again, the little boys will be able to come back to their mom."

"Sometimes, Boone, I think you are a really good guy." Crockett's hand rested on his shoulder for a moment.

"But then you rethink it, right?" Boone laughed, both embarrassed and pleased.

"You'll miss Chicago."

"It'll still be there, just a short flight away."

Crockett held his gaze. "Your life there?"

"The old one doesn't exist anymore, and I don't care about the new one." Boone could see the houses on the River Walk from this vantage point. Micah and Landy's big Victorian had a few shingles missing from the tower. A couple of Frisbees in neon colors lay on the roof of Eli's house a few doors down. "Actually, the new life doesn't exist anymore, either. As soon as I got back to the apartment after leaving here, I called the doctor who lived there through the summer. He's got himself a new wife who really loves the place. She was walking through with us and she pointed at the corner of the dining room and said, 'Oh, my piano would fit right there.' I swear, I felt Maggie pushing me from behind, telling me she wanted her to have the place. So I sold it to them."

Crockett grinned. "That's great news. Have you told Lucy?"

"Not yet."

"Does she know you're here?"

"No one does but you and Sims. How about you? You left two weeks ago just like I did and here we are, back like proverbial bad pennies."

"Only you and Sims know."

Boone narrowed his eyes. Nervous energy had been an integral part of his friend all through their growing-up years. As an adult, Crockett became more laid back and infinitely quieter. Boone always attributed the change to his faith—no, to his calling to the priesthood. He wasn't so sure anymore. And the nervous energy was back. "You're coming back to Taft, aren't you?"

"I don't know." Crockett shrugged. "I want to be here when Gert has her bypass surgery next week and my mind and heart weren't where they needed to be anyway, so I requested a leave."

Boone waited, then said, "So where are they?"

"Where are what?"

"Your mind and your heart."

"I don't know that, either," Crockett admitted. "My faith's not a problem, though I seem to be losing my ability to 'let go and let God,' which is not only a catch phrase but a necessary part of being a priest. All I can say for sure is that the only time I feel at home or feel any kind of peace is when I *am* home. Here, with my family."

"I'd like it…we'd all like it if you came back." *Oh, hell, yes.* Boone grinned slyly. "Thinking of giving up celibacy? That's one vow I know you really did take."

"And one I'd be happy to forsake," Crockett said ruefully. "But it's all a ways down the road. I haven't left the priesthood or Virginia yet."

Boone nodded. "But you will." He extended his hand. "Think Taft can stand up to having both of us back?"

"They'll have to change the sign."

"Ready to go home?" It was funny how quickly calling the Twilight Park Avenue house "home" had become comfortable again, even more so now that Crockett might be returning too. "We'll get there in time for leftovers from lunch. I haven't eaten since breakfast in Chicago and a little bitty package of some really hard things on the plane."

"Me, either. I wonder what kind of soup Lucy made today."

"Vegetable. I talked to her this morning. Aunt

Gert made chicken and noodles and mashed potatoes, too."

"What are we waiting for?"

Gert and Lucy were in the kitchen when they got there. Lucy was loading the dishwasher and Gert was counting receipts. After a flurry of hugs and an in-depth kiss between Lucy and Boone behind the pantry door, the men sat down with the hoped-for leftovers. They'd just progressed to pumpkin pie—shared straight from the pan without benefit of plates—when a knock came at the back door.

Lucy went to open it, and when they heard her cry out, Boone led the rush through the sunroom.

Stan Morgan stood just inside the doorway. Lucy was beside him with a small black and white cat in her arms. "Look." Tears flowed unrestrainedly down her face. "See who's home."

"She showed up over the weekend." Mr. Morgan reached out to scratch Kinsey's head. "Made herself right to home on the back porch. I fed her and all, but, you know, she just seemed so sad lying there. Then Jack, that boy that works for you, came by this afternoon on his way home from school. He stopped to help me rake some leaves, and the cat came off the porch and climbed him like he was her favorite tree. He told me, then, where she belonged, and I brought her back right away."

"Well." Gert blew her nose and petted the cat with a trembling hand. "Appears like everyone's coming home today. Come in, Stan, before these boys eat everything in sight, and have a cup of coffee."

"Don't mind if I do. My own doesn't taste all that good."

Kelly and Sims came while he was there, then Jack appeared in the back yard, raking and bagging more leaves. Tom, still in uniform, was the next visitor. He stood talking with Jack for a long time, then they both came inside.

Tom nodded to everyone's questioning gaze. "It's going to be all right. Kelly's his advocate, but I reckon you'll all work together at keeping him in line and well-fed." He glared at Jack. "You need help with anything, you know where my office is, right?"

"Yes, sir." Jack spoke with his mouth full, spraying cookie crumbs. "Sorry. Thank you, sir."

"And stop calling me sir."

"Yes, sir. I mean, yes, sheriff."

Tom sighed, taking the cup of coffee Lucy offered. "It's Tom. Just call me Tom, all right?"

"Yes, sir."

It had probably been, Lucy decided, rolling out piecrust at midnight, the happiest afternoon she'd ever known. Everyone she loved had been crowded into the kitchen, plus a few who'd gained, like the title of a favorite old movie, places in her heart.

She wondered once again what had happened to the jar containing her tips and dreams. There hadn't been that much money in it—she'd taken to putting it in the bank every month or so—but she'd been gathering the dreams, detailed on slips of paper, receipts, napkins and business cards, since she was sixteen. Some had been achieved, some abandoned when they were outgrown, and some…some still resided in her mental hope chest.

Make that emotional hope chest, she amended, dusting her hands on her apron and bending to pick up the cat who came to wind herself around Lucy's ankles. "I missed you so much," she murmured, and Kinsey bumped her chin with her head.

"How about me?" Boone's voice came from the bottom of the back stairs. Kinsey jumped out of her arms and ran to give Boone's bony feet a caress before leaping into the rocking chair by the window and settling into the seat.

Lucy loved how Boone looked, with his hair appearing decidedly slept-in and his dark brown eyes both drowsy and somehow brightly aware. He wore a pair of plaid flannel pajama pants and a gray T-shirt that had seen better days. He was smiling at her, his teeth white and straight inside the crooked quirk of his lips.

She loved him. For better or worse and forever. She knew that with all certainty, and if he didn't love her back, that was something she'd just have to learn to live with. Friends. They could be friends.

He was holding her jar.

"Oh," she said, smiling back at him. "I was just wondering where that was."

"Kelly took it home. She washed the jar and the

money and cleaned up the dreams as much as she could. With true lawyer-like obsessiveness, she even alphabetized them and put them in neat little paper-clipped stacks. I'm pretty sure there's a new database on her computer entitled 'Lucy's Pickle Jar' too."

Lucy spotted the new sign on the side of the jar and laughed. It was a sketch of Gladys Doyle rolling piecrust, and the words *Lucy's Dreams* were printed in a large speech bubble above Gladys's curly head. "Thank you." She took the jar and set it in its old place on the counter.

"What about me?" Boone repeated his question from behind her. "Did you miss me, too?"

"Yes."

"If I came back here. To live. To work." He spoke in fits and starts. "Would I get in the way of whatever's in there?" He pointed at the jar.

Lucy didn't think she could breathe. "No." Her voice didn't sound like her own, so she said it again. "No."

"I'm buying that building from Sims. You know, the old lodge building down by the river."

"Oh." She couldn't meet his eyes, so she just kept staring blindly at the pickle jar. "Will you live upstairs there? It's nice and big, isn't it?"

He cleared his throat. "Well."

When he didn't go on, she faced him, but kept her gaze on his chin. He needed a shave. "Well?"

"I thought I'd live here." He drew the jar closer.

"Hey, there's a new piece of paper on top Kelly forgot to alphabetize."

She took out the new note, recognizing the paper he drew on. There was another sketch of Gladys, sitting on a park bench in her apron. Beside her sat the stick figure Boone drew as part of his signature in his comic strips. In the bubble over their heads were the words, "Marry me. We can make each other's dreams come true."

Lucy swallowed hard. "That's pretty romantic for a guy with a coonskin cap tattoo who's the worst driver in three states."

"See there? I need you to keep people on the road safe. You can do the driving in the family. As a tradeoff, I'll feed that useless cat and wash everything she sheds on. I'll talk to her about birth control and tell her not to hang with tomcats because they'll take advantage of her, then leave like thieves in the night."

"Speaking of birth control, what about kids?" she asked. "I'd like—"

"—several," he finished. "Great idea. You can teach them to cook and to drive and I can teach them...something. We'll have to work on that." His arms came around her, settling her against him.

She smiled at him. "I love you. I'll love you forever."

"I love you, too." His gaze met hers in a delicious tangle of laughter and joy. "So, what do you say, Lucy John Dolan? Wanna make an honest cartoonist out of me?"

"I say yes." Her arms came around his neck. "Oh, yes."

He kissed her, long and lingering, then swept her into a two-step. They danced around the kitchen in the night, hearing their own music and moving in glorious, shining time.

* * * * *